Jayel
Hands of a Healer

Janet M. Gibson

ISBN 979-8-218-49702-6

Cover design is a painting by Elinor Leshinski, modified with permission

Library of Congress Control Number: 2018675309
Printed in the United States of America

Chapter 1

The winds of change blew down from the mountains beyond Denerow Woods, and on another planet, Master Librarian Azala paused her reading and smiled. The sage, the oldest member of the Endowed, rose from the chair, walked to the bookshelf, and reached for the volume on the history of the House of Leidra.

***

On Leidran, the outermost planet in the Onus One star system, Jayel hiked along the bank of the Bubbling Brook which cut through Denerow Woods. The stream, named by the Endowed because of its many ripples churning along the rocky bed, reflected the soft midday pale sunlight. Late autumn colors and crunching leaves underfoot contributed to the peaceful solitude the young woman enjoyed on the secluded lands of the Endowed.

Then the memory intruded, again, uninvited.

"No one is to suspect murder." Her father's voice sounded unusually cold and threatening.

Jayel instantly stopped before entering his private office. The words slapped her face, the skin stinging.

"They won't." The voice of his first-in-command, General Chrysic. It always sounded like he had oil in his throat. "They'll continue to believe it was an accident." After a pause, the general shifted his tone and remarked, "She was a most beautiful woman."

Jayel heard the riffling of paper. Perhaps they were looking at photographs.

"Yes. A delightful sense of humor, too. Good times." A pause. Her father sighed, his voice almost a whisper. "I loved her. It should never have happened."

"But it did." Another pause, the tone almost comforting. "You couldn't keep her, you know that. She chose your brother."

"Hmm."

Jayel again heard papers shuffling.

In a firm voice, the general said, "Keep these as a reminder that I know the truth. You must stay silent. It's imperative no one ever finds out, or you will lose everything."

"It's imperative no one ever finds out," her father repeated.

Jayel dared not look around the doorframe. Her heart raced with dread. *Her father, governor of Melandan, member of the Endowed, a murderer?*

Chrysic assured him, "We've made the best of the situation. I give you my word, I'll remain silent. Remember, I have your back."

Sounds of their bodies moving, perhaps getting ready to leave his private office, caused a new alarm. Jayel ran out of the outer room before they discovered she overheard them.

Jayel continued running for two standard years.

But the memory kept pace and reappeared now and then, unwanted, reminding Jayel that the beautiful retreat at the

House of Leidra offered only a temporary escape from reality. A day would come when she must act on what she knew.

The annoyance at reliving the memory again gave way when Jayel saw her destination ahead, the open glade surrounding a magnificent pine tree.

This awe-inspiring pine upstaged all nearby trees, boasting great height and splendid shape of massive branches thick with blue-green needles. No other tree grew under its shadow.

Jayel sat on the grass to rest from the hour's walk and inhaled the strong, pleasant pine scent. She loosened her scarf and fluffed her brown, shoulder-length hair beyond the jacket's collar. She leaned back on her arms and wiggled her long legs, loosening the trousers from their tuck inside the hiking boots.

As she appreciated the magnificent pine branches, long and heavy yet strong and sprouting new tips, Jayel's eyes caught approaching clouds overhead.

Perhaps a snowstorm is on the way.

Moments later, a brisk breeze pushed Jayel's hair into her face. She tightened the scarf as she stood.

Another breeze, colder and stronger than the previous one, caused the pine branches to wave from top to bottom.

Suddenly, her inner voice warned weather wasn't the only change coming. Jayel felt her heart rate increase.

I've got to get back to the House of Leidra now.

She zipped the jacket, and after a goodbye glance at the silent pine tree, Jayel selected a more direct path back. *I'll make it before it snows if I hurry.*

Jayel found the path that cut through the woods, away from the brook, and quickened her pace.

Too late did Jayel see a shape, much bigger than a twig, obstructing the path. She tripped, falling hard to the ground, her body pressing against crisp leaves.

"What the *flutz?*" Jayel cursed, shocked at her first fall since childhood. She twisted around and looked back.

It's a man.

He lay face down between two bushes. His left leg extended into the path. His clothes, suited for milder weather, were worn and faded brown, but Jayel saw no specific signs of trauma.

The body felt soft as she turned the man onto his back. His eyes were closed, and his near-shaven face appeared weary and strained. Droplets of perspiration covered his brow, and leaves mixed in his mahogany hair. He seemed around forty standard years old.

She sensed a familiarity in the cheekbones and nose, but Jayel didn't know who he was. *What's this stranger doing here so far from Quintar, and on the private grounds of the Endowed?*

"Hello? Can you hear me?"

No response.

Jayel took off one glove and touched his wrist to find a pulse. Suddenly, intense weariness and coldness passed through her fingers and up her arm.

She quickly withdrew her hand and shivered. Along with these sensations came the knowledge the man had been walking in a weary or confused state for a long time. Only recently, within the past hour, had he stumbled to his knees and fallen into a near-comatose sleep.

How do I know this from my touch?

Tentatively, Jayel held the man's hand again. Although his fingers didn't move, she felt as if he drew strength from her. Jayel clasped his hand firmly. His skin warmed, and the pulse increased though it remained below resting pace.

How could such a rapport be possible? Nothing like this experience happened to me in medical school. Yet, she couldn't doubt the transcendental feelings. They were intense, too strong to be denied.

A wet snowflake melted on her cheek. *Little time to think about these feelings now.*

Jayel shook his shoulders, but the man didn't respond, no moan, groan, or sigh. He wasn't going to get up and walk back to the cottage. She regretted not traveling by hovercraft.

Could she carry him? Perhaps ridiculous, but what alternative was there? Squatting, Jayel took one long deep breath, sat the man up, thrust her shoulder into his middle, and slung him over her shoulder, balancing his body against hers as she slowly stood. The man made no sound. Though she groaned, Jayel found she could support his weight.

She took two steps forward and spoke aloud, "Not bad."

For a tall, well-built man, his body weighed less than she expected. Or perhaps rural living for two years strengthened her muscles more than she knew.

Another snowflake melted on her face. Jayel clenched her teeth and set out for the House of Leidra.

Her breathing grew heavier towards the trek's end, and she was hot and sweaty, but as doubts about continuing formed, Jayel saw ahead the garden of the House of Leidra, and her strength renewed.

Moments later, Jayel entered the cottage, kicked the door closed behind her, and hurried to the quilt-covered bed located in the far corner. She let the man's body roll off her shoulders and easily straightened him out. Jayel peeled off her scarf, gloves, and jacket. Although she wanted one, a shower would have to wait until she saw to the man's health.

In the kitchen, Jayel selected herbs that might help relieve muscle tension and prevent fever. Jayel learned much from Endowed books on herbal medicine. She dipped a hand towel in a pot of boiled leafy greens, eucalyptus, honey, and ginger, returned to the main room, and laid the towel on the man's forehead.

The man's skin had warmed to the room's temperature. Snow melted in his hair, and she wiped off the excess water. He didn't move, save the rise and fall of his chest. Jayel rolled him from side to side and managed to remove his damp coat. As she shook the snow off, Jayel felt and removed from an inside pocket two pouches made of material like rawhide.

Fingering one pouch, it felt full, but Jayel found no opening or latch. She squeezed but nothing came out of unseen holes. These *borrells* were used to keep personal belongings from unfriendly eyes. Owners specified the seals, and only owners could open them. *Borrells* were rare and expensive. Jayel wondered what else this man concealed under a haggard dress disguise. If these *borrells* were his, he could hardly be poor. *Or perhaps he stole them?*

Her fingers trembled slightly as she held the pouches. What would the man do if he awoke and found her examining his possessions? Jayel watched his face, waited for him to suddenly open his eyes and accuse her of theft, but he didn't stir. The man slept peacefully, strain and weariness no longer visible upon his features. His breathing seemed deep and even.

Carefully, she placed the *borrells* on the end table, where he could see them when he awoke. Jayel found nothing else within his clothes to yield clues to his identity or place of origin. If he had carried other items before he collapsed, they were left behind. Too upset when she discovered him, Jayel hadn't thought to look around the area for other items.

"You rest now. Call out if you need anything."

Jayel added a large log to the glowing embers in the fireplace. She went upstairs to find dry clothes. Although living in the isolated cottage was primitive compared to city life, Jayel was, by no means, reduced to bare necessities, for the House of Leidra was a House of the Endowed, and as such, it met its occupants' needs. Storage rooms supplied clothes for men, women, and children, linens, and home goods, including dried foods and seeds to grow garden vegetables. Her explorations during the past two years uncovered an extensive variety of books, artworks, and useful supplies like telescopes and hunting gear. Curiously Jayel noted how although she daily consumed stored food and beverages, the shelves remained fully stocked.

After finding clothes for the stranger, she tended to her needs. Feeling refreshed after a shower, Jayel slipped on a comfortable robe over a tunic and slacks and returned to the main room.

She checked on the man. No change. "I don't know about you, but I'll be wanting a meal soon. I'll make us something to eat."

Jayel went to the kitchen and prepared a stew. While it simmered, she returned to the main room and relaxed in a rocking chair by the fireplace. Abundant tongues danced as the fire consumed the logs and cast a golden light over the room's lacquered wood furniture. The warmth provided comfort.

Jayel resumed reading a book begun yesterday, and her thoughts and concerns about the stranger receded.

One hundred pages later, the man stirred.

Chapter 2

Dareck, son of Harmond, member of the Endowed, found comfort under the warm blankets. Although he felt weak, the man's thoughts cleared. He recognized the House of Leidra, a cottage which in the past hosted retreats for the Endowed. He visited here twenty standard years ago with Neondra before they were married.

Without moving, his mind detected a young woman, not more than twenty-five standard years old, sitting nearby. Dareck tried to read her thoughts, but they were well-guarded. *Well, she doesn't know I am awake.*

The man turned his thoughts to recent events. He recalled arriving on the planet three weeks ago after receiving word General Chrysic was in the city of Quintar. Dareck kept tabs on Chrysic's movements in recent years, ever since becoming aware Chrysic made frequent trips to the planet Ondre in the Onus Two star system. Dareck suspected the general aided the war there. Any concern of Chrysic's in politically quiet Quintar aroused his concern.

Upon arriving on the planet, a flight deck manager informed him Chrysic's ship, the distinctive W4-C7-X2, left three days ago, but Chrysic wasn't on board. Dareck made further inquiries and learned the general left Quintar on foot, alone, in the direction of Denerow Woods, a vast unpopulated area of forests, hills, and valleys owned by the Endowed.

On foot, Dareck tracked the general, eager more than ever to discover Chrysic's intentions. After tracking him for more than a week, the Endowed member became convinced Chrysic was lost, as the general's path often doubled back or went in circles.

Dareck watched, hidden in the trees, as the general sat eating a noon meal in a small clearing. Chrysic wore no sign of uniform, status, or rank befitting a general, but rather, was dressed in a plain woodsman's garb, eating a simple lunch before a primitive campfire. Chrysic hadn't groomed his gray facial hair.

What classified mission was he on that he carried it out himself, alone like this? Dareck decided to confront him to find out.

"General Chrysic!" Dareck stepped out from among the trees and greeted the general. "What a pleasant surprise to find you sneaking around in a forest. Are the cities getting too mundane for you?"

Chrysic abruptly stood, acting startled and alarmed. The general turned to meet this intrusion. His plate fell into the fire. He quickly scanned the woods behind the figure, and seeing he was alone, assumed a threatening pose. "Dareck!"

"Now that we know who we are, what are you doing here in Denerow Woods?"

Chrysic's shocked expression melted with a smile, betraying relief Dareck didn't already know. "I'm on vacation, if you must know. But I'm surprised to find you here, Dareck. Your dear brother, Karsch, will no doubt find it, ah, interesting when I report it."

Right for the jugular. Chrysic knew Dareck's relationship with his brother was unbecoming of an Endowed member. He deflected the jab. "I doubt it. You know my brother and I don't keep tabs on each other."

"In case you don't know, then, the governor recently was named president-elect of the Systems' Council. We're extending our political clout across Onus One and Onus Two. He has a great future. No one will stop him, especially you."

Chrysic stood proud and tall. His gray eyes burned coldly, and his complexion wasn't fair. A lesser man than Dareck would tremble with fear under such a visage.

"Indeed, stop him from what?"

The general opened his mouth to argue, but Dareck cut him short. "Let's not discuss my brother's public, ah, service. Let's talk about why you're here. You don't usually travel alone without your bodyguards."

"Hah!" laughed Chrysic as he sneered, "My doings are my own business."

The Endowed member sensed the general's irritation and disappointment that his presence was discovered.

Chrysic added, "I will deal with the flight deck blabbermouth when I return to Quintar."

"Well, this is Endowed land. Have you become a member, Chrysic? Come, tell me!"

"Hmmph," mumbled Chrysic as he put his hand in his pocket. "You and your Endowed ethics. Your heritage means nothing to me." He spat and a glob reached the flames and sizzled, adding punctuation to his contempt.

"I could make you tell me, General."

Chrysic's face paled a shade, but his eyes remained fixed as glass. "I never liked you, Dareck. You're trouble wherever you go." He spat toward the Endowed member's feet. "You've no power over me, Endowed member. It doesn't take a mind reader to know how this will end. I plan to harm you here and now."

"Why must we fight? Just tell me what you are doing here in Denerow Woods, and we can go our separate ways. Besides, murdering an Endowed member is the highest offense in the system. Even my brother Karsch won't protect you if you kill me. You cannot get away unscathed. You know how it is."

Chrysic fingered the device in his pocket and stepped closer to Dareck. "I can think of at least one Endowed member's murder which has gone, ah, unavenged—about seventeen standard years ago … You know of whom I speak."

Dareck's eyes flashed, and he lost control. He grabbed Chrysic and began to beat and choke the general, his anger exploding after years of suppression. He wanted nothing but to crush Chrysic's life into bloody pieces.

The Endowed member could physically overtake Chrysic with one calculated blow, but intense anger made his fighting sloppy.

As Dareck's arms tightened around the general's neck, Chrysic removed from his pocket a nerve paralyzer he prepared for emergency defense. He reached up and thrust the needle into Dareck's upper back.

Immediately, the strangling hands weakened around Chrysic's neck, but they didn't go limp.

Chrysic freed himself from the loosened stranglehold, and, gasping for breath, grabbed his bag and ran.

Thoughts foggy and his balance unsteady, Dareck threw wild punches into space. Finally, he stopped moving and realized the folly of allowing his hatred to overcome him. Satisfaction replaced anger. Chrysic admitted he knew the fire and Neondra's death weren't an accident. Dareck long suspected his brother, Karsch, killed Neondra, and Chrysic admitted he knew.

Dareck stumbled from the campsite. He felt cold and hot

at the same time. Gray skies thickened, darkening the already weak light filtering through the tree canopy, further hampering his blurry vision. Dareck's thoughts rambled and bumped off the sides of his skull.

It was the drug, he reminded himself. He must maintain control. Sentences ran in and out of his mind without logical connections, without conscious direction.

What was Chrysic doing in the woods? He's still around here somewhere. No sun out. Probably headed back to Quintar. Follow Chrysic. Leave him alone. Sleep. A four-day walk back at the least. Sleep. I wonder if my brother knew Chrysic was here. The idiot, what was he looking for? Going west now. Snow soon. Sleep. Shelter. Leidra.

Dareck heard it now, through the numbness. Whispers of encouragement beckoned him to come to the House of Leidra. In his mind, he saw the clear, sharp image of the Ceremonial Evergreen tree, a source of strength to the Endowed. His legs felt alien, but he walked on. More time passed. How long had he been walking? He didn't know. The damn drug threw off his calculations. His thoughts craved sleep, but was he already dreaming? A moving sleep like a zombie. It was the drug, he reminded himself again. Dareck plundered on, relying on willpower to keep walking towards the whispers.

Eventually, blissfully, the knowledge he could sleep safely descended upon him. He knew he could relax the strained, numbed muscles, lower the heavy, brainless head, and release the connections of mind from thought. He found the protective custody of a power greater than himself.

As he closed his eyes, Dareck thought he could see the grand pine in the distance, but it could be a mirage. Somehow it didn't matter he didn't reach the safety of the House of Leidra. The shadow of the evergreen afforded enough shelter.

Dareck sensed the presence of another person, but as he struggled to meet this new danger, he felt warm hands, the sensation telling him this person was no enemy. Dareck felt a surge of strength pass through his body, a strength which eased his nerves' inflammation and soothed the strain. He gave way to the pull of slumber, to the hands and the strength they held.

Returning to the present, Dareck opened his eyes and moved under the blanket.

Chapter 3

Jayel immediately looked up when the man stirred. She rose and went directly to the bed. For an awkward moment, neither spoke, each sizing up the other as friend or foe.

"How do you feel?" Jayel broke the silence. But she could already tell he was better than the time she first saw him on the ground. Color had returned to his face.

"Much stronger, thank you. Do I have the honor of addressing the person who rescued me?"

Jayel nodded.

"Well, I'm indebted to you."

"Are you hungry? May I get you something to eat or drink?"

"I'm famished. I can't remember when I last ate. Do I smell stew? Wonderful. Bring me some and then talk with me awhile."

Jayel hesitated. The authority in his voice surprised her. *Did he just order me?*

The stranger was sitting up when Jayel returned with a tray holding a half-filled bowl of stew and a glass of water. She could tell from his manners he wasn't a lost hermit, and she doubted he lived in Quintar. *Perhaps he came from Melandan or Characta.*

The man grew tired before he finished. He handed the bowl to her with thanks and immediately fell back asleep.

Conversation would wait.

The next morning, Jayel planned to bring him breakfast in bed, but the man said he felt strong enough to join her at the table. After he groomed and dressed in clothes she laid out, the stranger looked transformed from a ragged wanderer to the master of his home. Jayel approved of the change.

The man buttered a slice of bread and started the conversation. "Well, you enjoy many comforts here despite your isolation."

"Yes. The house is modern despite its age. Energy panels convert light for power, and I recently harvested a good crop of vegetables. The woods provide game and an endless supply of firewood."

Jayel reminded herself to not talk so freely. She didn't want to explain about the Endowed and how this house belonged to them. *Find out more about this stranger.* He certainly looked and acted like a friend. But his brown eyes penetrated her thoughts, and she felt the need to keep her defenses up. Jayel poured herself a cup of tea.

The stranger's voice took on an innocent tone. "You're here alone? When did you come?"

Something about him told her it could be dangerous to lie. Those brown eyes remained focused on her.

"About two standard years ago. The solitude appeals to me."

"I see. A long time to be alone."

After an awkward pause, Jayel shifted the conversation. "I'd like to know what happened to you yesterday. How did you end up unconscious in Denerow Woods?"

Dareck swallowed and leaned back. "It's a long story and not as interesting perhaps as how you came to live here."

"I doubt it."

Dareck nodded. He swiped jam on a piece of bread. "Well, it would seem we're reluctant to share our stories … and our names." He chewed thoughtfully. "It's amazing the information we convey in a name. I haven't told you mine, and you haven't told me yours. Are we guilty or hiding?"

Jayel stared at him to meet this accusation, but the stranger wasn't looking at her. She noted the use of "we." *What was he guilty of?*

"Well, we must learn more about each other. I conclude you don't know who I am, and you're afraid I will ask too many questions. Am I correct?"

Jayel nodded.

"Well, I know this is the House of Leidra, a house of the Endowed. Yes, I know its name. I see you do, too. But you aren't an Endowed member, are you?"

"No, I'm not."

Dareck paused for a long moment. He reached for a fruit and then peeled it.

Jayel drew in her breath as she anticipated what he was about to say—*he was an Endowed member.* It would explain the charisma—who else awakes in another's house and assumes the identity of the master? She glanced out the window and noticed the swirl of snowflakes against the windowpane. It snowed overnight and was still lightly snowing.

Dareck smiled warmly. "Well, I sense your reluctance to speak openly, and I understand it. From your perspective, it's I who am the intruder, and it's I who owes you explanations. Therefore, I'll be the first to reveal who I am and how I came to be here. In doing so, I hope I'll ease your suspicions. But whatever you choose to share with me about your background, don't lie to me." He accentuated these last words as a warning.

He picked up a knife, cut the peeled fruit into slices, and

offered Jayel one as he swallowed another. "I tracked an enemy into Denerow Woods from Quintar. I thought he might be meeting someone, but I found him alone. We argued, fought, and he injected me with a drug. He meant to kill me, but here I am, almost recovered, thanks to you."

"You're fortunate I was there to find you. With the weather changing, I won't be at the glade for a long time." Jayel smiled. "The medicine has helped, too. You look much better than yesterday. You possess remarkable recuperative powers." She poured two cups of hot tea.

"Yes, well, I am no ordinary man."

I should say not.

The man paused again. "I think more than chance brought us together." He lowered his voice. "I wonder if he was looking for you."

"Who?"

"The man I fought in the woods. General Chrysic."

"Chrysic!" Jayel exclaimed. He was her father's first in command and a dangerous man.

"Then you know him?"

"Who doesn't?" Jayel's thoughts raced.

The man closely watched her face. "Tell me, is it possible he planned to meet you? Would you welcome his arrival?"

"As of yesterday, I wouldn't have welcomed anyone's arrival."

Distressed about what could've happened had Chrysic found her, Jayel muttered, "I thought I was safe here. Chrysic's not a member of the Endowed."

"Hmm, well, neither are you, and yet here you are. The powers of the House of Leidra do prevent unwanted visitors from finding it. If Chrysic intended to come here, he wouldn't have found it. It's why he wandered in circles for days."

Jayel sipped her tea. "General Chrysic is a formidable opponent. You're lucky to escape."

The man looked directly into her eyes and firmly spoke, "I don't think it was luck. I think the general was only a lure to get me to come to this house. I was meant to find *you*."

Jayel raised an eyebrow. "Me? I don't see why. I still don't know your name."

He smiled warmly. "My name is Dareck, son of Harmond, member of the Endowed."

Jayel felt the blood drain from her face. She suspected the stranger was an Endowed member but didn't expect him to be her father's half-brother.

"You've heard of me, then?"

Jayel barely managed a nod. She studied the man's face. His hair was lighter than her father's, more brown than black, but she saw similarities now. Though twelve standard years younger than Karsch, they shared similar hairlines and chins. Maybe the nose and eyebrows were slightly different. Jayel remembered how his face had seemed familiar. Now she knew why.

"You needn't fear me," Dareck said. "How much do you know about the Endowed?"

"There is much written about them, of course."

Dareck stood and looked out the window. "We're a group of men and women trained in superior techniques. We serve the people to develop their potential. We're powerful, but our power isn't domination. Our power is competence and wisdom."

Dareck turned around and smiled. "We're proud of our service."

"I apologize, Dareck, for not recognizing you at once."

"Members of the Endowed are people, not gods. Try not

to look so upset."

"If I may ask, why were you interested in General Chrysic's affairs?'

Dareck sat next to her and confided, "I suspect he's mixed up in corrupt political dealings. I've watched him closely for many years."

"He works for your half-brother, Karsch, doesn't he?"

Dareck looked surprised. "Yes. I see you're familiar with my life. Most laypeople don't know we're half-brothers. We aren't close."

"Is your brother also involved in Chrysic's corrupt politics?"

"I'm concerned he may be."

"Karsch is a member of the Endowed, like yourself. The Endowed aren't corrupt. You must be mistaken." Jayel focused on her cup as she sipped the rest of the tea.

"Well, I fear Karsch has let his ambitions overcome his wisdom."

"With the training required to be an Endowed member, is this possible?"

"Everyone makes mistakes. He's influenced by General Chrysic, who is an ambitious man. I wish I knew why Chrysic was in Denerow Woods, land of the Endowed."

"Never did I expect to meet you, Dareck." Jayel stood and moved away as if with distance came strength for self-disclosure. "You need to know my name. I am Jayel, daughter of Karsch, your niece."

Chapter 4

Dareck raised his eyebrows. He hadn't suspected her identity. Perhaps Chrysic's drug affected his usual perceptiveness. Although she blocked her thoughts well, she spoke the truth.

He said, "I regret my strained relationship with my brother caused me not to know his daughter."

"I regret not knowing my uncle."

Dareck stood and placed his dishes in the sink. He returned to the table but remained standing across from his niece. "Who knows you are here?"

"No one."

"Do you think General Chrysic was looking for you?"

"I hope not, but it's possible."

Dareck sighed. "Well, there's much we need to talk about, Jayel. I'm convinced we were meant to meet here and get to know each other. I have many questions, but I grow tired. We'll talk later." He left the table, stretched out on the bed, and slept the rest of the day.

***

After a dinner of leftover stew, Jayel carried a tray with two cups and a pitcher to the recliners in front of the fireplace. Dareck settled in after getting the logs to catch flame.

As she poured, Dareck began their conversation. "I'm puzzled. You said earlier you're not a member of the Endowed, yet you are the daughter of an Endowed member. I don't understand why my brother didn't train you."

"Perhaps he tried when I was younger but found I wasn't any good at it. Birth alone doesn't qualify one for membership."

Dareck shook his head. "The Endowed are proud, and it's unheard of that the child didn't receive training. Of the things I know about you—your living here in a House of the Endowed, your being at the right place at the right time to find me, your decision not to leave me in the woods, your healing powers when you touched me, and your strength to carry me—all these portend Endowed potential. I urge you to get training and become a member of our esteemed organization."

Jayel handed Dareck the warm drink. He sipped. "An unusual, interesting taste."

"I modified an Endowed recipe. It seems one of the past residents specialized in herb lore. I've been growing several varieties and experimenting with them. The herb *xyilac* encourages the release of endorphins to help alleviate pain."

"Do you have a background in medicine?"

"I spent a standard year in medical school at the University of Mena before I came here."

Dareck continued to sip the drink. "I'm concerned you choose to live alone when you should be finishing your studies and enjoying an active social life."

"Procrastination, mostly. I have decisions to make and hoped the peace of Leidra would help the process." Jayel paused a long time and kept her eyes on the fire. "I don't know whether or not to oppose my father."

"Oppose him?"

His niece appeared reluctant to continue. Dareck sipped his drink again and waited for Jayel to explain. He commented, "Two standard years is a long time to be away."

"When you say it aloud, yes, two years is a long time. Yet sometimes it seems like I arrived only yesterday. I like the privacy here." She turned to look directly at him. "See, I didn't want General Chrysic or my father to know I was aware of their crime."

"Crime? What crime?" Dareck put his cup on the tray, sitting up straight, and fixed his eyes on her.

Jayel pushed her hair back as if the action could deflect his gaze. "I'd rather not say, Dareck."

"If you know about Karsch's involvement in criminal acts, you must tell the Endowed or planet authorities."

"What I know is hearsay, and I foresee a cascade of consequences if I make accusations without substance. It must be done right … with care."

"Perhaps if you confided in me the details, I could help your decision-making."

Jayel put her cup down. "If what I heard is true, *you* should be the one to make the accusation."

"Why? Because Karsch is my brother?"

Jayel remained silent.

Dareck waited. He sensed an internal struggle to share. His voice encouraged her. "You can tell me."

After a long pause, she whispered, "My father murdered your wife, Neondra."

Dareck leaned back in his chair and closed his eyes. Then, without opening them, he said, "How do you know?"

"I overheard my father and General Chrysic talking … I could hear but not see them. It sounded like they were reviewing pictures and papers. They spoke about Neondra's death being a murder, not an accident."

Dareck opened his eyes and fixed them on her. "What kinds of papers?"

"I don't know, exactly. Documents or records concerning her death, I assumed. General Chrysic said no one would see this evidence as long as they stayed silent about the murder."

Uncle and niece watched the flames in silence.

Then Dareck spoke. "Long have I hoped I could prove Neondra's death was murder. Will you help me obtain these papers?"

Jayel wiped a tear from her cheek and sighed. "I believe you were meant to come here and prod me to act. I will help you."

***

Dareck remained in the recliner long after Jayel retired upstairs. The room was dark, save a weak yellow glow from the last log. He closed his eyes, relaxed his muscles, and allowed his thoughts to wander through interplanetary space. His awareness transcended the golden-echoed darkness of his eyelids. His mind contacted his apprentice on the planet Melandan.

"Ranthal."

"Mentor Dareck?" answered the young Endowed member, looking up from a desk as he worked on a report.

"Are you busy, my friend?" The shadow on the wall was long, but Ranthal's blue eyes were alert, and his smile genuine. Dareck noted the growth in his apprentice. When they would next meet, he would greet a master.

"Never for you, Dareck. I'm glad you checked in. But you sound tired. Are you ill?"

"I had a run-in with General Chrysic. I'm recovering well."

Ranthal searched Dareck's face with concern. "Where are you?"

"I'm safe at the House of Leidra. Chrysic traveled alone to the planet Leidran. I found him lost in Denerow Woods."

"Alone, on Leidran … without his armed guards," echoed Ranthal.

"Not a one. There is more. I found Jayel, daughter of Karsch, staying at the House."

Ranthal answered with interest. "I had forgotten your brother had a daughter. Let me see, about my age, isn't she?"

"Yes, a few standard years older. She came to my aid after my encounter with the general."

"Interesting. I don't recall her initiation into the membership. Tell me, Dareck, what is she like?"

"Jayel is a strong woman, a healer. But she is cautious, hard to read her thoughts even though not trained in the ways of the Endowed. I don't know much about my niece yet. In a few days, we will hike to Quintar, Leidran's only city. I'm not feeling a hundred percent, but I can handle the challenge. The weather, thanks to satellites, should be manageable despite the planet's move toward winter. This pristine land is beautiful, and its powers are restorative. I expect we'll arrive in the city within two weeks."

"It amazes me," laughed Ranthal, "how the fastest flyer in both systems can find pleasure hiking through desolate woods. It's why I love you, my mentor. You're full of refreshing paradoxes."

"Well, I'm not the only one. You revel in paradoxes, too, Ranthal."

"Really, Dareck, I think you know too much."

"It always seems this way to everyone but me."

They shared a laugh.

Ranthal sobered. "I wish you well, Dareck. But keep up your guard. Remember, she's the daughter of a man you don't trust."

As Dareck nodded, Ranthal signed off, "Health and wisdom, Dareck."

"To you also, Ranthal."

The image of his apprentice faded, and Dareck opened his eyes to find the room dark, save a shaft of moonbeam which pierced a frosted window. He rose from the chair and wearily slipped into bed.

His thoughts drifted to the last time he came to the House of Leidra, with Neondra, a lifetime ago, when everything about her enthralled him. Neondra's long hair cupped her breasts, and her smile swallowed his spirit. Dareck clung to the image, savoring it, and then let go. Time to focus on the future.

Chapter 5

The day before their departure, Jayel organized clothes and supplies to pack. Dareck returned from upstairs holding an armful of items.

"We can use this lightweight, portable heater when we camp." Dareck handed her the small unit. It weighed less than she expected. *Leave it to the Endowed to have the ideal gear.* She added it to the pile.

"These will come in handy, too. Better than sleeping bags."

Jayel took two tightly rolled blankets and placed one by each backpack. "Are we allowed to take these items from the House? I doubt we will be returning them."

"Yes, we may take them. I saw you left containers of seeds, canned vegetables, and fruits from your summer's harvest. You made a good trade."

Dareck walked to the table and glanced at a large, unfolded paper map. "I'm sure you found supplies never run out."

"I suppose. You're looking at the map I brought to help find this House," Jayel said, walking over to him. "I expect we want to find a direct route back to Quintar."

Her uncle nodded. "I'm curious, Jayel, how you learned about the House of Leidra and discovered its location. It's said no one can find the House unless one is an Endowed member."

"I read about it in a book years ago. Then, as I packed to leave my father's estate, the House of Leidra came to mind. I found this paper map in our estate's collection. I wasn't sure if my pad would work in the woods, and when it didn't, the map helped keep my sense of direction. From what you told me, though, I was lucky to have found the House because its precise location isn't marked."

"Hmm." Dareck studied the route she plotted two years ago from Quintar. "More than luck guided you here, or else you would have gotten lost in the uninhabited woods like our friend, General Chrysic." He folded the map. "Fortunately, I know a direct route to Quintar. With good supplies and my feeling close to a hundred percent, I estimate we'll need only a week to get there if the weather holds. A week to get to know each other better."

***

Early the next morning they set out on paths Jayel knew well from her two-year stay. By afternoon, they traversed the snowline and found a good pace over dry ground. Jayel felt sad to leave the House of Leidra behind but enjoyed the sights, sounds, and smells of Denerow Woods. The clover left a minty aroma. The breeze rustled autumnal leaves still hanging on branches, and small animals scampered among fallen leaves and ferns.

During a stop by a stream, Jayel caught a glimpse of the gaseous planet, Kelpar, low near the horizon. She pointed it out to Dareck. The light wouldn't be so bright again until its next transit.

"It took a long time for astronomers to agree Leidran was a planet and not a moon of Kelpar," Dareck remarked as they resumed their hike. "And even longer until technology allowed Leidran to support life. Without our complex satellite network controlling the northern hemisphere, the planet is much too cold and the gravity too weak for life. The city, Quintar, is the planet's only controlled environment."

"How did the Endowed get to own much of Leidran's land?"

"The first geological explorer was an Endowed member named Najule. He spent decades on Leidran in those early days. Najule built the House of Leidra and planted trees in Denerow Woods with seeds and saplings from several planets and helped them thrive. He worked diligently to breed them to thrive in Leidran's environment.

"Najule planted the grand pine tree, then a tender sapling, where you found me. The tree, legend says, took on its magnificence when he died, growing to the height and beauty you see today. Najule's spirit lives."

"And the cottage?"

"The land of Leidra is food for the soul, and the House provides respite and renewal. Only members of the Endowed know its precise location."

Jayel nodded. "Maybe its location is becoming forgotten. Members don't seem to use the House anymore. No one came while I was there … except you."

"Hmm, maybe. Leidran's location is ideal for four months of a standard year when the planet is uniquely positioned between the two systems. As the people of Onus One moved to tame the planets of Onus Two, the Endowed donated a large chunk of land for the System to build Quintar. The city serves as a relay station for travelers and commercial supply exchanges."

"I'm surprised people inside Quintar's city limits don't wander and explore Denerow Woods. It was difficult finding my way out of the city."

Dareck shook his head. "Quintarians respect the land of the Endowed and don't dare pollute it. It's against the law to leave city limits—unless you are Endowed—even to fly around for aerial tours of Denerow Woods. All spaceships enter and leave by the south."

Uncle and niece made camp when the sunlight faded. The portable unit heated the air, and a small fire provided light. Dinner consisted of fresh game supplemented with vegetables from the House of Leidra's garden.

When Jayel sat on the folded blanket Dareck added to their supplies, she smiled, delighted and surprised. The material responded to pressure like a mattress, and it felt warm, too. She relaxed and stared into the campfire.

Dareck sipped hot tea and leaned against his backpack, watching Jayel. When she returned his attentive stare, he said, "I'm concerned you have no training in Endowed ways."

Jayel looked down and finished sanitizing the plate. "I believe most members complete training in childhood, and their skills become part of their natural development."

"True, but there is no age requirement. I encourage you to begin training now."

"What does training involve? If I agreed, where would I start?"

"Well," her uncle replied thoughtfully, "I would lean towards practicing mental discipline. You already possess some skill. Too often we don't attend to our surroundings. Not everyone would look up at the sky and see Kelpar. You did. Start there and improve your concentration and attention."

"Yes, I would value improving my powers of attention. At medical school, patients who lost the ability to control their attention due to head trauma were easily frustrated and had difficulty with daily routine tasks."

Dareck added, "Endowed training will give you tools, and your frequent practice will reduce effort and cognitive strain when you use them."

"What would I have to do if I wanted to improve my mental discipline?"

"I can give you specific exercises. They require daily practice, but we have days until we reach Quintar. Some you can practice at rest stops and others while we walk. After this week, judge whether you want to continue."

Dareck pulled out a *borrell*, opened it, and took out a small, hexagonal-shaped object, smooth and dark, dotted with tiny, colored spots. It reflected the campfire light in myriad ways, like a prism.

"Let's see how good your concentration is. On this side, there is one pink design among all the others. No other shape on this side is pink. Find it."

"Sounds easy enough," Jayel said taking the object, "unless there isn't a pink shape to be found, and this is a test of how long I will persist on a hopeless task." Jayel caught Dareck's stern expression and sobered.

The tiny and close-spaced designs splashed randomly against a black field. Jayel saw various colors, but not pink. Shades contrasted, creating an illusion of pink until she looked deeper, and the color wasn't pink. She searched from corner to corner, top to bottom. No pink. She scanned again. About to give up, the background turned a lighter shade, and the contrast made the designs stand out, floating in the forefront, as if space separated them from the background. They grew slowly in size and brightness, then moved rapidly, floating, and swirling in a green-gray turbulent sea.

"There's something wrong with my eyes," Jayel murmured, and she closed them, knitting her eyebrows. The shapes danced before the darkness of her eyelids and then disappeared. All went black again.

"Open your eyes," Dareck said.

The object she held looked the same as when Dareck gave it to her, dark. Jayel handed it back to him.

"No pink," Jayel sighed, feeling she failed.

"I would be surprised if you found it the first time. For some trainees, it takes twenty trials. Tell me what you saw."

"About every color but pink. When the shapes began swirling, I had to close my eyes—it was too confusing; I felt cross-eyed and a little nauseous."

Dareck didn't look displeased and smiled instead. "Good. You have done well on your first attempt. When your concentration is stronger you will be able to keep your eyes focused, and you'll find the pink design … for I assure you it's there."

Dareck placed the hexagon back into the *borrell.* "You'll try again tomorrow." He yawned and wrapped himself in the blanket. "We've done well for our first day. See you in the morning. Good night."

Finding the heater provided enough warmth, Jayel poured water on the campfire. In the darkness, she unfolded the blanket and lay down. Indeed, it was firm like a mattress underneath and soft and warm like a comforter above her body. She put all worries out of mind and slept well.

***

Two days before reaching Quintar, the woods thinned to mostly birches and *malaches,* wildflowers. Their hike progressed smoothly without problems. Jayel felt more comfortable with her uncle and wanted to know more about his past.

"How long did you live on Orim, Dareck?"

"Until age fifteen. I studied at Orim's Northern Academy and joined an apprenticeship program where I gained experience at first-rate institutions across Onus One—the University of Ismus for physics, Cardan for ancient cultures, and Zyntarn for political science.

"But when I was eighteen, my father, Harmond, encouraged me to return to Orim, to home. It didn't take much persuasion. At the time, my father was a prominent figure in the Endowed organization, and I cherished working together."

"Our culture promotes children to be independent early," Jayel interjected, "to find a career and leave family behind. Many children on Melandan leave home by age ten, try out two apprenticeships, and then start a career."

"Well, soon after working with my father, we traveled to Melandan to attend a formal celebration being held for my brother who had been appointed Lieutenant Governor. At the gala, I met Neondra, the daughter of Ristan. When she entered the room, dressed in a stunning dark red gown, everyone's eyes were drawn to her." Dareck paused, eyes distant with a touch of moisture as if reliving the memory. "The light on her hair, her skin … Neondra was very beautiful."

"How romantic." Jayel mused. "You didn't know Neondra before then?"

"No. When our eyes locked that night, I knew we would marry. She was a member of the Endowed, and they say the love bond between two members is stronger than magnetic poles. We married months later. My parents were happy for us, but Karsch wasn't enthusiastic about our union."

"If I'm following the timeline, my father was already married to my mother when you married. I wonder why my father objected to your marriage."

"Well, it wasn't because he disapproved of her. In fact, Karsch already knew Neondra before I met her. They worked together at a biological research facility before he chose to pursue a political career, and I think he had a favorable impression of her. Though he disapproved, he didn't protest our marriage, but ...well, I think he ended it." Dareck's voice trailed off.

Jayel sympathized but remained confused. "I still don't understand how he could've done such a thing, commit murder. I've witnessed him risk his life for others ... stepping forward when others hung back. I don't understand the hostility between my father and you. Were you never close?"

Dareck clasped his hands. "Well, we didn't grow up together as he started his apprenticeships soon after I was born, so I didn't see him often. But perhaps we grew furthest apart after my marriage. I think my son's birth flared his jealousy. You see, my brother and I share the same father but different mothers. His mother was a commoner and mine an Endowed. Thus, I am the son of two Endowed members, and he is the son of one. My son, the child of two Endowed members, and his daughter, the child of only one."

Jayel looked at Dareck. "If Endowed membership meant so much to him, why didn't he marry a member of the Endowed? Why did he marry my mother?"

"His marriage to Mandel was arranged. Her father at the time was Governor of Melandan, a position Karsch holds now. Your mother's betrothal secured your father's political future."

Jayel said nothing. Something about her uncle's picture of her father didn't sit comfortably. But jealousy is a powerful emotion, and this would not be the first time it overrode reason. What Dareck said could be true. Yet, "jealous" wasn't a word she would use to describe her father. But then, neither was "murderer." The sting of betrayal, not knowing her father as she thought, made it difficult to think through the situation.

"I know your father is a brilliant and admired man," Dareck continued. "But in recent years, his political ambitions dominated his actions. I'm afraid he currently is escalating war in the Onus Two system, where his entanglements are getting nasty. I don't trust him or General Chrysic who does his bidding."

"War? I thought all the planets were at peace." Jayel felt dismayed.

"Ondre's young development was rushed, and two cities sprouted too close to each other. They fight over scarce resources and their mismanagement."

Jayel looked away. "Returning from a retreat is harder than I anticipated. I didn't realize my father might be causing problems for others."

"Only suspicions, I don't know for sure." Dareck sighed. He looked Jayel in the eye, and warned, "Getting the evidence of Neondra's murder and dealing with the consequences won't be easy for you."

Jayel shuddered as a stiff breeze pushed her hair back, chilling an exposed neck. She tightened her scarf. "I won't lie, Dareck. I am afraid of what might happen, but it's time to stop running."

Chapter 6

On the morning of their seven-day hike, Jayel saw the skyline of Quintar on the horizon. Eight hours later, its great height towered before them. When she left two years ago, Jayel never looked back to view its massive structure, but now the engineering marvel amazed her.

The well-designed city consisted of six levels above the ground and five below occupying two hundred square kilometers. From a distance, the layers lacked symmetry—a stratum's height was narrow in one part and tall in another. Throughout the city, urban designers scattered zones of natural light on every tier, including vast open spaces for parks and a small artificial ocean. A tall, thick stone wall surrounded the city, protecting residents within an encapsulated weather-controlled environment.

Jayel periodically could hear the roar of spaceships. Lights appeared in building windows as nightfall approached, but eventually, as they neared the city at twilight's ending, she could only see the imposing wall around the base.

Dareck guided her to the southwestern side. The stonework offered no entry points Jayel could see.

"It's a good thing you're here, Dareck, because two years ago I didn't think about getting back in. I focused on getting out. When I left, I rappelled over the wall."

"Not a bad idea, given sturdy rock surrounds the ground base and the city's few doors are always locked. Do you remember where you performed this feat?"

"I think I left on the east side of the city." Jayel paused. "You don't think the rope still dangles, do you?"

"Even if it is, it's on the other side and would take nearly a day to walk around Quintar's base. I have a different plan, and it doesn't involve rope climbing."

"Good, but I'm getting tired of walking."

"I want to enter the city unnoticed in case General Chrysic arrived before us. I prefer he didn't know I've returned or learn we're together. I know a secret way to enter unseen."

Dareck pointed to a section of the jagged boulders in the wall. "Between those two vertical gray stones, there's an entrance leading to the first sublevel of the city. It takes us near the warehouses. There shouldn't be any workers on the streets at this hour."

Jayel scanned the façade. Though well blended, she saw one rock was different from the others. "I think I can see the door's edge."

"Good. Your Endowed exercises are working already."

His trainee smiled. "Where do we go once we get in?"

As they approached the wall, Dareck said, "I know many people in Quintar. This fact is good and bad. If Chrysic arrived before us, he'll have people watching for me."

Jayel wondered what Chrysic would do if he found her. She felt a wave of fear.

"Do you feel all right?"

"What? Oh, yes. Just thinking about Chrysic, what could've happened if he found me before you did."

Dareck laid his hand on her shoulder. "I will protect you from now on."

His niece smiled.

"Do you know anyone in Quintar?" Dareck asked.

"No, I don't think so. I told no one about my coming to Leidran, and I spent only a day in Quintar without using my name."

"Good. I know a woman who will give us rooms tonight and not tell anyone we're staying there."

At the mention of a female friend, Jayel imagined a tall, dark, voluptuous young vixen. Given Dareck's status, good looks, and wealth, she suspected her uncle knew many women in every city on every planet in the Onus One and Onus Two systems.

Her uncle watched her expression and laughed. "She's an old mother *brearl*, who looks after me when I stop over between systems. We've been friends since my early student days."

They walked up to the quoin in the wall. Dareck pressed several areas in a preset pattern, and an unseen door in the rockface suddenly opened.

Jayel peered into the dark opening. "I feel like we're breaking in."

"We are. This entrance violates Quintar's law."

They slipped in, and the door closed. Darkness enveloped them, darker than outside, where at least the glow of city lights bounced off the clouds and brightened the landscape.

Gradually low-intensity lighting reduced the darkness. A long featureless hall on a slight decline spread before them.

Dareck said, "Programming brightens the passageway after the door opens. In five minutes, it'll darken again. Let's be quick." He led the way, and Jayel followed closely.

When Jayel looked back, the doorway had vanished into darkness. The light around them lasted long enough to see a few steps ahead of them, then faded. They walked for some time without encountering any clues as to where they were. The air felt chilly but not icy, and the concrete walls were silent, echoless. Jayel felt them closing in on her, and an image of suffocation crossed her mind.

"What's wrong?" Dareck stopped and turned around.

"After being outside for so long, this passage makes me feel claustrophobic."

"We're almost there."

Dareck continued walking, and Jayel shadowed. *Focus, hold it together.*

Minutes later, they came to a door, but Dareck didn't immediately open it. He stood listening to the sounds beyond. Jayel couldn't hear anything. Dareck stood very still. Then, the light around them darkened and she could no longer see Dareck in front of her.

"Leave our camping gear here," whispered Dareck. "I will arrange for someone to retrieve it tomorrow. I'd rather make our way through the city without backpacks."

They leaned their gear against the wall. Dareck opened the door, and they stepped out. Orange energy-saving streetlights revealed silent, empty sidewalks. Dareck closed the door and pressed an unseen lock.

"Follow me," he whispered. "Walk close and take my arm, as if we're lovers. Chrysic's spies likely won't be searching for a couple. Nonetheless, we'll take an indirect route."

Jayel reached for his arm, closing the gap between them, and followed his lead as he started walking. She focused on his body's movements and turned when he did as if knowing where they were going. *Almost like dancing.*

They walked beside three-story warehouses serving as storage and distribution centers for the city above. After moving up a hill, they came to a bridge crossing a waterway, and, after passing more buildings which led to an elevator.

Metal crashed and reverberated.

They turned sharply to find a cat jumping out of a storage bin. Jayel suppressed a laugh and felt Dareck's arm relax again.

She hoped they were nearing the end of their travel. They arrived at a commuter platform, and soon after, the tubular-shaped, high-speed train arrived. After entering, Jayel found it clean though, obviously several decades old, and sparsely occupied. Dareck chose seats behind a young man and woman.

Jayel felt relief to sit down again. They hadn't rested from walking since their afternoon meal. From signage on the buildings, she guessed they were now on the east side of the city.

Five minutes later, the train arrived at a platform. Dareck stood and led Jayel to the door. A couple from the other end of the car also got off. Dareck waited and watched them walk away before he guided Jayel down the street.

"It won't be long now," her uncle encouraged as Jayel tightened her scarf.

They walked two blocks through a residential neighborhood built in older-style architecture, two-story row homes with windows on either side of the front door and centered on the second floor. Small hedges and flower gardens adorned each building's entranceway.

"Look at the detail in the stonework," Jayel commented. "Images like you might see in park fountains."

They reached Dareck's intended destination. He pressed the buzzer on a green steel door of an all-brick house. Despite the late hour, the lock turned soon.

When the door opened, Jayel heard a soft voice. "Oh, it's you, Master Dareck. Come in, come in." The voice added, "And you've brought a lady friend."

Jayel smiled. Their host stepped aside, and they entered. In the foyer's lighting, Jayel got a good view of the woman. She was stocky, about 75 standard years old, and her blonde and gray-streaked hair was pulled back into a hairnet. She wore white pajamas with a red flannel housecoat, folded tissues sticking out of its pockets, and fuzzy slippers. Her blue eyes were vital and warm. Jayel took an immediate liking to her.

Dareck made the introductions.

"Jayel, this is Kathzerum Elesh. Kath, this is Jayel, my niece."

"Your *niece*!" The woman said, sounding half disappointed, half-surprised. "And here I thought you had found a new wife, Master Dareck."

Jayel blushed, and Dareck appeared slightly uncomfortable. Kathzerum looked keenly at them. Jayel pushed her hair back, wishing she had taken time to comb it before their arrival.

"Your niece, you say?"

The woman's expression relayed she knew about Dareck's relationship with his brother. Jayel smiled, hoping to allay any negative feelings Kathzerum might feel toward her.

"There's a story here, no doubt. But come, the hour is late, and stories can wait until later." Kathzerum Elesh locked the door.

"Thank you, Kath." Dareck kissed the woman's right cheek. "We're no trouble, I hope?"

"None at all. Never for you, Dareck, you know that."

The elderly woman led them up the moving walkway to the second floor. Two beautiful porcelain lamps lit the long and narrow hallway. Jayel thought they might be imports from the planet Orim.

They stopped at the third door. "This will be your room, Jayel," Kathzerum said, then turned to Dareck. "Yours is, as always, the one around the corner."

After saying goodnight, Jayel entered the bedroom. Spacious, it appeared freshly cleaned. The antique furniture gave the room a certain elegance. She found snacks and juice on the table as if Kathzerum Elesh expected guests.

Jayel stretched out on the bed, her back and feet relieved. Eventually, she got up and explored the room while chewing an apple-like fruit. The closet and drawers were full of clothes, and the private bathroom was fully stocked.

She enjoyed a long, hot shower and washed away the journey's dust. After changing into provided pajamas, Jayel slipped under the covers. The faint voices of Dareck and Kathzerum could be heard through the wall. She fell asleep before deciding to listen.

***

Jayel woke early, being used to getting up by sunrise. She slipped on a one-piece loungewear from the closet and went down to the first floor quietly, planning to repay her host's kindness by making breakfast for the three of them. But, upon entering the kitchen, Jayel found Kathzerum setting the table. The smells of frying eggs and meat, toasted bread, and coffee filled the room. Jayel couldn't keep her exclamation silent. "Yumm."

Kathzerum Elesh laughed. "Have a seat, dear. You're in for a treat. I'm the best cook this side of the system."

Jayel watched Kathzerum retrieve a tray of pastries from the oven and proceed to add icing. "May I help?"

"No, everything's ready. Please, enjoy." Kathzerum placed the pastries on the table and selected items for her plate.

Jayel sat and ogled the assortment of foods. She sampled every bowl and serving plate. All the tastes were delicious and satisfying. As she reached for a second pastry, Dareck entered the kitchen and greeted his host with a kiss.

"Good morning, Jayel," Dareck said. He sat between the two women and immediately filled his plate.

"Mmmppph," Jayel, mouth full, returned her uncle's greeting.

Finishing a pastry, Dareck smiled warmly at Kathzerum. "These turnovers taste marvelous, Kath. You must share your secret recipes with me." He leaned over towards Jayel and commented, "She never does."

Jayel added her compliments while smiling and swallowing. "You *are* the best cook this side of the system, Kathzerum. And this kitchen, I'm stunned. I see three ovens, two stovetops, two huge refrigerators, and three islands for workspace—indeed, the kitchen of a master chef."

Dareck finished his coffee. "Are these coffee beans from Ondre? A unique flavor, for sure. Yes, this breakfast surpasses your past ones, which I didn't think possible. I can hardly wait for lunch."

Kathzerum Elesh appeared pleased by their compliments. In a voice feigning humility, she said, "Thank you, both. Naturally, when two starved dogs show up at my door, anything would taste good to them. But now that they're sated, we'll see what they think of lunch."

“I can’t wait,” Dareck said, standing. “But, until then, I need to go out and assess the situation.”

Chapter 7

"May I help you clean up?" Jayel asked as Kathzerum stood and gathered the breakfast leftovers.

The elderly woman pointed to her left. "The dishes go in the sanitizer."

Jayel lined the dishes on the belt and pressed the button. The glass door slid closed. An arm extended and secured the items, and a second mechanism scraped all residue from the plates and flatware. After the crumbs were cleared to a back trough, the belt moved further along. Hot water laced with detergent power-washed all items as the arm rotated 360 degrees. A blast of heated air finished the job. The arms retracted, and the glass door slid open.

Kathzerum removed the dry items and returned them to cabinet storage, all but one cup. This one she placed on the table. "I'll brew a new batch of coffee while you go up and dress. No need to wear your traveling clothes today. Please, help yourself to anything in your closet."

"Very kind of you, Kathzerum. Are you sure it's no trouble?"

"My pleasure, dear." The elderly host smiled and paused. "When you come down, you might enjoy catching up on the news. I own state-of-the-art electronics, and Quintar's network connects to both systems."

A brief time later, Jayel returned to the first floor. She wore a loose-fitting blue tunic, brown slacks, and open-back shoes.

"In here," called her host.

Jayel entered the den, a large circular windowless room. Kathzerum finished pouring coffee and placed the cup on a table adjacent to the computer console. Several monitors displayed default home screens.

"Although I'm retired, I maintain access to numerous databases, universities, and news sites from both star systems." The woman pointed at the multiple screens. "You can run various applications on separate monitors or within the same screen. These are your visual and auditory controls, plus keyboard and voice commands. I tend to sit close, but your vision might be better than mine. Extend the table this way."

After Kathzerum pressed a lever, a wood surface extended from the wall. Jayel rolled a chair to it and carried over her coffee cup.

"I didn't realize until now how I missed being connected. I'm grateful, thank you, Kathzerum." Jayel put on wireless earpieces and sat.

"You have anonymous guest access," the woman continued. "But until we hear from Master Dareck, I suggest not doing any searches that might alert people to your whereabouts. Personal correspondence should wait."

"I understand."

"I need to go to the market to pick up fresh items for today's meal. Here's how to contact me if the need arises." Kathzerum pointed to an icon on a monitor and, when Jayel nodded, moved to the door, and left.

For two years, she hadn't missed the outside world but now felt eager to read the news. Jayel activated the local news site,

The Quintar Reporter, first. Jayel scanned major headlines of recent months. Short news videos played on the upper screens while she read text eye-level on the lower monitors.

Scans reviewed quite a flap concerning the war between Catana and Marshe in the Onus Two system. A few months ago, after the governor of Ondre's assassination, mayhem and battles escalated. Interestingly, despite the civil war, trade and travel between Ondre and other planets appeared strong.

Jayel remembered Dareck's comment about her father's possible involvement in the war. She requested photographs and paragraphs of top stories from Ondre's news site, *The Post.* Multiple photos instantly appeared on one window, and their linked stories lined up on another, making for easy side-by-side reading. The dual windows made for independent scrolling and zooming in for visibility when needed.

Yes, General Chrysic attended the governor's state funeral. Jayel searched further back. A dated video showed Chrysic on Ondre days before the assassination. After further searching, Jayel learned the general visited Ondre, specifically the city of Marshe, four times in the two standard months before the murder. *Why would he travel so far from Melandan four times in two months?* She could see why Dareck held suspicions of his brother's involvement. Karsch, through General Chrysic, might be influencing the outcome of the war or trying to gain the winner's support. *Having allies on Ondre would strengthen her father's power in the Onus Two system.* However, she found no evidence her father had visited the planet.

With additional scrolling through news items, Jayel discovered Dareck visited Ondre at least once a standard year for many years. She didn't know why he was interested in the planet—perhaps he traveled annually to all the planets in Onus Two.

What do I know about my uncle? A biographical sketch listed accomplishments in astrophysics, excellent piloting skills, and ongoing research projects with four think tanks. Although he didn't hold a political office like her father, government officials on every planet sought Dareck's advice. He influenced their decision-making. She noted that across images taken throughout the years, no woman appeared twice. He apparently never had a long relationship after Neondra, at least not publicly.

Moving away from the local press, she opened news sites from her home planet, Melandan. Articles prominently covered her father's achievements. As governor, he attended state functions and negotiated deals with major businesses to assuage economic concerns. Jayel nodded approval for his support of scientific research. More than a few agencies credited the governor's policies for Melandanians' high quality of life. She didn't see much in the news to suggest the war on Ondre concerned the inhabitants.

Other news focused on improvements to lower-level orbiting weather satellites. Many were over 100 standard years old and starting to malfunction. For the most part, errors caused only minor deviations from programming, but last month a cluster controlling the southeast continent allowed snow to pile up in city streets. Typically snow reserves are collected in rural areas. Scholars hoped replacement technology would include better atmosphere collectors to manage sulfur emissions from two active volcanoes. The planet's environmental commission pushed for the satellites' speedy manufacturing and installation. A recruitment call solicited volunteers to man the factories.

Jayel paused and finished her coffee. Melandan's volunteer employment system worked well. People rarely got bored because they could volunteer for diverse projects rather than work in dead-end jobs. The word "job" was becoming an archaic word. Starting early, children apprenticed to discover their interests, skills, and talents. Social altruistic practices became institutionalized and a way of life. People thrived in seeing projects finished. Jayel had no doubt the satellites would be replaced within a year.

Through Melandan's University of Oia site, Jayel learned her mother maintained an active work schedule doing anthropological research. The current project placed her on the other side of the continent from her father's estate. *I'm not surprised.* Both parents often lived and worked apart for extended periods.

Done with news sites for now, Jayel searched the graduates from the medical program at the University of Mena, specifically searching for the name Dorind Saerskind. A beep indicated he didn't graduate. Jayel frowned, checking her estimate again. He should've graduated by now. Something went wrong with Dory's plans.

A pang of guilt caused Jayel to shift her balance and lean back in the chair. It had been hard leaving Dory behind. Her departure had been sudden, but Jayel believed Dory understood. He should be busy completing his medical degree, and his lover's absence would help him focus. Surely, she wasn't the cause of his failure to graduate.

Dory will be the first person I contact when I can. She longed for his arms to hold her again. *We'll be together soon.*

Six fellow students graduated, and they were now working in medical centers scattered across the Onus One system.

A scan of Melandan's public social media displayed the milestones of childhood friends now young adults—several babies born, one untimely death from a fall, and many proud achievements. Jayel's youngest friend, Karden, won systems acclaim for an orchestral score. She was commissioned to write a piece for the next systems' Governor's Council.

Jayel stopped reading and began feeling the passage of time. *What have I done in two years?*

At that moment, Dareck walked into the den. "Not bad news, I hope?"

Jayel turned around and shrugged. "You caught me feeling guilty for not working these past two years."

He nodded but added, "You'll be contributing soon. No more watching from the sidelines."

They exchanged smiles.

Jayel stood. "Have you word of Chrysic's whereabouts?"

"Well, the general is in Quintar. I haven't found out where he's staying. However, he scheduled his private ship to arrive today."

"What does that mean for us? Do we leave before him or after?"

Kathzerum walked in as Jayel spoke these last words. "I hope you can stay at least one more day, master Dareck."

"Might be two days, Kath."

"Good," the elderly woman smiled. "I have a seafood lunch waiting. Let's put off making plans until you've sampled the best Quintar has to offer."

The three went to the kitchen. Kathzerum served them white chowder, hard-shellfish salad, and baked flatfish.

"Kath, you spoil me. The seasoning on this fish is better than I've ever tasted," Dareck said, kissing her cheek.

The elderly woman beamed. "I enjoy trying out new recipes. The *charmike* was flown in alive from Uamong."

After they emptied every serving dish and plate, Dareck pushed away from the table. "I'll be busy for the rest of the day and probably tomorrow." He turned to Jayel. "I'm sure Kath will keep you company while I'm out."

Kathzerum lowered her coffee cup and frowned. "A young woman like Jayel should get out, Dareck. I understand the need for caution, but I'm sure she can go somewhere without fear of being spotted by the general's spies. They are looking for *you*, not her."

"I agree, Kath. It's up to you, Jayel. Away so long, you may be eager to see Quintar. Maybe go listen to live music at a pub or see a show."

"I could go with you if you like," Kathzerum offered.

Jayel suppressed a laugh at the idea of a 75-standard-year-old escort. "Thank you, Kathzerum, but I don't need a babysitter or a security guard. A pub does sound inviting."

"I recommend *The Thirsty Boots*." Kathzerum looked at Dareck. "It's a nearby tavern, small, but has a local band each night. The clientele is mostly neighborhood residents."

Dareck nodded. "Small and local sounds good. Very well, but keep a low profile, Jayel." He reached into his pocket and pulled out a phone wallet. "Use this cash card for expenses and this phone if you need to contact me."

"You'll find appropriate clothes in your closet, Jayel." Kathzerum added, "And here's a key to my house. No need to knock. Just let yourself in."

"Live music after two years of digital, a delightful way to return to city life. What could go wrong?"

Chapter 8

From a dimly lit corner of the tavern's lounge, he watched Jayel enter and choose a booth towards the back, off to the side of the dance floor and sound stage. A wise choice, he thought. She could see the room but not be seen by others whose focus would be on the stage or bar. Not unlike his decision to deflect attention. His dark work clothes and overcoat draped over his shoulders blended in with the clientele, indistinct, and not worth anyone's attention.

Before seven, most customers in *The Thirsty Boots* came directly from work before going home. It was six o'clock, and two small groups occupied tables in the middle of the room. Two men sipped drinks seated apart at the bar. A small crowd for now.

The band, comprised of the typical assembly of four-octave wood strings, one six-octave metal strings, one reed wind, an electronic laptop, and a set of *plantar* drums—finished testing their equipment and started to play. The lead singer had a good voice. She warmed up the crowd with two songs, and soon most sitting at the tables were on the dance floor, laughing and enjoying the fast-paced rhythms.

The two men at the bar didn't seem to notice the change in activity, but instead stared into the mirror behind the bar, outwardly lost in their thoughts.

The man watched one of the tavern's two servers, a woman in her thirties, approach Jayel's table.

"What can I get you?"

"I'll have an Orim Orbit."

"Tonight's two for one. One tall glass, okay?"

Jayel smiled. "Sure. Add a bowl of salted bread chunks, too." She handed her the cash card Dareck gave her.

The server pressed it on the pad, returned it, and left. Jayel sat back and watched the dancers.

From his position, the man could tell Jayel was used to sitting alone by how comfortable and unassuming she looked. Had he not been looking out for Dareck's niece he might not have noticed her.

Her mind was closed to him. He could read everyone else in the room. Good. Her guard was up. However, the man didn't need to be a mind reader to see the young woman enjoyed the music. Jayel sat as if bathing in a waterfall of music on a hot summer's day, soaked and lathered in the notes.

After the server placed the blue foamy drink and a bowl of salted bread chunks on Jayel's table, she walked to his booth and asked if he wanted a refill.

She scrolled the bar tabs on her pad. "What's your name again?"

"Mick." Not his real name, but it was the one on his cash card.

"Gotcha. Another ale?"

"Yes, please."

The night shift came on at 7:30. The ordinary lighting darkened, and vibrant colored bulbs along the cornices cast a splash of color against the glasses and well-lacquered tables. The booths filled with couples of various ages. Three female servers, wearing flashier, sexier clothing than the "after work" shift circled the crowded pub. The band played a mix of contemporary music from across the systems to encourage more dancing, drinking, and merriment.

The two men sitting at the bar remained when the after-work patrons went home, but a third man soon entered and sat between them. Mick briefly attended to their thoughts. The man on the left worried about a problem with recent imports. The man on the right needed to choose between two lovers, his wife and his boss. The new arrival was worried about his young wife. She wanted to leave Quintar before the planet moved farther away from the orbits of the inner planets, and she would be stuck, her words, on this frontier post, also his wife's words, for another eight months. He wanted to stay because business was good.

A conscious warning caused Mick to return his attention to Jayel. Her posture didn't seem as relaxed as before. He saw Jayel's eyes follow one of the new servers. Despite the lighting, Mick caught recognition and concern in her eyes.

The man studied the server of interest, who seemed oblivious to Jayel's attention. The woman wore a dark blue sparkle shirt and a tight skirt with skin-tight boots hugging her lower thighs. She wore two rings on her left hand, and a shiny necklace drew attention to her cleavage. The server looked about 30 standard years old, but perhaps the clothing made her look younger than her true age. He guessed the woman rebelled against aging or had discovered such dress resulted in better tips. She served tables with the ease of one who enjoyed the work and knew her customers and how to manage them. The woman smiled continuously and talked with the club's patrons to keep everyone's spirits high.

The server caught Mick's gaze and walked over to him.

"You're not my table, but do you want something? Can I get you another drink?"

"No, but if you will, sit and chat for a minute." His voice exuded charm he knew would make his request hard to ignore.

The girl slid into his booth across from him and smiled. "Okay, but only for a minute. We're allowed to mingle with customers, but not too long, if you know what I mean." She winked.

Mick smiled. "What's your name?" He searched the woman's face for any sign of deception.

"Ruchelle. And I'm 30, single, and no."

"No?"

"If want to know if we can meet later and have sex.'"

"No, nothing so bold," he laughed, and, putting the woman at ease, she laughed, too. "I noticed you're good at your job. You have everyone up and dancing. Have you worked here long?"

Ruchelle turned her head and looked at the dancers. "Less than a local year, but, yeah, I like the people here. Good customers."

"The pay is good?"

"Good enough."

"Do you know everyone here?"

"Except for you," she said and leaned to get a good look at all the tables. She stared long and hard at Jayel who was watching the dancers. When Ruchelle looked back at Mick, the smile was gone, and her eyes lost their sparkle.

"No, not everyone. Look, I must get back to work."

Ruchelle stood, walked past the tables, and went behind the bar to draw the man's draft. Closing the tap, she glanced at Jayel again. This time Jayel smiled as she met her eyes. Ruchelle looked away. She handed the mug to another server, indicated

Mick's booth, then turned around and busied herself with empty bottles stacked in the selector located under the mirror. Ruchelle pushed its button, and the shelf receded and brought up a new row of inventory. She rearranged bottles, though obvious to Mick the woman wasn't working but trying to look busy.

For the rest of the evening, Ruchelle avoided the area near Jayel and the man. By eleven, the band finished and packed up. Recorded music played through ceiling speakers at a much lower volume. No more than a few patrons remained.

The other servers cleared empty tables and took glasses and flatware to the kitchen's sanitizer, leaving Ruchelle at the bar to handle any last calls.

Mick saw Jayel prepare to leave. He moved to the monitor near the door and pretended to read the headlines of *The Quintar Reporter*.

Jayel walked to the bar and sat on a stool.

Bent over, Ruchelle arranged newly cleaned glasses under the counter.

"Ruchelle? Is it you? What are you doing working in Quintar of all places?"

The server stood and ignored Jayel's question. Her eyes, easy-going and friendly before, were smoldering. "What the hell do you want, Jayel?"

Jayel was taken aback. "What's the matter? We're friends, aren't we?"

"I don't know how you found me, but just go away. I never want to see you again."

Jayel reached out and touched her arm in friendship. "Please, Ruchelle. Will you explain what's wrong?"

The woman quickly pulled away. "Hah! You're the one who needs to do the explaining. You destroyed my brother, Dorind.

I'll never forgive you."

"Dorind? What's wrong with Dory?"

"He didn't finish medical school, thanks to you. After you left him two standard years ago, he quit and joined Chrysic's command."

Jayel gasped. "No! I can't believe it. Why would he work for General Chrysic?"

"Believe it, sister. You destroyed the only man I loved. My baby brother became a hateful, soulless person. After a few months of training, I no longer knew him. Dorind now desires power and cares not the cost it takes to climb the general's ranks. He's mean and cruel. And it's your fault."

"I don't know how I'm to blame, Ruchelle. I love Dory, you know that."

"Some love. Dorind did it *for you.* My brother said you left him because he couldn't satisfy your father's expectations. Dorind felt he wasn't good enough for you because he's not from a family of Endowed members. He believed he would gain your father's approval by working for someone your Endowed papa respects. That's why Dorind chose to work for General Chrysic."

"Chrysic!"

"Everyone knows Chrysic's the governor's number one man. After a few months of service, my brother changed, and became cold and ruthless. You killed all that was good in him."

Jayel leaned on the bar. She felt sick.

Ruchelle continued, "I thought *you* were different, Jayel. I thought you cared little for Systems power and rank, didn't care about public boasting of status like the damned Endowed who make sure everyone knows how better they are than the rest of us."

Jayel swallowed.

Shaking her head, Ruchelle paused. "If only you hadn't gone away suddenly without telling him where you went. You left him when my brother needed you most. You abandoned him."

"Where is Dorind now?"

"I don't know. He's in Chrysic's secret forces. I haven't heard from him in over a standard year. I try not to think about it, it hurts too much. I hate what's happened to him, and I … I hate you!" She picked up a tray and went into the kitchen.

Jayel stood alone and stared across the bar into the mirror. Mick sensed her thoughts. *Didn't Dory know I loved him? Didn't he know I could care less what my father thought of our relationship? Did I cause him to quit medical school?*

Then Jayel noticed him in the mirror, and her mental guard prevented Mick from continuing to read her thoughts. She abruptly left the pub.

Mick waited several moments, then followed at a safe distance. As Jayel walked to Kathzerum's house, her guard dropped, and he read her mind. She grumbled about the cold and wondered why the weather satellites couldn't add another ten degrees. Her anger simmered. Anger for contacting someone after knowing she was supposed to stay quiet. Anger for choosing to leave Dorind to come to Leidran to find peace. Anger at losing it.

A block away from Kathzerum's house, Dareck's niece remembered she wasn't supposed to walk directly home. Jayel looked around. Shadows speckled the street, and she didn't see him or anyone else. She made a few right and left turns, adding another ten minutes to her return.

As she entered the house, Mick sensed she raised her guard once again lest Dareck might hear. She closed the door immediately behind her.

The man scanned the street and waited ten minutes. Satisfied no one followed them from *The Thirsty Boots*, nor was anyone watching the house, he walked to his car parked a block away. He was intrigued by Dareck's niece who, despite little Endowed training, had learned to guard her thoughts from him so well when she wasn't upset, better than most. Tomorrow's surveillance would provide opportunities to learn more.

Chapter 9

Jayel entered the kitchen a little past ten the next morning, sleep noticeable in her eyes. "Any hot coffee?"

Kathzerum motioned for Jayel to sit. "Dareck left, but I just made a fresh pot." The older woman smiled and poured the hot liquid into a cup. "Did you like *The Thirsty Boots*, dear?"

"Yes, the band was great. The locals danced well, too. Fun to watch." Jayel paused. "Do you mind if I go out for the afternoon? I want to see Quintar's synthetic ocean."

"It's worth a trip, I agree. You have a key in case no one is home when you return." Kathzerum pushed a plate toward her. "Here, eat a pastry. I so enjoyed making them for company."

"They're delicious. Are you sharing recipes? I'll trade spices packed from the house of Leidra for the recipe of this superb coffee cake."

"Done. But don't tell Dareck. He's been after my recipes for years, but your uncle never thought to offer a trade. Jayel 1, Dareck 0. He hates to lose."

By early afternoon, Jayel rode Quintar's tubular train to the tourist area. Magnificent hotels, restaurants, and shops lined the street at the seawall. On all six levels, the buildings' windows provided a beautiful, scenic view of the vast ocean.

A technological marvel, the ocean looked, smelled, and sounded natural. Green-blue water stretched to a pale blue horizon. Rolling waves, strong enough to show white caps curling to shore, lapped onto an ample sandy beach. The small Onus One sun peeked through thin clouds overhead. Unseen pumps circulated warm air to reduce the early winter's chill.

This is exactly what I needed.

Jayel took off her shoes, rolled up the pant legs, and walked to the water's edge. The sand felt cool and soft on the toes but firm on the soles. She didn't know which planet the sand was imported from, but it was the right kind for strolling. She walked ankle-deep in the warm water along the shoreline. Waves capped and turned, foam swirled to the beach, and water ebbed out again, sometimes leaving a strand of seaweed behind. A strong ripple of seawater splashed her knee, and a droplet caught her lip, tasting salty.

She smiled at this delightful experience. It revived nostalgic childhood memories of when her family spent their vacation at Sarranzo beach on Melandan. F*eels like a lifetime ago.*

After walking a long stretch, Jayel saw a group of rocks ahead—a breakwater perhaps—piled back to the seawall. She climbed some boulders and rested.

She looked back in the direction she came from. The starting point, a tall yellow ten-story hotel, was no longer visible. The beach wasn't crowded. Jayel saw only one man walking on the sand in her direction, too far away to discern any features. She looked to the left and saw a couple holding hands about to walk past her, and farther up the beach a scattering of blankets and families.

She listened to the waves. They harmonized with the cries of seagulls and distant children's playful screams. The breeze caressed her skin.

Déjà vu washed over Jayel like a wave upon a fragile shell. The way the sunlight hit the water, the distant sounds of children's voices, and the drowsy roar of the waves all told her she had been in this setting.

Jayel found the memory. It came from a summer vacation at Sarranzo's beach, with her best friend, Johnlon. He made up fun imagination games. Johnlon was eight, and she was five. He was the brother Jayel didn't have but always wanted.

It was a day just like today when Johnlon splashed into the gray sea laughing and full of life until a large wave crashed upon his small body. Jayel relived the fear and alarm she felt sixteen standard years ago, alone, searching the sea for a sign of her friend. Yes, even now Jayel heard his screams for help echo in her mind. She saw frantic arms in the surf, reaching for a lifesaver which wasn't there.

Suddenly, Jayel became aware the waving hands and cries for help weren't from memory. They were happening now. She opened her eyes. Further up the shoreline, a child had waded too far out, and the current pulled him offshore.

Someone rushed by the rocks and shouted, "Come help me save the child." It was the lone approaching walker now running past her, pointing toward the water.

She climbed off the boulders and ran into the ocean behind the man. Jayel hadn't been in an ocean since the day with Johnlon long ago. Sensations flooded her as chilly water crashed against her body. The water, warm at ankle depth, was much colder shoulder high. To reach the boy, the two rescuers forced their bodies through curling waves.

"There he is!" Jayel shouted to the man. She pointed to the flailing arms just barely visible.

The deep water's current threatened to suck the child beneath the surface. *Why did they make an artificial ocean with such a strong undercurrent?*

With effort, they reached the sinking body. The man lifted the child's head into the air, and Jayel pulled him toward her chest. The boy went lifeless in her arms.

"Johnlon!" she said aloud.

The man caught her attention. "We've got to get him to shore."

Jayel nodded, but it was easier said than done. They struggled against the strong undertow, and they exerted effort to keep themselves and the boy afloat. With one free arm, they stroked against the outflow and surged forward with the inflow. Finally, reaching shallow water where the waves were smaller, their feet and knees found support. Their tired legs trudged out of the surf as their soaked clothes increased their weight.

They carried the child's body beyond the water's edge. Jayel dropped to her knees and checked for breath as the man straightened the boy's legs to ready the resuscitation procedure. His skin was turning shades darker. The dark shade of a cold death.

"No respiration," Jayel announced. She blew four quick breaths into the boy, felt for his ribs, and pushed down on his chest. "Come on, breathe."

A crowd gathered around to watch. One person reported they had called for help. Soon, the air ambulance arrived, and two medical personnel took over. When the boy coughed up water, the small crowd cheered.

Suddenly, the distressed parents pushed through the crowd and hugged their child. The boy sat up and cried.

One EMT stood and assured the parents, "Our scans show all is well. A good rest is all this skipper needs." The medic handed the father an electronic pad. "If you would complete our records… Do you need a ride to your hotel? We can drop you off."

The other EMT gathered the equipment, and the parents, with the child hugging his mother's neck, followed them. The crowd dispersed. Only Jayel and the man remained.

Exhausted, Jayel lay back, seawater drenched, sand coated. *We rescued a child … a rescue that didn't happen eighteen years ago.*

Someone had given the man a towel. He sat near her and dried his shoulders and arms. Jayel turned, seeing the stranger clearly for the first time. He had the physique and skin of a thirty-five-standard-year-old, his medium-length hair dripped onto broad shoulders, and his eyes sparkled in reflections from droplets on his face. The man's breathing had returned to resting rate, and he looked calm, patiently waiting for her to start the conversation.

She sat up and stated matter-of-factly, "You've been following me. I saw you at *The Thirsty Boots* last night."

"I'll explain if you give me the time." He smiled with encouragement.

"Time…" Her eyes moved to the ocean. Johnlon's memory lingered and resisted forgetfulness. Jayel sighed and weariness flooded through her.

He handed her the towel. "Some rescue … huh. Let's sit and talk awhile." The stranger spoke in a kind voice, soft and gentle.

Jayel forced a smile. "For a minute, I wasn't sure we could save him. We nearly drowned ourselves."

The towel couldn't remove all the sand glued to her skin. The salted water made the scalp feel sticky. She felt irritated and wished the stranger would go away.

Instead, he encouraged her to open up. "Yes, but it's only one of the reasons you feel weary."

She looked at him, puzzled.

"Tell me."

Her mouth opened to challenge this assumed intimacy, but the depth of his eyes stopped her. All fear and suspicions dissipated, and she realized this stranger was an Endowed member. He possessed an ability to read her thoughts, like Dareck.

Because it was the path of least effort, Jayel didn't block him.

Five years old, a best friend, a wild ocean. Alone at the time, I had been unable to pull his body from the deep water until it floated into shallow water. Even then, after I had dragged Johnlon onto land, I didn't know life-saving techniques. The boy died, on the beach, alone with a five-year-old girl who didn't know whether to go for help or to stay with the friend. Eventually, someone took her away.

She shivered from the memory.

But this wasn't all. No one afterward understood her experience. Her father was angry at his daughter's incompetence. She should have saved Johnlon. Karsch later took back words he spoke when he saw the intensity of her grief, but he gave up, seeming disgusted, when she refused to learn life-saving techniques or take swimming lessons, even when he sent his assistant, Chrysic, to instruct her personally. Did no one realize the girl was afraid of drowning, of being in the water? The loss of friendship at a tender age without mature interpretation…

Jayel broke the connection. She stood and brushed the sand off her arms and clothes with the towel. "I must get back and change into dry clothes."

"I'll take you, Jayel. I've transportation nearby. It'll be much faster than the train, where you'd look too conspicuous traveling through Quintar thoroughly soaked."

"How do you know my name? Who are you?"

"My name is Brusch. I am, as you've already realized, a

member of the Endowed, and, more importantly, a friend of Dareck's."

"Then I'll give you what you asked for."

"What is that?"

"Time to explain."

Brusch smiled. They walked off the beach and down three blocks to Brusch's vehicle.

Jayel gasped. "This is your car?"

It was an exquisite hovercraft from the luxury Galaxy Wormhole series, capable of vertical lift without the need for forward momentum before rising into the air.

"It was the only rental I could find, the last car available."

Jayel admired its sleek body, then shook her head. "Our wet clothes, the sand. We can't sit in it. We'll ruin the seats."

Brusch opened the door. "I'll get it cleaned tomorrow and add the cost to Dareck's expense report."

***

Dareck stood in Kathzerum Elesh's foyer, having just arrived himself, when Jayel and Brusch walked in.

"You look like a duo of half-dried river rats," Dareck joked.

Jayel grinned, pushing the damp sticky hair from her cheek. "It's a long story, Dareck, but we're okay. Brusch can tell you about it. I want to shower, get into warm clothes, and go to bed. It's been a long day."

Dareck watched Jayel ascend the moving stairway, then turned to his friend. "Don't tell me she fell into the ocean!"

"Far from it."

Brusch's facial expression told Dareck they hadn't been in danger from General Chrysic but there was a story to be told.

Dareck clapped his friend's shoulders. "You should see what you look like. And is this seaweed in your hair? Come, let's go to my room. You can shower and put on dry clothes.

Kath keeps a full wardrobe. I'm curious why you made contact and why you took a dip in the ocean."

As they passed Jayel's room, Dareck glanced at her door.

Brusch remarked, "Don't worry, my friend. Today, we saved a life. I'll tell you all about it after you lend me those dry clothes. I'm shivering cold."

Chapter 10

In the evening, Jayel quietly came down from her bedroom and paused a moment in the foyer. She heard faint laughter and voices of her friends coming from the kitchen. She silently opened the front door and stepped outside, wrapping the warm scarf across her face. She dashed to *The Thirsty Boots.*

When Jayel entered the tavern, loud music from five string instruments swept over her. Lines of patrons danced in coordinated motion. Jayel saw two servers working the room, neither of whom was Ruchelle. To the right, a male bartender chatted with a middle-aged man. Two other customers at the other end of the bar nursed beers, their coats matched the ones Jayel saw last night.

She loosened the scarf, walked to the bar, and attracted the barkeep's attention. He stopped speaking and lifted his head as if to say, "What do *you* want?" but didn't speak.

"I'm looking for Ruchelle."

The bartender frowned, and his face darkened. "Shez quit on me. Last night," he spat. He glared, lowered his eyes, and resumed the conversation with his customer.

Jayel sighed and stepped back. She watched the crowded dance floor and considered staying for one drink, maybe even joining in the line dance.

Instead, Jayel left *The Thirsty Boots* and rushed back to Kathzerum's house, slipped in as quietly as she left, and went up to her room.

***

"Good morning, Jayel," Dareck welcomed his niece as Kath moved a tray of freshly baked pastries from the counter to the table. *She looks rested. I wonder how she will take the news.*

"Good morning, everyone. Mmm, these look grand." Jayel sat beside Brusch and reached for a cake.

Kath, smiling, filled Jayel's cup with hot coffee. "More for you, Brusch?" The older woman poured a refill before he answered.

Dareck said, "I have news of importance, Jayel. We're leaving Quintar tonight."

She put down the coffee cup, nearly choking on the pastry. "Tonight?"

"Yes. I must go to the planet Ondre immediately."

"Ondre? Isn't it where the war—"

"Yes, the planet Ondre in the Onus Two star system. I've received word I'm needed to assist with an intelligence issue."

Brusch buttered a slice of toast. "Also newsworthy, we think General Chrysic left last night and flew to Melandan, in the opposite direction of where we're going."

"Then you're traveling to Ondre with us. I'm glad."

Dareck added, "I found us a ship, a 64-A22, the same model as the one I own."

Jayel nodded, finished chewing, and sipped the coffee. "While I'm sorry to be leaving Kathzerum and her wonderful baking, a side trip before returning to Melandan sounds ideal. I haven't decided yet what to say to my father when we return, so I appreciate a delay." Jayel looked at the clock and turned to Kath. "I have some research to do before we leave. May I use your computer?"

After Jayel left the room, Kathzerum sat back. "If you ask me, and I noticed you haven't, I like her, Dareck. I see a lot of you in Jayel when you were her age. I think she will help you in more ways than you expect." Kath gave him an I-am-wise-and-know-all look.

Smiling, Dareck touched his former mentor's hand. "I agree. In fact, Kath, I'm counting on it."

***

As they approached the spaceport, Jayel heard the roar of a ship's engine overhead.

Quintar's port occupied the southeast side of the city. Until Leidran's annual orbit pulled it away from the Onus Two solar system, company representatives and tourists came here to meet or buy goods without needing to travel deeper into the other system. Huge cargo planes transferring imports and exports between systems dominated the berths. Commercial passenger ships, some small, some jumbo, peppered the landscape.

Smaller, private crafts carrying fewer than a dozen passengers docked at the terminal adjacent to the main complex. After Brusch returned the rental car, they took an elevator to this terminal's first floor. The glass-lined hallway provided excellent viewing of the parked spacecraft.

"I think I see our ship." Jayel pointed to the far end of the terminal. The 64-A22's height, width, and engine size appeared mammoth compared to the other private crafts.

"Yes. You know about spacecraft?" Dareck sounded surprised.

"Somewhat," she answered vaguely.

As of yesterday, I knew little about them. But in the afternoon she studied the manual on 64-A22s. Kathzerum's exceptional computers offered instructional packages on piloting spaceships. Jayel crammed as much knowledge as she could. *It felt good to be a student again, though it wasn't medical information.*

She asked, "Will you and Brusch be the only pilots?"

"Yes," Dareck answered. "We'll have a crew of four trustworthy aides from my estate."

"How convenient."

"What do you mean?"

"This isn't your vehicle, correct? But your employees serve as crew."

"Yes, well, after I arrived a month ago, the crew flew my ship to Characta, my home planet. Knowing I was now ready to depart Leidran but wanting to keep my flight secret from General Chrysic, my crew flew from Characta to Orim, boarded this craft, and flew it to Leidran. They only arrived this morning and hopefully with no trace of a direct connection to me."

Brusch warned, "The general is resourceful. He could connect the dots. I wouldn't put it past him to review all ships coming and going from Quintar within a two-week window."

"True. I'm hoping our flight plan to Ondre, instead of to Characta or Melandan, allays any suspicions to further investigate this ship's crew."

Jayel checked her wristwatch. "One thing I know is this is a fast ship. We should reach the planet Ondre in about thirty hours."

"We should —" Dareck's voice sounded uncertain.

"Do you expect trouble?" Jayel asked, worried.

Her uncle shrugged. "I feel a sense of urgency. I wish I knew Chrysic's exact position. There are no reports yet of the general back on Melandan. And General Chrysic doesn't enjoy leaving battles unfinished. I'll feel better when we're off Leidran."

They arrived at their gate. The craft, sleek for its size, had large windows, four engines, two jumbo fuel cells, and one solar antenna. A flat moving walkway allowed them to enter the ship just aft of the command bridge.

Brusch thumbed the pad in his hand. "All is well, Dareck. We received clearance to leave."

"Good. Let's be on our way. Jayel, please go to your cabin for takeoff."

Dareck went forward to the command bridge. Brusch exchanged smiles with Jayel and followed him. A crew member escorted her through the lounge to an elevator, taking them up to a corridor of private rooms. The aide opened the second door, nodded, and left.

Jayel walked into a spacious cabin, complete with a bed, bureau, sink, and standard buckle-in chair used for takeoffs and landings. A large window extended to part of the ceiling, allowing for overhead and side views.

Inside the closet, she secured her rucksack and a basket of baked *snuffets* Kathzerum made for their journey and closed the door.

"Take off in two minutes," Jayel heard from the speaker on the wall. The slight vibration beneath the feet as the engines warmed urged her to sit and secure the straps.

Belted and waiting, Jayel looked out the window. The scene began to move to the right and downwards as they surged into orbit. Quintar grew small, and the trees of Denerow Woods blurred to green and brown land, the mountains mere ripples in the tapestry. As they accelerated, she felt pressure against her chest and face, but the feeling soon passed as they entered orbit with only a minor noticeable change to the gravitational pressure. The artificial gravity lived up to the 64-A22's reputation for excellence.

They left orbit, and the window viewed only blackness. Space without atmospheric distortion was hypnotic. There was so much to apprehend in the vastness, arousing philosophical thoughts. *Were people living in any other solar system in the galaxy, in the universe? Did they have artificial satellites making their planet livable?* No such evidence yet existed, as all people in Onus One and Two traced their roots to the planet Orim. Only through technology, the barren planets of both systems bore life.

For a moment, the darkness heightened the cabin's illumination and created the illusion she bathed in dazzling light. Jayel felt exposed.

Someone in the cold darkness outside could see her in this large spotlight. She imagined someone seeing her face in the window, saying, "I see you, but you can't see me."

Blood drained, causing a moment of lightheadedness, and her heart beat faster.

She knew then. Jayel knew General Chrysic was out there. She scanned the blackness and looked for his ship's lights. Deeper she searched, like searching for shapes on Dareck's hexagon.

She felt as if the vacuum of space enveloped the room, cutting off the oxygen.

She unfastened the belts and hurried to the intercom.

"Dareck, what do the ship's sensors pick up in the N-5 sector?"

"N-5?" he echoed. "What's the problem?"

"Don't ask how I know this, but General Chrysic is there." Her skin turned cold and clammy. "He's waiting for us."

Chapter 11

Jayel listened to Dareck question Brusch. "What's in Nan-5? I can't get a good optical view from this angle."

She waited. *At least Dareck would look.*

"Captain," shouted a bridge crew member, his voice audible over the intercom. "I do have a bogey in sector Nan-5 … and approaching fast, on an intercept course."

"I'm coming up." Jayel didn't wait for Dareck's reply. He wouldn't want her there, but she needed to be involved.

The elevator rushed Jayel to the lounge. She quickly made her way to the command bridge.

"What action will you take?" Brusch asked Dareck as Jayel walked in.

"Well, I know we can outfly him," Dareck commented, not looking up from his panel.

"Outfly him?" cried Jayel, moving up to the front. "Don't tell me you aren't going to fight."

Dareck shook his head. "I've already had one encounter with General Chrysic. I don't want another."

Emotions high, Jayel wanted to argue but instead pressed her lips.

The crew member in front of a scope spoke. "Readings show it's a private vessel, a W4-C7-X2, cargo and passenger class but equipped with arms usually used for blasting small asteroids or space junk."

"Yes," Brusch added, "we must determine if the vessel is Chrysic's before we act. We don't *know* this ship is his."

Jayel read the doubt in Brusch's eyes. "You two are the Endowed members. Don't ask me to explain, but I looked out the window and knew Chrysic was there, waiting for us to break orbit."

The two men exchanged glances. Dareck studied the scope's image and frowned. Finally, he stood and faced Jayel. "Look at me."

She looked up into his brown eyes. They were deep and intent, inviting her mind to open before him. Jayel didn't look away. *What could he hope to read in my thoughts when I don't know how I'm certain Chrysic was out there?*

Dareck held her eyes for only a short time. He turned away and sat at the controls. "Chrysic is there."

Brusch raised an eyebrow but remained silent.

Dareck sighed, then said decisively, "We will fight. But I won't destroy his ship and litter space. It's to our advantage to prevent the general from following us. We can render the vessel harmless and continue our course to Ondre."

Dareck issued orders. "Brusch, you will help maneuver our vessel with me. My crew can manage the engines and weapons. Jayel, go back to your cabin."

Dareck returned his attention to the panel, but Jayel leaned in. "I can be of assistance in navigation. You and the crew will be busy handling ship operations. I can plot the best course to take regardless of our position."

Before Dareck could respond, Jayel opened the floor hatch. "I'll use the auxiliary control room."

His niece disappeared through the hatch.

Dareck turned to Brusch. "Do you think she knows navigation?"

Brusch smiled. "At my suggestion on the ride home from the beach, your niece spent most of today on Kathzerum Elesh's computer to study navigation controls for this craft."

"Hmm, Kath does own ultramodern simulation software. Well, good. Let's hope we're intact and able to continue to Ondre after this encounter with the general."

Brusch finished downloading battle strategies into his console and added, "She has personal reasons for wanting General Chrysic out of the way."

"We all do," Dareck remarked.

Their eyes met, and Dareck smiled. "Thank you, my friend, for supporting my decision not to destroy his vessel. There will be another time, another way to deal with Chrysic. Our revenge shall be sweet."

Below the command bridge, Jayel concentrated on the panel's screen. The display matched the training simulation. She slowed her breathing, relaxed, and grew calm. When ready, Jayel established communication with the control room.

Dareck reprimanded her. "It's about time, Jayel. Your first step should have been to establish contact with the control bridge, then prepare your console."

"Acknowledged, Captain," she answered, trying not to reflect the smile in her voice. *At least my uncle didn't tell me to get out of here.*

Brusch added, "The coordinates to Ondre now appear on your screen. As you can see, Jayel, we want to reach the M corridor. It's your job to get us back to M after our confrontation. Familiarize yourself with the surrounding routes. We don't want to get lost."

"Acknowledged." Jayel displayed the space map of nearby star systems, including Onus Two. She plotted multiple routes they could travel to the M corridor, a slipstream enabling the spacecraft to reach Onus Two within days instead of months. If calculations were off even a shade, they could end up in the wrong solar system. Having just learned to read three-dimensional navigation charts, Jayel checked her calculations again.

"Target in range," a crew member called out.

"Establish radio contact," Dareck ordered.

Before the crew member could acknowledge contact, General Chrysic's voice blasted through the speakers. "I should've killed you before, Dareck. But today will have to do."

"General Chrysic, I intend to file a complete report when I return to my estate. You will have to answer for your recent actions against me."

"An optimist to the end, Dareck. *If* you return." Chrysic ended communications.

"Not much for talking," Brusch laughed.

The two spacecraft maneuvered into position. Jayel waited as the vessels danced like boxers in a three-dimensional ring posturing for an opportunity to knock out the opponent. The fight required a good deal of maneuvering, speed, and timing. Navigation was key because there was no bottom in space to help maintain your bearings. If lost, you could run out of fuel if you didn't find solar wind channels to reach a spaceport. Coordinates rotated on the display.

As the computer's simulations taught, Jayel programmed the panel and interpreted the three-dimensional charts. Planetary bodies weren't a current concern, as their vessel now flew in the far regions of the Onus One solar system on a different plane than Leidran.

The ship quickly changed direction and speed, and the gravitational system's adjustment lagged, throwing off Jayel's equilibrium, and she swayed. Jayel gripped her hands on the console for balance and kept her eyes fixed on the panel. It displayed the position of the two ships and the main reference point, the Onus One star.

Jayel listened to the exchange between Dareck, Brusch, and the crew. Chrysic's vessel had a larger weapon energy store than theirs. The general's military experience increased the odds he could hit them at least once, even with Dareck's renowned pilot skills. Timing was everything.

Dareck repeated the intention to disable but not destroy Chrysic's ship. Everyone knew their jobs and reported ready.

They traversed thousands of kilometers of space within the metaphorical boxing ring. Dareck used defensive tactics and exploited the 64-A22's advantage in maneuverability and speed. Chrysic used his aggressiveness to taunt and jab.

Finally, Chrysic made his power shot, a missile straight down the center of the boxing ring.

Dareck anticipated and swerved. The missile surged into empty space. Dareck aligned his torpedo ports with Chrysic's engines.

The general erred and didn't follow through with evasive actions.

"Fire!" Dareck ordered.

Seconds later, Chrysic's ship floated adrift, appearing to have lost maneuverability and speed. They had him on the ropes.

A crew member looked up from his panel and reported Chrysic's engines were damaged, but life support was intact.

Jayel hoped Dareck would swing around for a final blow but knew he wouldn't. She found the coordinates for the M corridor and plotted a flight path. Although the fight moved them away from the Onus Two star system, and therefore they had more distance to cover to get to Ondre than if the fight hadn't occurred, they had enough fuel for the thirty-one-hour flight.

"Affirmative on the route," Brusch said after checking the calculations. "Come on up, Jayel."

She climbed up the ladder. "Well?"

The men attended to their consoles and received reports from all stations.

Dareck turned and said matter-of-factly, "The general's ship is disabled. He won't be in pursuit, and it will take time for him to return to a spaceport on battery reserves."

Jayel relished the euphoria of victory. "You got Chrysic without him ever hitting us."

Brusch interjected. "Oh, he made a few jabs, but due to Dareck's deft maneuvering, we were out of the way before those shots reached their target. Dareck, you flew superbly."

"Well, thank you, Brusch. But what were you doing while I did all the superb stuff?" Dareck smiled warmly at his friend.

"Everyone including the crew should be congratulated. I'm glad to be alive." Jayel ran her fingers through her hair, pulling the bangs away from the forehead.

Her uncle asked, "Navigation wasn't a problem? I'm impressed."

"I think my medical training, the brain courses in particular, helped me think in three dimensions and interpret the navigation charts. Neural pathways are like miniature solar systems."

Dareck nodded. "Well, we are lucky the general wasn't flying his flagship with stronger armament and full crew. Otherwise, we likely wouldn't be having this conversation."

“We have a bitter enemy,” Brusch reminded them.

A bridge crew member announced, “M corridor ahead, as scheduled.”

Their spaceship tilted sharply as it turned into the corridor and adjusted to its increased speed.

Jayel put a hand out against the wall, unable to keep her balance. “It takes a while to get one’s space legs, I suppose.”

“Go below and get some rest,” Dareck suggested. “Later, we’ll talk about what to expect when we get to Ondre.”

“You get some rest, too, Dareck,” Brusch said, seeing him yawn. “I’ll take the first shift.”

“Very well. Call if you need me.”

Chapter 12

Jayel leaned across the lounge table while pouring two glasses of *switchya*, a hot beverage like coffee containing alcohol. "You can count on me to be discreet."

Dareck reached for the last of Kathzerum's *snuffets* and didn't speak until finishing half of it. "When Neondra's 'accident' occurred, they reported my young son died in the fire, too. But it wasn't true. Because I suspected murder, for his safety, I hid my son."

"Wow." Jayel stirred the *switchya* and waited for her uncle to continue.

"Layon was raised on Ondre since he was nearly three standard years old."

Jayel slowly nodded. "Are we going to Ondre to see your son? Does he need your help?"

"He's not directly involved in the civil conflict. I don't know how familiar you are with this war between the planet's two major cities, Catana and Marshe. The Marshets were losing the war, some say badly, until the assassination of the Catanan governor a standard year ago. Since then, the Marshets have strengthened their forces and intensified attacks."

Jayel commented, "Sounds like outside help intervened."

"The Catanan government also thinks so. The planet's

other cities aren't strong or organized enough to give aid on the scale necessary for Marshe's success."

Stirring the *switchya,* Jayel asked, "Doesn't Systems law forbid interplanetary interference for civil wars, except humanitarian aid?"

"Yes. Military support from another planet is a criminal offense, subject to stiff penalties. However, the Catanan government doesn't know who's supplying aid to Marshe. Despite hostilities, both cities continue normal trade with other planets."

Jayel looked out the window. Although they had entered the Onus Two solar system about an hour ago, the view out the window remained unchanged. "I can guess who in Onus One you suspect is helping the Marshets. My father has an interest in this war, doesn't he?"

"Yes. Karsch strongly holds political power in Onus One. In the Onus Two system, his current influence is weaker. If your father can gain a stronghold on Ondre, his influence could spread more quickly to other planets in the Onus Two system. It would certainly be to Karsch's advantage if he can influence the outcome of Ondre's war to his liking."

"Does my father openly side with the Marshets?"

Dareck paused as he emptied his cup. "The evidence is circumstantial. In recent years, your father's ambassador often visited the Governor of Marshe, and twice this year, General Chrysic has made appearances."

"But how is Marshe receiving the aid?" Jayel asked.

"That's the big question. My son works in a politically neutral organization charged with investigating this issue. Traffic among the planets hasn't increased—so how are the shipments being made? I plan to examine their data and offer solutions. They may have overlooked the obvious."

Jayel finished her cup of *switchya*, the satisfying taste lingering on her tongue. "Why the sense of urgency to go to Ondre now instead of later?"

"Intelligence reports indicate imminent threats. They hope my discovery of how Marshe receives military supplies will reduce them." Dareck leaned back.

After a short break in the conversation, Jayel suggested, "Tell me something about your son."

His eyes glistened. "I saw him a few months ago. Almost eighteen standard years old, Layon is trained in the ways of the Endowed, but membership eludes him until he can reveal his identity. He can't declare publicly he's my son, as he's presumed dead."

Dareck looked at her. "With your help, Jayel, I can finally uncover what happened to Neondra, find justice, and my son can join the Endowed."

He paused and poured the last of the *switchya* into his cup. "Meanwhile, Layon does computer and neuroscience research. He's been content growing up on Ondre, but he's a young adult now, eager to make public contributions. He's been working on an invention which, according to Brusch, will soon be ready for mass production."

Dareck stood and in the galley put on a fresh pot of *switchya*. When he returned, his voice carried a tone of caution. "I don't think my son will be happy to see you, Jayel, once he learns who you are. Layon knows the name of his mother's murderer, and I don't think he'll welcome the murderer's daughter with open arms. You'll have to charm him with your dazzling personality, as you have charmed me."

"Have I charmed you? I thought it was the other way around." She flashed a quick but genuine smile. In the two weeks spent together, they had built a strong friendship.

Dareck sipped his *switchya.* "I hope to persuade Layon to leave Ondre with us."

"Aha!" Jayel leaned her elbows on the table. "Now we have the true reason we are going to Ondre. Without you, they will eventually find the source of Marshets' military supplies. You're going to Ondre now to take your son away. Is Layon in danger because of the war?"

Her uncle smiled. "You're as perceptive as an Endowed member. I worry he wants to break free of my protection and prove himself on the battlefield. It's increasingly difficult for Layon to remain neutral, even though he lives in neither city."

The ship slowed its speed, the drag barely noticeable. Jayel looked out the window and saw the green-blue planet in the distance. They'd soon be in orbit.

Dareck took a *borrell* from his pocket. "You promised discretion. You mustn't refer, imply, or hint to anyone that Layon is my son. Even though my aides work with Layon, they don't know I am his father. They think he's my pupil, my prodigy."

"I'll remember."

He removed a small metallic object from the pouch. "Take this."

"What is it?"

"A pin, identifying you as a member of my party. If we get separated, my men will know you may enter where others may not."

Jayel looked at the small gold insignia, shaped like an oval *oilwood* leaf with detailed veins.

Dareck stood and gestured for Jayel to do the same. He attached the pin to her tunic's collar.

Sitting again, Jayel said, "Because we are no longer worried about General Chrysic, I presume I don't need to hide my identity."

Putting the *borrell* back in his pocket, he said, "Well, an interplanetary visitor wouldn't be surprised my niece traveled with me. Still, we won't make an official announcement and thus not attract attention to your presence."

Jayel nodded. "What am I to do while you investigate the arms supply?"

"Well, you could explore the facility with Brusch, maybe visit Catana. Parts of the city boast modern architecture worthy of a tour. And you should continue working on your Endowed exercises. You've progressed well, and I'll give you more advanced challenges."

They shared one more cup of *switchya*, then, hearing the chime from the command bridge, Dareck stood. "Go to your quarters and get ready for landing. We'll be on Ondre soon."

Jayel walked toward the elevator, turned around, and asked, smiling, "Are you sure you wouldn't like me to land this ship? I could use the practice."

***

The spaceport outside the Catana city limits served private vessels only. To land here, pilots must know the proper codes and patterns. With the war on, security was tight. However, Dareck's ship received immediate clearance.

After a smooth landing, Jayel joined Brusch and her uncle on the command bridge as they prepared to disembark.

"We expected you yesterday," controller Samsen greeted Dareck over the speaker. "Your transportation awaits at gate 23."

"Thank you, Samsen. When you're free, let's get together and talk. I'll be staying with Layon."

"Looking forward to it. Have a nice visit, and, of course, welcome to Ondre."

The crew stayed on the ship to complete procedures. Dareck, Jayel, and Brusch made the transition to Ondre's gravity as they walked to gate 23. They entered a six-seater, low-ground, single-engine hovercraft.

Although system satellites helped to control the weather, Ondre was a planet of hot temperatures. Buildings outside the city limits were located underground for efficient cooling.

As they traveled, Jayel saw the countryside as a splotchy grassy plain, spotted with different colored roofs sticking up out of the ground like cabbage heads. Animals grazed lazily beneath strong sunlight. As a newly cultivated planet, technology and nature lived side by side.

There were no signs of war. They passed a freshwater lake. Children played from neighboring cabbage-head houses. The orange sun glowed high above them. On first impression, Jayel liked the planet because it differed from cool Leidran.

Dareck pointed. "Layon works over there. It's a research facility, staffed with interplanetary personnel. Its acronym is ICID, which stands for *IndalSycalImpalDenesta* in the secular tongue. Yes, long names here on Ondre. Located far from the cities, most staff live at ICID, too. I hope you don't have claustrophobia. You may not get to the surface often."

As far as her eye could see, tiny buildings, air vents, scopes, and antennae pimpled the ground, evidence of the facility's immense size underneath. ICID spread underground like the roots of a grand *oilwood* tree. *Not cabbage heads but icebergs.*

"Impressive, isn't it?" Brusch asked, leaning to look out her window.

Their car slowed and entered an enormous above-ground garage. After parking, they walked to ICID's main entrance where a welcoming committee received them.

Dareck shook hands with the group leader, an older man

dressed in a military Systems uniform. They talked in the customary greeting of an Endowed dignitary and as reunited friends.

Jayel scanned the fifteen people in the group. Her eyes skipped over the women and older men. One of four young men might be Layon, but she couldn't be sure.

Then, a tall, young man stepped off the elevator and joined the group.

Jayel recognized him immediately.

Jayel's heart pumped faster. He had short, brownish-black hair and vibrant eyes, with a strong jawline complimenting his manly profile. He dressed casually in contrast to the group's formal business attire.

His beautiful eyes drifted away from Dareck and met hers. Their eyes locked.

A powerful wave of emotion past through her. An attraction, a bond of indescribable force, was immediately established between them. If this man were anyone else, Jayel would've smiled, inviting him in, but she was troubled by her physical response to a cousin.

The young man's eyes sparkled, and his expression said he felt it, too. His interest in her doubled. Then, after holding each other's gaze, his eyes drifted down to Dareck's pin. His expression darkened, and he looked away.

Jayel suppressed a laugh. *He thinks I'm Dareck's romantic partner.*

When the young man looked at Brusch, his face brightened, and he smiled.

Jayel felt more confused. *I've seen this smile before.*

Her thoughts were troubled. The resemblance was unmistakable. *Was Dareck aware of it? Was Brusch?*

Jayel tried to squash the growing suspicion, but the seed

already sprouted into an *oilwood.* Layon didn't closely resemble her uncle, Dareck. Instead, he looked like her father, Karsch.

Chapter 13

Jayel caught Brusch looking at her and doubled efforts to hide all thoughts. *Now was not the time to raise concerns.*

Soon, the welcome formalities ended, and the group dispersed. Layon led Dareck, Brusch, and Jayel to a private lounge.

While pouring four drinks, Layon asked, "Did you experience an easy flight?"

"We had a run-in with General Chrysic," Dareck replied, sipping his drink and leaning back. "I hope we left him lost in interspace beyond the Onus systems, unable to get back to his men for a few days."

"Are you saying Chrysic flew without his bodyguards?"

"Yes, most unlike him," Dareck agreed. He motioned to his niece. "Well, allow me to introduce Jayel. She is … going to help me obtain the evidence on Melandan we have long sought."

Layon raised his eyebrows and looked at Jayel with renewed interest.

Before Jayel could think of something to say besides "hello," Dareck continued, "We can talk about the matter later. Tell me, what's new with the war?"

"The conflict doesn't go well." Layon sighed and returned his eyes to Dareck. "Escalations might lead to massive destruction of people and the ecosystem. Catana needs ICID to soon identify Marshe's source of military supplies."

"I'm eager to look over the data and offer suggestions if I can," Dareck said.

Layon smiled. "Your arrival has improved morale. Commander Eidelnim has collated reports for your perusal and plans to meet you in his office after lunch. His staff scheduled a meal for you and your party in an hour."

Jayel looked at her watch to see if it automatically updated. It did. Ondre rotates once every 22 hours with respect to the Standard Time Satellite, making for 55-minute hours.

Layon put down his glass and stood. "I'll show these two to their rooms. Dareck, you're in the usual VIP quarters."

Dareck nodded and left.

Layon escorted Brusch and Jayel through a maze of corridors.

As they walked, Brusch said, "I'm eager to see how your invention is coming along, Layon. May we see it after lunch?"

Layon flashed a smile. "I would like that. You're welcome to join us, Jayel. I would value a third opinion."

After more turns than Jayel could count, they walked down a long corridor with numerous closed doors. She surmised they reached the dormitory section of ICID.

"This is where you'll be staying, Brusch." Layon stopped a third of the way down the hallway. "I'll be back after I get Jayel settled, and we can catch up."

"Sounds good." Brusch left the door ajar for Layon's return.

Layon motioned for Jayel to follow. Her room was near the end of the long corridor. The light from Brusch's open door was barely visible behind them. He handed her an electronic pad. "Here's a newcomer's map of the complex to help you from getting lost."

"Thanks." She pocketed it and entered a spacious room beautifully decorated in pale blue and gold. It included a computer desk and a private bathroom. Though windowless, two large prints hung on the wall imitating windows with a view, and the strong artificial sunlight in them gave the space a less claustrophobic feel. Her rucksack stood on the floor by the bed.

Layon added, "ICID provides a variety of clothes for your use. Feel free to choose anything in your closet during your stay."

"Most kind."

He lingered. "I need to ask, Jayel. Are you Dareck's girlfriend? I see you wear his pin."

"No, I'm not his girlfriend."

Layon smiled and relaxed his shoulders. He moved closer and swallowed. "When I first saw you at the welcome ceremony, I felt a wave of emotion as our eyes met." Layon paused, and his eyes scanned her face. "Ah, then you felt it also. I feel I have always known you."

Up close, Jayel could see subtle differences in his facial features from her father. His brows were more arched, and his eyelashes longer. *Perhaps my suspicion is wrong. A half-cousin, not a half-brother.*

"I would like us to be more than acquaintances," he whispered. Layon impulsively leaned forward and kissed her wetly on the lips.

No one had kissed Jayel since she parted from Dorind two standard years ago, and a yearning awoke. She fought the momentary desire to kiss him back.

"Layon, stop." She moved away and held up her hand for emphasis. Jayel added, "I think it's best if Dareck tells you who I am."

Layon stepped back but said with encouragement, "Very well. Hopefully, you'll spend some time with me while you're visiting."

"I look forward to seeing your lab," Jayel offered a compromise.

He looked down the hallway. "Brusch is waiting for my return." Layon sighed, then turned, and walked briskly back to Brusch's room.

Jayel closed the door. *Once Layon knows who I am, the daughter of his mother's murderer, he will feel differently.*

She put troubling thoughts aside, took a shower, and studied the closet contents. Jayel selected pleated black slacks and a burgundy polo top from the closet. She attached Dareck's pin to the collar. Jayel checked the time, found she had taken longer than intended, and hurried to Brusch's room.

"There you are." Layon stood as Jayel walked in. "I thought you were lost already. I was about to send out a search party."

"Very funny. I can find my way down a straight hall."

Brusch, sitting at the desk, concentrated on a sheet of formulas.

Layon filled Jayel in. "He's working on algorithms for my invention. He couldn't wait."

After a moment, Brusch looked up and smiled. "This project is the main reason I came along to Ondre—I hold little interest in a war, though, of course, I hope it ends soon." He turned to Layon, "Since we last talked, you've made tremendous progress, Layon. I'm impressed. I have some ideas for increasing efficiency. We can discuss them after lunch."

"I look forward to it," Layon said.

The three left Brusch's room.

Jayel asked, "What is the invention?"

"My device is a thought imager. It can take thoughts—pure brain waves—and digitize them, reproducing speech and imagery on a multi-modal monitor—sights, sounds, smells, tastes, and tactile sensations. Imagine the mind as camera and director, creating clear sensory details to share with others as they observe."

Brush quipped, "Gives a new meaning to 'tell me what you're thinking' or 'what do you have in mind?' One can answer without words."

"Incredible," Jayel exclaimed.

On her home planet, Melandan, they were starting to manufacture digital devices that provided smells with sights and sounds from files, but these devices were very artificial, too mechanical, and unable to capture all the nuances of aromas. Interplanetary chefs who initially backed the technology were horrified. She wasn't aware of any devices capable of reproducing novel thoughts or getting code directly from the brain.

"You wrote the software and created the hardware?"

"Yes," Layon replied. "With important technical assistance from my mentor, Brusch. I've overcome a major barrier in capturing thoughts and coding them for a sophisticated computer I designed to reproduce. However, the detail isn't there yet, and I must admit, images are indiscernible at times because of the inefficiency of digitizing. Too much information overloads the system. Thoughts changing with time are even less clear."

"I look forward to seeing a demonstration."

They entered a brightly decorated room with five large circular tables covered with elegant tablecloths, set for a formal lunch. Dareck sat at the head table and conversed with men and women wearing various uniforms. Jayel assumed they were the high brass from ICID intelligence. Three servers circled the room and poured drinks.

Layon whispered, "Why don't we skip this luncheon and go to my lab now? I can order sandwiches to take with us."

"Sounds good to me," Jayel said, liking the idea of avoiding questions about her background.

"Brusch agreed and said, "I'll tell Dareck where we're going."

Layon spoke to a server. A minute later, lunch bag in hand, they left and descended to the lower levels of the complex.

While they walked, Jayel saw offices, recreation facilities, libraries, eateries, and greenhouses. But the more they discussed Layon's invention, the less attention she paid to the surroundings and became immersed in the role of a research scientist.

Brusch asked, "Do you know how accurate the image is? For example, when you think of a flower, does the same flower appear on the screen, or is it a general form of a flower—like another variety, color, or perspective?"

"So far, the thought imager identically copies my thoughts of simple objects held in consciousness for at least five seconds. But it's challenged by complex scenes or abstract ideas and feelings. Hopefully, with more efficient programming, I can speed conversion issues."

Jayel imagined public acceptance of such an invention. "I can see multiple uses. It could even become an art form. I mean, think about it. In the past, people converted their thoughts by painting, writing, sculpting, or filming. But information gets lost in reproduction. We typically don't possess the talent to express our thoughts as clearly as we think. With this device, we get results without skill or proper brain-to-muscle coordination."

Brusch agreed. "Writing or speaking takes much more time than thinking. Sometimes, we get to the end of a sentence or paragraph and forget what we initially were thinking. Imagine now, with Layon's device, we could replay our forgotten but device-captured ideas."

They took an elevator down two levels as they continued brainstorming possibilities.

Jayel added, "After a person suffers brain damage, say from a stroke, their thoughts, which might still be intact but no longer able to be expressed in speech or writing, or perhaps memories stored but unable to be retrieved, could now be digitized and shared with others."

After more thought, she added, "I wonder if the device could help diagnose brain disorders, perhaps identify unusual or impaired thinking."

"Interesting." Layon thoughtfully nodded. "I've been thinking in the brain-to-monitor direction, but what we observe on the monitor could inform us of what is going on in the brain. The device would know the location of brain areas contributing to any impaired signals and might help physicians know where in the brain to investigate further."

He led them around another corner. "Of course," Layon lamented, "the device doesn't clarify our muddled thinking on its own, at least not yet. One day, I would like to press a button and make the machine show me what I meant all along but couldn't conceive."

Dareck was right, Layon would become famous when he marketed this invention.

She asked, "Layon, can you record dreams as well, thoughts from our nonconscious mind? People could wake up and play back dreams they don't remember."

"A dream recorder is a definite spin-off of the main invention. The current device digitizes only conscious thoughts, but if we tapped the appropriate sites showing activation while sleeping, I think the principles of digitizing remain the same."

Brusch cautioned, "Could people use the imager to read the mind of an unwilling participant, a dark side to this invention? The Endowed, who can read the thoughts of others, follow ethical restrictions. Can a machine? Would owners of a thought imager use it ethically?"

Layon led them down an empty corridor. "Yes, I've wondered about implications for law. Scientists already know most memories are distorted by how the brain assembles encoded experiences. Would eyewitness testimony be improved with a filtered digital record, or would the thought imager reinforce beliefs in false recollections or, even worse, add more distortions? A missing or erroneous added detail could be critical in eyewitness testimony."

They reached the laboratory, located in an isolated section of the lower levels of the complex. Layon paused as he turned the knob. "Remember, you're sworn to secrecy."

Brusch and Jayel nodded, and Layon opened the door.

Chapter 14

As they entered, the dark room automatically brightened, revealing a small, four-walled square devoid of furniture and wall decorations. One broom leaned on the wall to their right.

Layon closed and locked the door.

"Very impressive," Jayel teased. "The camouflage is quite good. I would never know this broom closet is a laboratory."

Brusch smiled.

Ignoring her, Layon squatted by the corner of the opposite wall and placed his hands on it. Speaking into an unseen receiver, he said, "Layon. At your service."

Instantly, the wall he'd touched moved backward several feet. Layon stood and turned to face them. "Precautionary measures in case anyone got in, despite the lock."

"Good idea," Brusch commented. He and Jayel followed him through the opening.

They entered a large room more to Jayel's expectations of a research lab—tables, computers, miscellaneous audio-visual equipment, and walls covered with plans and notes. She also saw to the side a kitchen, bath, and sofa.

The wall behind them moved back.

Layon went to the kitchen area and filled a water pitcher,

brought three glasses to the table, and took sandwiches out of the bag. However, his guests couldn't be persuaded to eat first. "Very well, I'll demonstrate now. I need a volunteer."

Jayel pointed at Brusch, but the Endowed member shook his head. "Go ahead, you do it. I remain a skeptic of young Layon's boasts and prefer an objective viewpoint."

After looking scornfully at Brusch, Layon asked Jayel to sit in a well-padded chair positioned in front of a large blank screen bordered by speakers.

He wheeled over a tripod with attached head sensors. "Now, this instrument captures your brain waves. It doesn't need to touch your hair or skin. But try not to move around too much or bump the sides or top." Layon adjusted the height of the pole. "Comfortable?"

"Yes. So far, so good, I like it already. I'm not required to wear a helmet nor feel scalp pricks."

Layon walked over to a set of dials on the side of the monitor. Lights blinked on. A console on their right also displayed lights and text on a monitor. He explained recent upgrades to dials and buttons to Brusch.

"Okay." Layon turned. "The display screen is on, and we are ready for input. First, let's start simple. Don't think of anything too complex. Hold the image for five to ten seconds."

With Brusch and Layon focused on her, she tried to pick something they would recognize. They talked about flowers earlier. Jayel generated a mental image of a long stem *ebbie.* The men focused their attention on the monitor as a dim shape appeared and sharpened into two green leaves, a stem, and a fresh pink blossom.

"Yes, exactly what I'm imagining. Wow." Jayel moved forward, and the image disappeared. She leaned back and chose a different item.

"What's this from?" Layon pointed to the image of a grand pine tree.

Brusch piped in, "I know, it's Najule's tree. It grows on the grounds of the House of Leidra."

"Yes," she studied the screen. "The image looks much like what I'm imagining. Look, you can see the sky and other trees at the glade's edge to give perspective. Amazing."

Brusch prompted her, "What about motion? Imagine something moving."

Within seconds, the screen displayed a 64-A22 spaceship taking off. The image blurred as the ship sped across the airstrip, then upward in flight.

Layon made notes on a pad. "I've yet to solve the time differential. See, our thoughts review a process such as a spacecraft's flight much faster than the actual event. The moment-to-moment details are only temporarily held in mind. It's a challenge to add accurate details the person doesn't remember precisely."

Nodding, Brusch agreed. "Users won't like waiting minutes for digital material to appear." He put his hand on his chin. "I think we can interpolate missing details on the replay, though, and clarify the picture."

Layon typed commands on the console next to the monitor and then played back the last segment. The ship's details were sharper, and its flight seemed less erratic.

Brusch nodded thoughtfully. "We may be able to use Jango's classic algorithm for data crunching on your knowledge files and reduce built-in redundancies. I have current ideas gleaned from reviewing papers at a recent AI conference. I think they'll help assemble the images faster."

He slapped Layon on the back. "For now, I must say I'm impressed with the quality of the images already. You have done well. Sharpening the picture should be the least of your concerns. Can we add another modality?"

"The pine tree scent," Jayel suggested. She brought back the memory of standing in the glade, focusing on the strong and pleasant scent.

Layon twisted dials. "What do you think? Close to the real thing?"

The emitter was in front of the headset. "Yes, I can smell it, but it occurs to me there's another problem. If it's an unpleasant smell, I don't want it in my face. And you told me not to move my head too much, so there's no escape. I think the user needs control over scents."

"Good point. Eyes can close or look away, but noses can't turn off." Layon wrote on his pad. "Maybe smells can be modulated like volume. The user would increase or decrease the intensity.

Brusch commented, "Hmm, perhaps the user could release another scent afterward to neutralize the current one, similar to how we cleanse our palate in taste-testing."

After a long pause, Jayel added, "In medical school, I read how people vary in their ability to create mental images. If they can't imagine a scent, could this device generate it for them?"

Layon smiled. "I like your idea. Enrich the recording and the experience when replaying vague memories. If you see it in the mind's eye but can't imagine the pine scent, the imager could add it based on knowledge of pine trees."

"Intentional false memories," Jayel noted. "But for pleasure, not to distort the past."

Layon continued writing while Brusch added, "Perhaps make it a choice, a parameter setting for the user telling it how much the imager should copy what they're thinking or enhance their thoughts."

After Layon finished writing, he flipped a set of switches. "Put your hand on the screen. Feel the pine branch."

Brusch touched the screen first. "Remarkable."

Jayel leaned forward, but the picture disappeared.

"Oh . . . keep your head under the sensors," Layon reminded her. "Let me move your chair and headset closer so you can see better."

She thought of the evergreen tree again, reached out, and touched the screen. Hundreds of tiny sensors filled the surface. Her fingers could discern the needles from the empty spaces. "Wow, it does feel like pine needles."

Layon explained, "The program interprets which skin areas on your fingertips need to be stimulated, and activates corresponding brain areas, triangulating thought-activated areas. Because you know they're pine needles, you interpret the stimulation to fit, instead of, say, sandpaper. It works on the same principle as categorical color perception—we imagine the red of fruit because we know the fruit is red even if the shade is physically different—or like speech perception—we hear words from sound waves once we know the language."

Brusch nodded. "So far, we've seen images Jayel deliberately concentrated on. Surely, she has thought of more than these three things in all this time. It seems to me the user of this machine has good control over captured thoughts. It's the safest way to program for now. Don't capture all thoughts, only those the user wants to share, by requiring the user to hold the thoughts in their mind for at least three seconds. A speedier, but still slow, conversion process may prove best."

Layon teased her. "If you're having indecent, fleeting thoughts about me, the monitor won't give you away unless you want it to."

Jayel blushed and leaned forward, moving her head away

from the instrument's range.

"Let's eat those sandwiches now," Brusch interjected. "Tell us more about the experiments you've planned."

Layon rolled the tripod away from the chair, and they walked to the table. "I've designed many tasks." He handed Brusch a pad. "And the user can report how well the monitor captured their thoughts while completing them."

"So many different directions you could explore," Brusch noted as he scrolled the list. "Soon, you will be ready to patent your work."

Layon beamed.

"Keep in mind, my friend, you don't have to do everything yourself. Other scientists will explore how the brain generates thoughts and how brain areas work in concert. Others will improve your hardware and software once word gets out. I suggest you focus on accuracy and speed. Conduct one experiment and compile its results. Then provide the data as an example when you present your prototype to research firms for funding further development."

"It's taken the last four standard years to get to this point." Layon sighed, leaning back in his chair. "I admit it's hard to let others work on my project."

Brusch smiled. "I'm honored to be the first."

"Thank you, Brusch." Layon leaned forward. "Your support throughout this project has meant much. I was discouraged early on by failure and overwhelmed by obstacles, but your encouragement and suggestions, though from a solar system away, helped me persevere and succeed."

Layon quickly entered commands into his pad, giving Brusch password permissions to all his files.

Finishing the last of her sandwich, Jayel offered. "If you need a research participant for data collection, I volunteer to help."

"Thank you." He added their permissions to enter the lab on his pad, then looked at the time. "I'll check upstairs and see what the schedule holds for us."

A minute later, Layon put the electronic pad away. "Dareck is busy for the rest of the day in ICID's intelligence center. I have tomorrow off, and Dareck suggested you might like to go to the surface and see Ondre's sights. We could start working on the research now if you're willing."

"Why not show Jayel around ICID now," Brusch suggested. "I'd like to continue working here on formulas and code before you start data collection. You and I can look over my modifications early tomorrow, and by midmorning, Jayel could begin providing data. Then, after a few hours, take a break and see Ondre."

Layon smiled at Jayel. "Just the two of us for an afternoon tour of the facilities."

She met Brusch's eyes. *Is he in a rush to program, or is he deliberately putting the two of us together?* Jayel wondered if Brusch had any idea of Layon's advances earlier or her suspicion Layon was more than a half-cousin.

Brusch returned an innocent look.

"A tour of the facility now is agreeable," she said.

Jayel watched Layon open the wall to the broom closet. When she stepped into the hallway, the contrast felt like going from oasis to desert, from science fiction to reality.

"Letdown, isn't it?" Layon remarked, looking at the bland hallway. "I frequently experience the contrast you just felt, between a boring present and an exciting future into the unknown."

Jayel nodded. "Guess you don't need a thought imager to know my thoughts."

After they walked to the elevator, he lowered his voice. "I want to apologize."

"What for?"

"My attitude earlier. I first thought you were Dareck's lover, and then I hoped you would be mine. It was silly of me only to see you that way. I appreciated your comments today about the imager, and I'm glad you'll work on the project with us tomorrow."

Jayel smiled. "I will enjoy being in a research lab again. It's been a long time."

"I … I still feel I've known you all my life and hope we can become close friends. Very close friends."

She remained silent, and they entered the elevator. Layon spoke their destination. Seconds later, they stepped out into a large lobby.

Layon led the way. "Come, let's begin our tour of ICID."

Chapter 15

"Vroom!"

"Oh," Jayel stepped back into the elevator's entrance.

A toddler wheeled quickly by, yelling with delight. A woman emerged from the nearby play center and ushered the child back into the large room where other children rode three-wheelers.

Jayel laughed and walked out of the elevator again.

Layon looked annoyed. "Sorry. The complex divides into two main sections. The east section consists of mostly business and research facilities, and the west accommodates private and recreational needs. As you can tell from our young joy rider, we are on the west side of ICID."

They began walking through the complex, past shops and restaurants.

"Psychologists told ICID's architects most people desire to be close to the surface," Layon continued, "so they designed everything on the first two levels. Operational and mechanical equipment occupies level three. Storage is on level four. It's why my research lab is on the fifth level—nothing else is, hopefully for a long time—they built it in case of future expansion."

"I'm not sure I would like to live underground. Is

claustrophobia a problem here?"

"Rarely. See the lofty ceilings here," he waved his arms, "and the elaborate landscaping to breathe life into spaces. With the war on, residents don't travel to Catana or Marshe as often as they once did. Fortunately, ICID offers a variety of activities to keep personnel from feeling confined."

Jayel imagined what it must be like living underground, not just here but in most places on Ondre. "Is the fighting limited to the cities? Coming in from the spaceport this morning, I didn't see any signs of war."

"We are a neutral organization and untouched so far. It might be worse if we were between Catana and Marshe, but we're located a half-hour flight south of Catana, and Catana is two hours southeast of Marshe."

"It's unusual for two cities to be so close to each other."

"Yes. Planners did well in Onus One where cities were built above ground. When they designed the cities on Ondre, they didn't fully appreciate the difficulties of underground formations and speedy growth towards each other. Within decades, the two cities were disputing property rights and resources."

"Is there a possibility ICID's neutrality may change?"

Layon shrugged his shoulders. "It's possible, but I wouldn't worry about it. We do our best not to offend either side or, at least, to offend both sides at the same time."

Jayel laughed but then remembered Dareck's fear of his son's inclinations to become involved. "What about you, Layon? How do you feel about the war?"

He paused. "I lived on Ondre all my life, so naturally I find it hard to sit by and watch two cities I know well destroy each other. Both cities are wrong to settle contract disputes through violence. If pinned down, I'd have to say I favor the Catanans.

Fortunately, Dareck will help us investigate the military aid Marshe is receiving. We're certain it comes from an outside source."

"I wonder how the wheels of diplomacy will spin when the source is named." *And will my father be the supplier?*

They took an escalator to the first level. Jayel toured a large greenhouse, wide and long, filled with rows of flowers and vegetables, hydroponic bays, and aquafarming tanks. Here and there, direct sunlight peeked through skylights at the end of small carved tunnels.

Soon they walked to the east side of the complex and came to the Research Information Center.

Layon said, "This is the RIC, where I work. It's here where we monitor the war activities."

Unlike the rest of the complex where Jayel and Layon moved freely from corridor to corridor and level to level, the RIC restricted entrance to staff and approved visitors. Armed uniformed guards stood at the hallway entrance, a reminder ICID wasn't a hotel or resort.

As they approached, one guard, a middle-aged man, said, "Hello, Layon. Working hard today, huh?"

"Ambassador duty, Marcum. I'm taking this beautiful woman on a tour."

Marcum's eyes checked Jayel out. He looked back at Layon. "She wears Dareck's pin and has clearance."

He handed Jayel an electronic pad. "Please indicate your entrance for our records." After she placed her right index finger on the pad, Marcum took the pad back and motioned for them to enter the opening smoke-colored glass doors.

They walked past various offices and conference rooms. She recognized one large room from Kathzerum's computer newsfeed, where the president of Onus Two had spoken last year after the assassination of Catana's governor. Flags of each planet lined the assembly room's wall.

At the end of the corridor, they walked into a large foyer.

"Oh, this is interesting," Jayel pointed to an enormous sculpture suspended from the ceiling, a model of the two solar systems' planets and their moons. Each system contained four inhabited planets—Orim, Melandan, Characta, and Leidran in Onus One, and Ondre, Vandera, Uamung, and Xarim in Onus Two. Additionally, one gas giant, Kelper, dwarfed the other Onus One planets. She stared at Melandan the longest. *Home.*

"The detail is exquisite," Jayel said as she studied the display. She noted the southern mountain ridges of Leidran, the enormous ocean of Xarim, and the rings of weather satellites around the moons and planets. The display also included the relatively very small Standard Time satellite in the outer space of Onus One.

Layon commented, "The sculpture slowly moves, imitating the moons and planets' orbits. Although the distance between isn't true to scale, you get the feel for how far apart the planets and two systems are from each other."

Eventually, they turned and walked into a different hallway. They passed a glass-walled room where Jayel noticed Dareck speaking with two generals. He saw Layon and Jayel and waved for them to enter.

As the generals stood, Dareck reached out to Jayel and drew his niece into their circle.

"Generals, allow me to introduce a member of my entourage, Jayel."

She knew their names from the newsfeed. Foxtrend oversaw the investigation of the source of Marshe's military aid, and Eidelnim oversaw ICID.

She shook both their hands. "General Eidelnim, Layon just

gave me a tour of your facility. I'm impressed."

"Thank you. We are impressed by it, too, though overwhelmed might be a better word for it. No other government research installation is like this one—weather, astronomy, geology, and agriculture. We study it all. Of late, however, we have focused more on military and political intelligence. I'm hopeful, with Dareck's arrival, we can de-escalate Ondre's planetary conflict."

"Any luck?" Layon asked.

"Some," Dareck answered. "We've excluded the planet Vandera, Ondre's nearest neighbor, as a suspect. We found no violations of systems' trade laws."

Dareck pointed to a glass map, suspended in the middle of the table, depicting the two solar systems. He pressed a button, and the planets moved along their elliptical orbits around their suns. "Planet Uamung is possible but not probable. Its orbit puts it on the opposite side of Onus Two for the last nine months. It's more likely supplies come from Onus One. It's the most direct path."

Jayel studied the map and watched the planets spin counterclockwise around their suns. A supply ship from Onus One needed months to travel through the vast space to Ondre unless it used the M corridor.

Dareck noted, "We've examined flight frequencies to Ondre during the past twelve months. Nothing is out of the ordinary."

"And the inventory of ships verified," General Eidelnim noted.

The map also showed moons orbiting their respective planet. Jayel asked, "What about flights to Ondre's moons?"

Layon answered, "Neither moon has a strong atmosphere for protecting life from solar radiation." He told the computer to zoom in. "Alkre moon serves as Ondre's storage area for fuel and radioactive elements. The other smaller moon, Bayre, doesn't yet serve any purpose to the people of Ondre. See, Ondre itself was only populated about a hundred standard years ago after terraforming supported life. Marshe and Catana are the main cities on the southern hemisphere's continent. But, like our northern hemisphere, Bayre's terrain remains too rugged to occupy, the temperature too hot."

General Foxtrend commented in a deep voice, "Alkre rotates slowly, about once every three standard days. Bayre doesn't spin on its axis and always has the same face turned to us. You can see its shape isn't spherical; its terrain on both sides is very rough, with mountain ridges and extreme lava formations."

"Hmm." Jayel nodded. "It seems to me the hidden side provides a good place to secretly receive supplies." After giving it more thought, Jayel pointed at the map. "A ship from Onus One could fly toward the Onus Two sun this way, deviating from the M corridor here, be obscured by the star's glare and radiation, then pilot this way to Bayre without anyone noticing."

Dareck turned to General Foxtrend. "I assume you checked out this possibility?"

"Ondre's moons were evaluated first." He pressed the intercom. "Dabs, bring me the report on Bayre Moon."

While they waited, Layon spoke. "As I think about it, the dark side of Bayre is an excellent location. The map shows the flight paths of traffic coming from the Onus One System. They don't intersect with Bayre. Thus, our investigations focused on traffic in the opposite direction. We could've overlooked ships flying through the back door so to speak to Bayre moon."

Soon, a young, uniformed woman rushed in. "The reports

are ready, sir."

General Foxtrend glanced at the pad, nodded, and uploaded the data to the glass screen for all to view. Dareck scanned matrices of numbers.

"Well," Dareck said, nodding. "We found an oversight. ICID did investigate activity on Bayre, but only on the side facing Ondre. Perhaps they assumed it unnecessary to check the other side due to its extreme temperatures." Turning away from the screens, he speculated, "Well, I suppose today's cargo ships could tolerate a close flyby to Onus Two if they took the path Jayel suggested."

Foxtrend nodded. "We better check this possibility right away." He ordered Dabs, "Get information on traffic behind Bayre. If supplies are being left there, someone must be picking them up." He turned to Jayel. "Thank you! I hoped we would discover just such an oversight. Bayre may turn up nothing, but I'm encouraged."

"And if Bayre is the supply base?" Jayel asked.

Foxtrend sighed and rubbed his beard. "We need to discover who delivers the arms." He turned to Dareck. "I'll get data reports to you on traffic from Onus One. See if you can find a pattern through the noise, find those deviations from the M corridor."

Dareck suggested, "Three things you must do before making any official report to Systems Headquarters. One, you must determine if anything you find is a war arsenal, not just a toxic waste dump. Two, you must show that Marshe knowingly and willingly is picking up those supplies. Remember, they deny accepting aid to explain their military victories. Lastly, you must identify the supplier before they can cover up."

"Yes," General Eidelnim agreed, "And do all these steps without losing neutrality or getting drawn into the war."

Concerned, Jayel asked, "Would Marshe attack ICID if they learned we discovered what they've been doing?"

"It's unlikely," Dareck replied. "Marshe could never withstand the power of two solar systems. An attack on ICID would likely bring in Systems retaliation. What is one-third a continent against seven planets?"

"Right," Eidelnim concurred. "I wouldn't worry. We've top men at ICID who can calm any angry escalation."

General Foxtrend nodded and left the room with Dabs.

Jayel looked at the remaining men's solemn expressions and asked, "What's next?"

General Eidelnim broke a smile and answered, "Dinner. You must attend my party tonight. I planned it even before I knew Dareck was coming. It will be more festive with your company."

Layon returned the smile. "Sir, we are honored. Your dinner parties are famous for excellent food, music, and dancing."

"Good," the general glanced at his watch. "I must go. See you at eight."

Dareck congratulated Jayel on her help. "Fresh eyes often make for the best problem-solving. Tonight, we celebrate what I hope is the end of our mission. I'm looking forward to Eidelnim's dinner party."

As they parted, Layon whispered to Jayel, "And I'm looking forward to a dance with you."

Chapter 16

Jayel surveyed the blouses in the closet and selected a creamy white tunic speckled with soft blue dots. She slipped on form-fitting dark blue pants with creamy white belts around the waist and ankles. The silk-like material accentuated her feminine qualities.

As she chose earrings from a tray, a knock at the door sounded.

"You look lovely, Jayel," Brusch greeted her as he entered.

"And you look rather dapper in your long white dinner jacket."

"Like magic, how clothes appear in the closet. AI, you know. They profile the room's occupant and stock what they think is needed."

"I'm glad you made it out of Layon's lab. I wouldn't want you working all night and missing the dinner party." Jayel returned to the mirror and attached the earrings.

The Endowed member sat at the table and watched her reflection. "No one misses General Eidelnim's dinner parties," he laughed. Then, Brusch became serious. "I came early because I'm worried about you."

She turned around. "Worried about me? Why?"

"If the Bayre moon checks out, Dareck's mission to Ondre

is complete. It's conceivable we'll leave soon. As Layon scheduled a full day with you tomorrow, I hoped we might talk tonight."

Jayel moved to the table and sat. "Is anything wrong?"

"I sensed a change in you after we arrived. You've been … preoccupied."

She stiffened slightly, not eager to share her suspicion about Layon's father.

Brusch narrowed his eyebrows. "You're disturbed about Layon. Am I right?"

Jayel bit her lip. "You're good friends with Layon, aren't you?"

"Yes. I've known him since he was six standard years old, and I've mentored his research. I'm the only Endowed member who knows Layon is Dareck's son."

Looking down, she confided, "I knew the moment I saw Layon, like how I knew Chrysic's ship was in the N-5 sector, so it was when I saw Layon. But it can't be. It doesn't make sense."

"What? What did you know about Layon?"

Jayel took a deep breath. There was no hiding from him now. "He's not Dareck's son." She paused. "He is Karsch's son. He is my brother."

Brusch gasped. "Karsch's son!" He stood and walked across the room.

Jayel waited.

Finally, he turned, came back to the table, and sat. "You knew this when you first saw him?"

"Yes. I felt a bond when we looked at each other, like old friends meeting again, only much more intense. Layon felt it, too. He told me so."

Brusch murmured, "The bond between Endowed

members can be very strong, and the brother-sister bond powerful."

"He thinks what he feels is sexual attraction."

"Yes, I sensed his feelings and thought that's what troubled you. He doesn't yet know you are his cousin."

"He's in love with his half-sister," Jayel corrected him.

"All these years, it never occurred to me he wasn't Dareck's son."

"You don't want me to say anything, do you?"

"No, not until we learn more."

Brusch walked to the window print hanging on the wall and appeared to look out. "It does provide a motive for Karsch's killing Neondra and attempting to kill Layon, however. Perhaps he knew Layon was his son. Karsch could have been jealous she stayed with Dareck and hid Layon's parentage, or perhaps Karsch was angry his son was being raised by his brother."

Jayel frowned. *My father intentionally tried to murder his son. I can't believe it.*

She stood, walked to the mirror, and finished putting on her jewelry. She liked the new haircut she got an hour ago and tucked hair behind both ears to let the sparkling earrings show.

Turning toward her, Brusch said, "I know a friend of Neondra's. She may be able to answer our questions. I'll contact her in the morning."

He walked over and stood behind Jayel's shoulder, speaking to her reflection. "Everything you've told me is confidential. Forget about it for now. Tonight … tonight we relax."

Their eyes met in the mirror. *Agreed.*

Brusch moved to the door. "We should go now, or we'll be late."

They walked down the long hallway to an elevator and soon

found the party suite.

Cocktails were being served when they entered. Layon, dressed in a one-piece black suit, opened at the neck, held a green drink, and smiled widely when he saw her.

A moment later, Dareck joined them. He stopped a passing waiter and handed them drinks. "Eidelnim serves wines from all the planets. Enjoy."

Jayel scanned the crowded room. "Should I worry if anyone knows who I am?"

"Well, I already checked the guest list," he replied. "Don't worry. Besides, if anyone here knows who you are, uncle and niece together shouldn't be deemed unusual."

General Eidelnim announced it was time to eat. Layon accompanied them to Eidelnim's table and sat next to Jayel.

The main dish featured succulent *knashori*, drizzled with spice sauce. On the fruit plate, Jayel found sliced *ovatons,* grown only on her home planet. She asked the server how they managed to get fresh *ovatons* from Melandan.

He replied, "This fruit comes from Marshe. They had a good crop this year."

Turning to Layon, Jayel asked, "Is it true Marshe grows *ovatons*? I thought the fruit was too delicate to thrive in any environment other than the northern hemisphere of Melandan."

"Maybe he meant Marshe imported them. Or maybe this is a similar fruit. Have you tried the *ebos*? Now, there's a delicacy for your taste buds." Layon handed her a plate of cheeses.

She doubted Marshe grew the fruit. *If my father is supplying Marshe with military supplies, food shipments could be the cover.*

About an hour later, with guests singing the praises of General Eidelnim's chefs, the jubilant crowd moved into an adjoining hall where a sixteen-piece orchestra waited. The dance floor occupied half of the spacious room. Tables, chairs, and a bar filled the remaining space. At the host's signal, the orchestra began playing, and dancers moved onto the floor.

Jayel quickly discovered Layon was a favorite among the women. Several approached him as soon as he entered the room. He seemed embarrassed by the attention in front of Jayel, but he didn't turn them down. The women whisked him away to the dance floor.

The remaining three found a table and ordered white dessert wine. The music erased Jayel's preoccupation with Layon's bloodline and her father's involvement with the war. The sound from the orchestral instruments blended harmoniously with the room's excellent acoustics, bringing a smile to her face and nostalgic memories of dancing with Dorind. They had entered and won local competitions.

She watched Layon dance three slow numbers, each with a different partner. *He's good—fluid movements, proper posture, and confidence. His grace made him the best dancer on the floor.*

Dareck leaned over. "As you can see, Layon has attended General Eidelnim's parties before."

"Yes," she smiled. "He is an excellent dancer."

At this point, a woman Jayel's age, with hair tied up with sparkly ribbons, asked her uncle to dance, mentioning how much fun it had been last time. He waved his hand and murmured, "Maybe later."

"Layon isn't the only one who is well-liked by the ladies," she laughed.

Brusch took a swallow of his drink. "Jayel, Dareck is an excellent dancer. Don't pass up an opportunity to experience his skills firsthand."

She glanced at Dareck to see what he thought of the suggestion and caught him winking at his friend as if to say,

"Good idea. I owe you one."

Her uncle stood, pulled her chair out, and led Jayel to the dance floor.

For the waltz, he held his niece about half an arm's length away, placing his left arm around her waist. His right arm on her shoulder felt protective, and he masterfully guided her about the room. She focused on the music and enjoyed the dance.

During the orchestra's break, Layon joined them at their table.

When the musicians resumed, they played the opening stanzas for a popular, fast-paced, more modern dance, the *Halaranza.*

"Jayel, may I have this dance?" He stood with his hand out.

She recognized the melody and knew the steps but said, "The *Halaranza* is a tough dance."

"Surely you're not afraid," Layon jested.

"Afraid? I don't want to show *you* up in front of your friends."

"Hah! Now there's a challenge I accept. Esteemed Endowed members, if you will excuse us?"

Most dancers sat this number out, as only the skilled ones could keep up with the tempo and complex steps. Once other dancers saw Layon and Jayel take their positions, they gave way, and Layon and Jayel had the floor to themselves.

The pair stood four feet apart, facing each other. The first chords blared, and the two began to move. The steps called for the male to begin, and the female followed. After the sequence repeated twice, the female led, and the male shadowed. The steps increased in difficulty with each change in the lead.

Layon started simply. As soon as Jayel took the lead and increased the difficulty, he smiled. The dance progressed, their steps executed perfectly with flair, each dancer mirroring the other, interpreting the increasing tempo—crisp turns, precise footwork, on the beat, in sync.

The tempo of the song, after a rapid pace of three lead changes, slowed for an interlude of soft, slow, rhythmic music. Layon extended his right arm, and Jayel placed her left hand in his. Immediately, as their hands touched, a powerful warm sensation passed through her arm and flowed through her body. Jayel felt strong satisfaction as if reuniting with a long-lost friend.

Time stood still as they gazed into the other's eyes, his reflected intrigue but also confusion.

The music continued, and they swayed back and forth, together, then apart.

The tempo picked up again, and percussion punctuated the beat. The dancers circled the floor, repeating earlier sequences, only this time their arms remained joined.

The finale consisted of flashy quick steps and arm movements, and abruptly ended with Jayel bending backward over Layon's arm, his face lowering towards hers.

They held the pose, and the room echoed with applause. The distance between the dancers' faces grew shorter and shorter, their eyes locked, and their lips inches apart. But just before kissing, Layon straightened, raising Jayel for a bow.

They returned to the table, breathing hard with excitement and exertion.

Brusch clapped as they sat. "Fantastic. Excellent, both of you."

"Yes," Dareck agreed. "It looked like you practiced for many hours together."

Jayel's gaze drifted to Brusch. *Had he noticed the pause in their dance, the moment when they touched?*

Layon caught the attention of a passing waiter. "A round of iced wine, please."

"Well," her uncle remarked, "You didn't learn the *Halaranza* at the House of Leidra."

"True. My friend Dory and I performed it in med school competitions … and won."

Layon frowned. "I should have known."

"Yet," Brusch remarked, "It isn't often two people, though separately good dancers, can perform so well the first time together."

The drinks arrived, and Jayel didn't return Layon's gaze nor acknowledge their dance had special meaning.

Brusch raised his glass for a toast. "To an enjoyable evening and things to come."

Chapter 17

Jayel heard the buzz of the intercom, interrupting data collection for the third experiment. She glanced at the clock. *Had more than two hours passed?*

Earlier, when she arrived, Jayel had found Layon at the desk, dressed in a RIC uniform.

He stood, pad in hand. "Thank you for coming, but I must report to work. We sent a probe to Bayre Moon, and I need to be at my post to monitor the information it sends back."

"Should I stay or leave?"

"Stay if you're willing. I finished implementing Brusch's new programming earlier this morning. He's already in the RIC to assist my team." He handed Jayel a pad. "I've outlined experiments for you to do. The directions should be clear but call me if you have any problems."

She quickly scanned the instructions. "I think I can manage."

"If you get bored or need a break, leave everything as is. I'll shut the equipment off when I return."

They walked to the thought imager tripod and reviewed how to work the controls. Opening the lab door, he said, "If I can get a lunch break around one, I'll come down. I'll let you know."

After he left, Jayel felt relief she had escaped any discussion about last night's dance. She loved him as a brother already and wanted to tell him.

The experiments were interesting, and Jayel made specific notes about how well the imager captured her directed thoughts. When she heard the intercom buzz, the clock displayed 12:47 p.m. *Where did the time go?*

As Jayel approached the intercom, its light changed from blue to green. *Maybe it was Layon announcing he was on his way for his lunch break.*

"Hi, Jayel. Layon here." His voice sounded distant. "I won't be able to get away for lunch."

"Do you have news?"

"There's nothing specific to report yet, but we're investigating further to make sense of the probe's findings."

He shifted the conversation. "How are the experiments coming?"

"I'm more than halfway through the tasks. I made notes about what I was thinking at each recording. The imager's detail is remarkable. It's much faster than yesterday."

After a brief pause, Layon suggested, "Listen, it might be best to stop data collection and go to at least the second level. Activity in the RIC is picking up. The rest of the experiments can wait until tomorrow."

"Do you expect trouble?"

Layon hesitated. "It's too early to tell. We might need to do more than glimpse what is on Bayre Moon. Complications make my superiors nervous, and then I get nervous."

"Hmm, I have nothing else to do, so I might as well stay down here. Okay?"

"Very well, then. I'll contact you later."

In the kitchen area, Jayel assembled a sandwich wrap but

considered leaving as Layon had suggested. But because working in the lab made her feel productive, she decided to stay.

After eating, Jayel returned to the imager and followed instructions for the next task. It involved simultaneously using all five senses. Jayel found it easier to imagine the sound of ocean waves than the smell of salty air. Concentrating on each image, she forgot about the probe and the war.

A loud noise shook the room followed by muffled deep booms.

A cup fell off the table and rolled loudly across the floor. Alarmed, Jayel pushed the imager tripod away and stood.

The intercom buzzed three loud alerts. "This is a top-priority alert. All ICID personnel are to report to the first floor except those with a five classification. Those employees report to your supervisors. Again, this is an emergency. We are under attack!"

Jayel swallowed. *Who's attacking us? Marshe? The moon base?*

Another quake shook the walls.

Jayel took several deep breaths. She drew on medical training for emergencies and looked around the lab. *How best to protect Layon's equipment?*

Spotting a closet, she moved the imager tripod, portable computers, and other devices into it. Dust fell from the ceiling. Jayel threw the cot's blanket over the equipment and secured the closet door. She put other small desktop objects in drawers.

The intercom blared, "Intruder Alert. We repeat, Intruder Alert. Hostile forces have invaded the complex. All personnel report any intruders ..."

A call to Layon didn't go through. Her pad was blank.

Another vibration.

More dust in the air.

It didn't feel safe to stay. *Time to leave.*

Jayel looked about the room for a weapon and grabbed a fire extinguisher and pocketed a kitchen knife. She picked up the electronic map, and with one last look around, left the lab.

Cautiously, she entered a silent hallway, as expected. Jayel rushed to the elevator but found it was out of order.

Of course, with the threat of fire or to impede the mobility of intruders, they shut down the elevators.

The only way up was by foot.

The hallway lights flickered and went out. The electronic map no longer provided a screen glow. *The network is down.* She pocketed the map and gripped the knife.

Look for a stairwell. Jayel felt the hallway wall with her elbow and walked slowly until she found a door. She turned the knob. The door opened.

Boom.

More dust floated in the air and into her mouth. She coughed.

Jayel entered the dark stairwell and began climbing the steps. *Why did there have to be so much space between levels?* Before long, her legs tired, and she paused twice to recover. She felt hot, and a trickle of sweat dripped onto her neck.

After reaching the top landing, Jayel discovered this stairwell didn't go beyond the fourth level. She'd have to enter the hallway and find another staircase.

The door opened inward, and Jayel stepped aside and peered out.

Silence. Faint emergency lighting helped prevent the space from appearing pitch black, but shadows obscured the path.

Jayel caught a barely noticeable glow of a blue light far in the distance to her right. She felt the way toward it, hugging the wall, trying to avoid disorientation in the darkness. Her fingers grasped the knife in one hand. With her other hand, Jayel pressed the fire extinguisher against her body.

I wish I paid more attention to this engineering section during yesterday's tour.

Where are the workers? An eerie silence enveloped her, a silence so thick it was like walking through water. Jayel's heart pounded in her ears.

After reaching about half the distance to the blue light, Jayel discerned the hum of massive machines pumping air through the complex. The sound calmed her. Life support remained operational even with the network down.

Jayel remembered the Endowed exercises to control the breathing and continued walking, feeling the wall.

Nearing the blue glow at the end of the corridor, a weak white light, floor level, from inside a corner office caught her attention. Jayel peeked in the doorway.

Three flashlights scattered on the floor pierced the shadows, their beams revealing three ICID uniformed men lying face down, their bodies surrounded by pools of blood.

She put down the fire extinguisher and checked each man for a pulse. They were dead.

Jayel picked up one flashlight and scanned the office. She saw an intercom on the side wall, but it didn't turn green when she approached. Tapping it had no effect. It was dead, too.

Damn. She turned away from the intercom and started to return to the doorway. *At least I can use this flashlight to see my way up.*

Her heart stopped when she heard footsteps approaching the entrance.

Jayel froze, unbelieving who stood in the flashlight's beam with her weapon drawn.

***

Jayel slowly walked along a corridor on level two. She couldn't remember her last thoughts nor how she got from engineering's fourth level. She felt disoriented, like waking up and not remembering ever going to sleep.

There was better lighting now, and she could see debris further ahead. A huge section of the ceiling filled the hallway. She pushed aside several chunks to get through the rubble.

Something on her left moved, and she reflexively took a step back.

A young child, a boy of two or three years old, huddled among the fallen debris. He saw her and began crying.

Jayel approached and whispered words of comfort. He was covered with splattered dust but otherwise seemed uninjured.

When she patted the boy's head and shoulder, her strength transferred to him. His skin warmed, and his face relaxed.

The toddler focused on her face and stopped crying.

Jayel wiped away his tears and picked him up. The boy locked his arms around her neck, wrapping his knees tightly around her waist. She winced.

"It's all right, now," she cooed, stepped over rubble, and continued walking.

A few turns later, they reached an open atrium filled with broken planters and benches. Despite the mess, Jayel recognized being here with Layon yesterday and knew where she was. She saw the non-moving escalator across the way, that went up to ICID's first level.

As Jayel approached the escalator, four ICID guards somewhere from her left called out, "Stop!"

Jayel waited at the base of the escalator while they approached.

The group leader, his uniform covered with dust, immediately looked at Dareck's pin on her collar, smiled, and nodded approval. "We're looking for intruders. Have you seen any?"

Jayel shook her head.

"Did you come from the greenhouse?"

"No, I … I came from over there." She pointed across the atrium to a hallway. "I found this boy hiding in some debris and want to return him to his parents."

"I see. Don't go up to level one right now. We're sending residents to the medical center located here on level two. It's not far." He pointed to the right. "We set up a security shelter there where you can check in."

Jayel thanked him and made her way to the shelter. The boy didn't loosen his grip around her waist.

Soon she could hear voices, not loud but many. Passing through the doors, she found the shelter's large room crowded, filled with civilians and their families, ICID uniformed personnel, and staff in blue and white medical garb. People were standing or milling around, shock and concern colored their faces.

She continued forward in hopes of finding the checkpoint. *I'll assist the medical staff once I find the boy's parents.*

She heard a familiar voice and quickly turned.

"Jayel! You made it on your own. Good." Brusch rushed to greet her. "Are you injured?"

"It's good to see you, Brusch. Are you okay?"

"Yes. Did you have any trouble reaching level two? Who's this child?"

With a blank look in her eyes, Jayel replied, "I … walked up because the elevators were out … I … found this frightened boy sitting in a pile of debris not far from here. I'm hoping his parents are here."

Brusch's concerned eyes turned to the child.

The boy clung tightly to Jayel, but he looked at the man and whimpered, "Mommy! I want my mommy."

Jayel asked, "What's happened? Is the attack over? Have you heard from Dareck or Layon?"

"The worst is over, I think. Dareck is out with the ICID space patrol. He's their best pilot. Layon is in the RIC at his station."

"I thought ICID was diplomatically protected."

"We were naive. Obviously, our probe stirred up trouble."

Brusch studied her face and frowned. "You look pale, Jayel. Are you feeling well?"

"A little in shock, I suppose … The elevators didn't work, and it was dark. I had to feel the wall to find my way." Jayel didn't mention not remembering how she made it to level two from engineering. *What's happened to the fire extinguisher? I don't remember dropping it.*

At this moment, the child pointed at a blonde long-haired woman approaching.

"Mommy!" the boy wailed, kicking his legs into Jayel's side multiple times.

Jayel groaned. He still held tightly to her neck.

A young female lieutenant, with tears of relief, reached out for the boy. "Merg, Mommy's here."

The boy exchanged Jayel's neck for his mother's and seamlessly wrapped his legs around the lieutenant's waist.

Jayel felt a wave of fatigue but smiled as she explained, "I found him in a hallway near the atrium, scared but uninjured."

"Thank you so much. Merg, let Mommy take a good look at you. … What's this? Oh no, your shirt and legs are covered with blood."

"What?" Brusch quickly helped the mother examine the skin beneath the child's dust-covered clothing. "Odd," he said, "there's no wound, yet the blood is wet."

Jayel looked down at her blood-soaked tunic and gasped. "It seems I'm the one who's bleeding," *Strangely, I feel nothing at all.*

The room's lighting brightened to a fiery white. Jayel vaguely saw Brusch's astonishment as she slumped to meet the rushing floor.

Chapter 18

"Shot?" Dareck exclaimed as he stood in the hangar of ICID's defense port. He had just landed when Layon met him with the news about Jayel. The excitement from flying the victorious mission quickly abated. *I'm never in the right place when I am needed.*

"Brusch is with her now."

"What happened? Take me to them at once."

Layon led the way and told Dareck what he knew. "Brusch kept an eye out for Jayel while he helped the medical staff with casualties. She arrived from my laboratory about a half hour after the attack started, and they talked for a few minutes as if everything was okay."

Dareck frowned. "Did she mention encountering an intruder?"

"No. According to Brusch, she fainted from the blood loss before saying anything."

Dareck pressed his lips together, suppressing his anger. *If I hadn't brought her to Ondre, Jayel would still be happily living at the House of Leidra. Was I too eager to have her help me get evidence of Neondra's murder?*

Dareck followed Layon onto the moving walkway. "The irony is that Jayel found the base which brought on this attack.

ICID generals believed we were safe from retaliation if they investigated. They were wrong."

"At least the attack is over." Layon stepped aside on the landing and allowed Dareck to walk in front of him.

They made their way through the crowded hallways, passed wounded personnel in hallway beds, and entered a quieter section of the medical center.

Brusch leaned against a wall looking pensive and smiled upon seeing them. "The doctor is with her. We should soon hear how the surgery went."

Dareck saw the concern on his friend's face. "You're not telling us something."

Brusch frowned. "I'm telling you what I know. If I look worried, it's because of what I don't know."

"Which is?" *It wasn't like Brusch to be indirect.*

"I sense her injury isn't merely physical. I'm afraid there's a deeper wound involved."

"Were you able to read her thoughts?"

"No. Her defenses were too strong. When Jayel arrived, she didn't mention an injury. It's as if she didn't know she'd been shot."

At this moment, the doctor came out of Jayel's room.

"Hello, Dareck, Layon," the doctor said.

"How is she, Dr. Cranger?" Dareck asked.

"The projectile missed the vital organs and didn't cause major damage. The danger is the loss of blood. We've replaced two pints. Our blood supply for her uncommon type is low, and—"

"I'll be happy to donate," Dareck interrupted.

"What is your blood type?" the doctor asked.

"C."

"I'm sorry, but she has type D—"

"I'm a D, Doctor Cranger." Layon began to roll his sleeve.

"Ah, good. You can come with me."

Brusch asked, "What's Jayel's prognosis?"

"An inch in any direction, and there might have been organ damage. No, the muscle and tissues will heal quickly now we've administered treatment. She went into shock from the blood loss, but we've checked those symptoms, I think. If her body responds well, she'll be tired and sore for a few days at most." The doctor looked at his pad. "If there's nothing more, gentlemen, it has been a busy day. Layon, come."

Layon and Cranger left.

Dareck and Brusch entered Jayel's private room which Brusch managed to get even though space was at a premium. Dareck smiled thanks, but his friend's expression was fixed on Jayel.

Dareck approached the side of the bed and studied her condition. Jayel's face was pale, and her respirations were not very deep, but they weren't labored. He looked into his niece's mind but couldn't read any thoughts. Usually, when a person slept, it was easy for him to do so. With Jayel, he hit a brick wall. *She's a cautious one with her feelings.*

"You may be right about her injuries," Dareck said. "She's not resting."

Dareck impulsively took her hand and closed his eyes. He remembered when the situation had been reversed, when she had touched him near Najule's pine tree and healing sensations passed between them. Perhaps his touch would comfort her.

Her hand was cool and unresponsive. Dareck felt nothing and frowned.

***

About half an hour later, Layon returned. He found Brusch in a chair by the foot of the bed and Dareck sitting close to her side, his hand still holding Jayel's. It was obvious his father loved her. *But why? If she wasn't his father's lover, then why did he care about her?*

Layon spoke and caused Dareck to stir. "I must know, who is she? Jayel wouldn't tell me until I talked with you first. What is your relationship? I can see you love her. Even Brusch has shown a strong affection for this woman. I must know who she is."

The two Endowed members exchanged quick glances. Brusch looked away and let Dareck make the decision.

Dareck released Jayel's hand and stood. "Well, let's talk now. Not here, in my quarters. I've heard they weren't blown up in the attack. Brusch, you will notify us if her condition changes?"

"Of course."

Father and son left the room.

***

"Karsch's daughter!" Layon couldn't believe it.

Dareck smiled tenderly at his son. "I was surprised, too, yet I managed to contain my emotion."

Layon was on his feet, visibly upset. "Are you sure, Father? Can there be any error?"

"None."

"You should have told me this before. If I'd known she was Karsch's daughter, I wouldn't have—" He broke off.

"Wouldn't have what?" Dareck pressed.

"Wouldn't have fallen in love with her!"

Dareck laughed softly and waited for Layon to sit. "Well, love is a complex emotion, to be sure, often misinterpreted. You are cousins. The bond between cousins can be strong."

Layon thought about it and agreed. He liked the idea of

having a cousin. He studied his father's face. "You look unhappy."

"I feel responsible. If I hadn't brought Jayel to Ondre, she wouldn't have been shot."

"What kind of reasoning is that? Don't be so hard on yourself. But before we lament our misfortunes, please explain some things. You said you met her at the House of Leidra. I don't understand. I thought Jayel wasn't an Endowed member."

"I can't explain why she was permitted to stay at the House of Leidra. I'm certain my brother would be proud for his daughter to enter the membership. But strangely, Karsch seems to have ignored her training completely. I don't know why."

"Do you mean she hasn't received *any* Endowed training?"

"She was reluctant to talk about it. But I've given Jayel exercises to sharpen mental discipline. Perhaps one day she will apply for membership."

Layon scanned his father's face. "There's more you haven't told me."

"Yes. It concerns your mother and the fire. Two standard years ago, Jayel overheard her father and General Chrysic discussing Neondra's murder. They had paper documents. As you can imagine, Jayel was upset to learn her father committed a murder. To hide her thoughts from him, she retreated to the House of Leidra until deciding what action to take, where, only by chance, I met her."

Layon shifted his posture. "Chance and fate often are misunderstood for the other. Was it chance or was it fate you two met? You say she lived there for two standard years?"

Dareck nodded. "The Endowed power of the House of Leidra is strong. Time passes there as in no other place.

However, Jayel learned many things from the Endowed books and records. She's done well with the exercises I gave her for developing mental discipline."

Layon sighed. The shock of Jayel's identity eased, and growing suspicions filled his thoughts. "But can you be sure Jayel is as innocent as she seems? What of Chrysic's visit to the planet? Perhaps their meeting was prearranged, but you foiled it. Or he had already been there and was returning when you encountered him? Or perhaps Karsch planted her at Leidra? Maybe she intends on destroying you instead of helping you."

"I had similar suspicions, but I've studied her these past weeks. The evidence says she's innocent. I know the power of the land and House of Leidra. Chrysic would never have found it—the idiot had been walking in circles when I encountered him. Nor could Jayel have found it if she'd been in cahoots with him."

Layon nodded. Dareck continued, "Further, she had opportunities to injure or kill me. Instead, she saved and healed me."

Dareck sat back. "And, we have Brusch's opinion. He trusts her, too."

Layon let out a long breath. "Now what happens? Is the plan to go to Melandan and confront your brother?"

"Not exactly. Jayel agreed to look for the documents Karsch possesses and give them to me after finding them. No confrontation with my brother happens until we see whether the evidence does indeed prove murder."

Layon leaned in toward his father. "Do you know what this means for us if Jayel succeeds? All these years, we hoped to find evidence Mother's death was not an accident, and finally, we learn such evidence exists."

Dareck placed his arm on his son's shoulder. "I know

only too well. It means your day has come. Soon, you shall claim your rightful identity and its rewards. As for me, a nearly twenty-standard year-old quest will have ended. We'll not be whole until then."

Father and son looked deeply into each other's eyes.

Layon questioned, "And what of Jayel? What does she get? She will have betrayed her father and destroyed his position on the Governor's Council. How can she do it?"

The two men sat in silence.

Dareck sighed and stood. "I'm going to check on her. Are you coming?"

"First, I want to go down to my laboratory and see how it faired. I'll come soon."

Father and son parted.

ICID elevators were functional again, and, as Layon returned to the fifth level, he felt increasingly happy. He understood his feelings now, why he sensed Jayel felt their bond but didn't return his romantic overtures. Not lovers, but cousins.

Layon smiled. Hidden on Ondre, away from family, he tried to ignore the void, the loneliness. *How wonderful I'm no longer alone, almost like having the sister I yearned for.*

Chapter 19

While Dareck and Layon talked, Brusch remained at Jayel's bedside. The medicine coursing through her veins assisted the healing process, and Jayel's facial muscles and breathing seemed more relaxed.

Brusch tried to reach her mind and encountered several gates, but he skillfully passed through them. Eventually, he entered her personal space, a mental image of a small stone cabin in the wilderness, the door locked, and its sole window barricaded. Peering between boards across the window, he saw a dimly lit bare room. Jayel sat on the floor near the far corner, her back to him.

Brusch called out Jayel's name, but she didn't appear to hear him. He pulled away one of the boards and knocked on the dusty, cobweb-filled window, but Jayel didn't—or wouldn't—turn around. Not giving up, he broke the pane with the board.

At the sound of breaking glass, Jayel turned around. She didn't seem to see him or know who he was. Instead, she slowly stood and backed away.

"Unlock the door, Jayel," he suggested.

No answer.

"Please, Jayel, allow me to enter. Trust me. Think about the beach when we connected. You know you can trust me."

After a long pause, she sighed and mumbled, "I … you will find the door unlocked."

Brusch left the window and went to the door and turned the knob. The door creaked as it opened. He entered, footsteps echoing as he walked across the room.

"Thank you for letting me in. I'm here to help you."

Jayel kept her head down, arms crossed. Although she didn't move toward him, she didn't back away either. He could tell she was afraid. *What is she afraid of?*

"You're safe now" Brusch assured her. "Let me help you. Tell me what you're feeling."

Still not looking at him, Jayel answered, barely above a whisper, "Nothing."

"Nothing?"

"I'm empty of all emotion."

"Why?"

Jayel shook her head as if she didn't know but looked away and said, "I have failed."

"Failed? How have you failed, Jayel?"

She didn't answer.

Brusch frowned but added warmth to his voice. "Come, let's go outside. Get fresh air and take in the sunshine."

Jayel didn't resist when he led her out of the musty room.

Outside, the sun shone upon the freshly cut green grass. A light breeze brought air to their lungs, the smell of rainwater nearby lingered in the air, and the sound of birds echoed from distant trees.

They walked up the hill and sat on a stone bench.

Brusch waited while Jayel soaked in energy from the sun.

Eventually, she looked at him, clearly seeing him for the first time.

"How did you get here, Brusch? I thought this was my sanctuary, where no one could find me."

He smiled. "It's one of my Endowed abilities, to communicate with another person this way. To put it modestly, I'm more than a mind reader. This communication is unique. You and I share a special connection. It began when we rescued the drowning boy. You can know me as no one else can, not even my wife."

"My dear Brusch, I didn't know you were married."

"I don't make it public knowledge. Dareck and a few others know. My private and public lives are two galaxies apart."

"I'm jealous of her," Jayel teased, half true, half happy for him.

"No need to be. You and I share a relationship she would envy."

Jayel attempted a smile. "Forgive me. I seem to have forgotten the value of friendship."

"What do you mean?"

"What? I don't know why I said that. Sorry, I'm tired."

"Hmmm." He paused, but when Jayel didn't add anything more, Brusch asked, "Do you remember what happened to you, about being shot?"

She seemed startled by his question. "Was I shot? Odd I can't remember. After leaving the lab, it was a dark, long climb up to the second level." Jayel paused. "Was I shot? I don't feel any pain. I feel nothing except weakness. Yes, I feel spent."

"Strength will come," he encouraged her. "You lost blood, but the doctor expects a full recovery. Remembrance will be easier when you're stronger. Give it time. Being shot is traumatic."

"'Give it time.' You asked me for time once before, on Quintar's beach."

Brusch nodded. "We learned many things about each other." He placed his hand on hers.

"Yes, and I remember Dareck's expression when we walked in the front door, our hair soaked, water still dripping in our eyes."

They laughed softly at the memory.

"Remind me to record the scene on Layon's thought imager," Jayel mused.

"I'd like to see Dareck's version of it," Brusch laughed. "He probably remembers us as swimming through the front door."

"To be sure." She laughed at an image of ocean waves crashing through Kathzerum's entranceway when they walked in, foam swirling around Dareck's feet.

A short silence passed.

Brusch began to stand. "You look better. I'll leave you to rest."

"Wait, don't go. If you do have the time, stay with me a while."

"Come here," Brusch whispered and opened his arm. Jayel leaned in, and he placed her head against his shoulder.

Brusch felt Jayel gather strength from his support. The time-suspended moment was a most unusual experience. Closing his eyes, a tear melted silently onto his skin.

***

Brusch stirred, startled by the closing of the hospital room's door.

"My friend, how is she?" Dareck asked.

The memory of holding Jayel still strong, Brusch gathered his thoughts and became aware of his current surroundings. "She's sleeping now, healing, finally. How did your talk with Layon go?"

Dareck stood on the other side of Jayel's bed. "He took the news fairly well."

"Where's he now?"

"Gone to his lab to check on his equipment." Dareck paused. "Did you learn what happened to her?"

"No. Maybe we'll find out tomorrow. Why don't you fill me in about the attack? In the confusion, I've yet to learn how things stand."

Dareck nodded. "I should report to General Eidelnim first. I'll meet you in your room, say in an hour. You look like you need rest. I daresay you've had as stressful a day as any of us."

"Sounds good. I could use a hot shower … if the pipes work. Ah, I hope my bottle of *crosex* hasn't broken."

"What standard year?" Dareck asked, a smile of interest on his face.

"4305."

"Excellent, aged exactly right. I like mine slightly chilled."

***

The two friends sat in Brusch's room an hour later, sipping slightly chilled *crosex*.

The complex reduced the energy output to complete main generator repairs, thus dimming the light in the room. However, the amber glow was strong enough to make out each other's expressions. They sat and relaxed for the first time today.

"What's the damage report?" Brusch sipped his drink and swallowed slowly, savoring its exquisite taste. The smooth texture lingered on his palate.

Dareck sighed. "Forty ICID personnel dead. Billions of monies in damage to the complex."

"For what? How did this happen?"

"Unfortunately, our probe's appearance at Bayre Moon coincided with the arrival of a supply shipment to the hidden base. They discovered the probe and immediately comprehended its purpose. Perhaps they thought Catana sent it. Fighters from the base deployed. It wasn't until the probe practically returned to ICID that they realized their error. Instead of the enemy city, they found they were attacking a neutral Systems' organization."

Brusch nodded as he imagined their surprise.

"Well, catching them as we did," Dareck continued, "must have upset them because they waged an attack on ICID rather than retreat and call it a mistake. I guess they hoped to prevent anyone else from learning about the base before ICID relayed its information. Naturally, we retaliated. They found us capable of defending ourselves."

Brusch interjected, "I'm sure those ship fighters didn't expect to find ICID protected by Dareck, famous space pilot and member of the Endowed."

"No, and we destroyed their fleet and stockpiles. The base is no longer operational."

"And the intruders? Did they get into the RIC?"

"We think there was only one squad who infiltrated ICID's defenses, about six members. They attempted to hack engineering but were unsuccessful. ICID lost some personnel down there. Fortunately, no intruders ever made it into the heavily guarded RIC."

Dareck refilled their glasses.

"So, we took no prisoners?" Brusch asked.

"None. We're still unclear where the supply ship came from. It was blown up, with nothing left to incriminate the suppliers. Marshe claims ignorance."

Silence fell between them, each thinking of the problems the planet must manage in the weeks ahead.

"What can you tell me about Jayel?" Dareck asked.

"I'm surprised she made it to the medical center on her own power. Jayel didn't realize she was injured."

"My niece can be strong when the need presses. Remember, my friend, she carried me for more than an hour."

"True." He paused. "I initially thought she responded well to the attack, but I was wrong."

Dareck took a long sip of *crosex*. The flavor of the aged wine lingered on his tongue. "Were you able to read her mind?"

Brusch stood before he answered and poured a third round of drinks. "I did."

"And?"

Brusch sighed. "Jayel doesn't recall being shot. She has repressed memory of the event."

Dareck watched his friend's face intently. He waited for Brusch to choose his words.

"She spoke of failure."

"Failure to do what?"

"I don't know. Maybe failing to get out of the way. Maybe Jayel feels getting injured was a failure. You said no intruders were found. Or maybe she meant she failed to stop an intruder. Or maybe failing to prove herself. Remember, she believes her father doesn't think her worthy of Endowed membership."

"Whatever the meaning, failure is hard to handle. As a medical student, Jayel might not have had many failures in her studies. I'm still annoyed by my failures, as you well know."

"There are many types of failure," Brusch added, "not all bad. In trial and error, we must fail. My love of learning has cultivated a strong appreciation of failure … and patience."

Dareck smiled at his friend. "I bow to the master. I aspire to have your patience, with myself and with others. Well, Jayel is resilient, and I'm hopeful." He stood to leave. "Let's get needed rest. Tomorrow the wheels of diplomacy will roll over rocky roads, and I'm expected to keep all parties on track. Goodnight, my friend."

Alone, Brusch finished the last of the *crosex*. The alcohol content of this rare fine wine worked to lift the tension of his muscles but kept the mind clear.

His thoughts focused on the friend who just left and the difficulties yet to come. How would Dareck take the news if indeed Layon was Karsch's son? *Or was it only a coincidence that Layon's blood type matched Jayel's, and Dareck's and Layon's didn't match?* Medical science identified many types and possible ways genetic traits combine. Perhaps blood type D came from Layon's grandfather, Dareck's father.

He slipped under the bed's covers. The sheets felt cool against his skin. At least, everyone would be busy for days, cleaning up the complex and untangling forthcoming political spats, leaving no time for further revelations on his part. Brusch inhaled deeply and relaxed. His thoughts floated away, and his body slept.

Chapter 20

Jayel stared at the ceiling above the hospital bed. Brusch's visit, whether it happened in fact or only occurred in a dream, supplied needed strength. She felt almost normal again except for the lack of memory. The clock revealed it was midafternoon of the day after the attack.

She looked at Dareck sitting in the corner, eyes closed. His appearance hadn't changed since fifteen minutes ago, but Jayel knew her uncle was awake.

"Why are you sitting here keeping vigil as if I were dying?" Jayel asked. "You deserve a good night's sleep in a comfortable bed."

Dareck sat forward. His eyes showed no weariness. Indeed, they were deep and warm.

"I was concerned. How do you feel?"

She exhaled deeply. "Much better, thanks. And you? You weren't hurt, I hope?"

"No. Brusch, Layon, all three of us escaped injury. Others weren't so fortunate."

He moved the chair closer to the bed. "I wish I had never brought you to Ondre. My foresight has been lacking lately."

"Nonsense, Dareck. Did you pull the trigger?"

"Do you remember being shot? We think it happened in Engineering. The same weapon killed other personnel on the fourth level."

"No, nothing yet. But I feel I could walk around today, honestly." Jayel sat up and winced.

Dareck leaned in to fluff the pillow. "Don't be in such a rush. The doctor, and only the doctor, will say when you're to get up."

"Yes, oh tyrant!" Jayel laughed, and Dareck smiled.

A momentary silence followed.

"Jayel," Dareck began, "I'm glad we have some time alone."

"I'm listening."

"Well, I understand if you no longer wish to help me obtain the evidence against my brother. You're free to go, no regrets."

Jayel shook her head. "This injury changes nothing. My life can't take another path until I resolve my father's role in Neondra's death. If he is a murderer, I can't let him escape justice. It's my responsibility as his daughter to hold him accountable … and help him find absolution."

"It could be dangerous, and I don't want anything to happen to you."

"I appreciate your concern." Jayel leaned back on the pillow.

After a long pause, Dareck said, "I had a private discussion with Layon. He knows who you are."

"Oh."

Dareck smiled gently. "You're afraid he hates you now."

"Yes."

"Well, put your fears aside. Knowing who you are hasn't diminished his feelings for you."

"His feelings for me? Did he speak of them?"

"He loves you."

"And I love him, but does he *love* me, or is he *in love* with me?"

"He's happy to have a cousin," Dareck assured her. "I didn't realize until we talked how much he yearns for family."

Two shapes appeared in the doorway. When they approached the bed, Jayel clearly saw Brusch and Layon, their faces full of concern. Layon placed a small bouquet of colored lightbulbs on the table and turned it on. He said, "These will brighten this room."

Brusch smiled. "You look much better, Jayel. Good."

"You had us worried," Layon added. "How are you feeling?"

"I feel good enough to get up, but they insist I stay put. Did your lab escape damage?"

"Yes, although I could only do a quick check, as I had to put in hours at the RIC. No real damage, just a lot of dust. Thanks for protecting the equipment."

"Dareck was starting to tell me about the attack. I want to know what happened."

Layon stepped towards his father. "General Eidelnim wants to see you at your earliest convenience."

"Well, no time like the present." Dareck smiled goodbye and left.

Brusch took Dareck's seat. Layon sat on the bed and reported on the probe's discovery and the attack's outcome.

Jayel smiled. "I'm relieved ICID is no longer in danger."

Layon continued, "They probably waged a full-scale attack to stall for time to erase evidence on Bayre moon. They destroyed their own base."

"What?" Brusch leaned forward, surprised by the news.

"This morning, General Eidelnim learned a massive bomb, detonated from under the surface, obliterated any evidence of a supply base."

"Drastic but effective," Jayel admitted.

Layon noted, "However, twelve minutes of the probe's transmitted data remain available. Our computer records weren't damaged even though the attackers destroyed the probe. The Systems War Committee is enroute to examine the data and investigate who supplied the base."

Brusch asked, "When are they expected?"

"The first ship is due later tonight."

"They work fast," Jayel noted.

"Dareck has clout," Layon responded. "Ondre's civil war demands more attention from the Systems' council when an Endowed member is involved."

Brusch sat back and crossed his legs. "I'd like the Committee to get Marshe and Catana to come to the table. Neither city wanted ICID involved, but now that it is, maybe they can discuss mutual concerns and peace."

"Yes," Layon agreed. "And without those supplies, Marshe has little chance of winning the war now. It's a stalemate. Everyone knows it's time for compromise and resolution."

A knock sounded on the door. Their heads turned to find Dr. Cranger scanning three solemn faces.

"What gloom! Gentlemen, this patient needs rest, not boredom."

"Us boring? Never." Layon stood, faking indignance.

Jayel let out an exaggerated yawn.

Brusch laughed and stood. "We'll be on our way." He patted Jayel's hand and said tenderly, "You look stronger. I'm glad."

"Thank you for stopping by." She smiled gratefully.

"Now, then," the doctor said after Brusch and Layon left, "Let's look under this bandage."

***

The next 22 hours passed quickly. Dareck and Layon kept busy at the RIC while Brusch worked in Layon's laboratory modifying programs and testing equipment. Jayel, ordered to spend one more day under medical supervision, went to the nearby community room. She needed to prove she could be up and about without problems.

Several patients and visitors played card games. Jayel saw a Puzzlecraft game and sat to play.

Puzzlecraft involved a jigsaw puzzle to be constructed on the second level of a three-tier platform. The game required mental rotation and spatial reasoning, as missing pieces on level two could be found jumbled on either the bottom or top level. To add challenge, players could only see the top level from its underside, the side without picture cues.

Players could move only one piece at a time from either the top or bottom level. If they put the piece in the wrong place, the middle plane's border lit blue, but if placed correctly shown yellow. A built-in program kept score.

Jayel turned on the game. The 500-piece puzzle appeared to be a scene of Orim's five-century-old Hallowbrook Bridge. Previous players had completed about a third of the puzzle on the second level. They had constructed the easy parts—the border and the bridge towers.

The proper placement of the pieces was not easy to figure out. After a careful comparison of the three levels, Jayel selected one from the left side of the top tier, predicting it would fit into the right corner of the tower. When the border turned yellow, Jayel smiled. *This is fun. Like one of Dareck's training exercises.*

In an hour, she had fit sixty pieces correctly on the first attempt, and another twenty on the second try. The digital score labeled her progress as "master" and showed less than 50% of the puzzle remained.

Layon stopped in after his shift and joined her. Together, they finished the puzzle.

***

The next day, Jayel convinced Dr. Cranger to release his patient. She was eager to attend to the memory loss of being shot now that her wound was healing well.

In her quarters, after showering and putting on comfortable clothing, Jayel brought out her rucksack and unpacked herbs from the House of Leidra. She planned to use an Endowed homeopathic remedy known to stimulate memory.

Jayel sorted through the various pouches and withdrew the amount needed, using five different herbs. She sprinkled cut leaves in a mug filled with hot water. A strong, pleasant scent filled the room. Jayel turned down the lights, drank the sweet-tasting potion, and lay on the bed.

She guided her thoughts to the afternoon of the attack. Soon, images appeared. Jayel saw herself climbing the steps in the dark to the fourth floor.

Sensations flooded back as she remembered walking through Engineering—dark, silent of others' movements, a barely audible hum from machines in the distance, and an occasional thud from an explosion above. Her heart rate increased as she felt alone in the darkness again.

Apprehensively, Jayel approached a light from an open doorway and peered in. The flashlights exposed three bodies sprawled on the floor. The pungent smell of their blood stuck in her nose. They were dead. *Intruders had been here.*

The memory slowed. Every second stretched. Jayel's feet dragged her body to the wall. The intercom was dead.

Footsteps approached.

Sounded like one person.

Jayel picked up the fire extinguisher.

The light showed the feet of someone standing in the doorway.

Unable to move, her heart pounded. She could barely breathe. Jayel forced her eyes to look up, to identify who stood there. The man wore a uniform she didn't recognize.

Jayel came face-to-face with an intruder.

Not quite. She needed to look the man in the face, to meet his eyes. Her fear resisted the attempt, but the herbs were powerful. Jayel's eyes slowly moved from looking at the weapon—the end still glowing from recent firing—to his chest and then to his face.

I don't believe it.

His beautiful face, so familiar, glowed in the flashlight's beam. His brown hair playfully peeked out from his cap as it always did, framing smooth skin around full, pouty lips.

"Dory!" Jayel gasped. Her chest tightened. She felt she couldn't breathe.

He didn't speak, though his lips which often kissed her on school nights not so long ago parted as if he would.

Jayel wanted to hug him, but when she realized he wasn't happy to see her, she remained paralyzed.

Dorind stood motionless, eyes cold and devoid of any affection.

"Dory, it's Jayel." She intended to say more, but her throat tightened, and speaking was difficult.

If he could see me better … Jayel forced reluctant muscles to move and took a step forward into his light. The dead bodies on the floor blocked an easy path.

Dorind's eyes lowered to her tunic's collar and focused on Dareck's pin shining in the flashlight's beam. Stone-cold eyes burned with renewed hostility, piercing her heart again.

His jaw muscles tightened. His fingers pressed the trigger.

Sharp pain slapped Jayel's side, and sickly warmth soon began dripping down her hip. Jayel dropped the fire extinguisher, the noise loudly echoing as it rolled. She leaned on the desk for support.

In her bedroom, Jayel stopped the memory and scanned the scene again. Did Dorind lower the weapon before firing? Had he experienced a moment of indecision, a moment of regret? Did Dorind mean to kill or only injure her? Jayel couldn't tell. Perhaps the extinguisher, cradled in the right arm, caused him to shift his aim.

Dorind was there, then not there. Whether he walked away or ran, Jayel didn't know. She had closed her eyes and when she opened them, he was gone.

Leaning on the desk, Jayel cared nothing about the pain in her side. Dory had pierced her soul, their love oozing out, releasing all emotions and life. She felt numb.

Jayel opened her eyes in the bedroom and sighed. Ruchelle's warning hadn't prepared her enough for the change in the man she loved. *Dorind. My Dory.*

The absence of love in Dorind's eyes saddened her. *Will I ever see him again, hear his beautiful voice, and hold him in my arms?*

The loss opened the floodgates, and Jayel cried. The released tears filled the mind with emotions again. Better to feel sorrow and loss than feel nothing at all.

Jayel stood and heated a pot of *switchya.* It was time to figure out how this happened and why Dorind was on Bayre Moon. Time to piece together what she knew.

Sipping a cup—*ah, this hits the spot*— Jayel considered information Ruchelle relayed at *The Thirsty Boots*, the news about Ondre's war from Kathzerum's computer concerning her father's and General Chrysic's connections to Marshe, and lastly Dorind's behavior. Once the dots were connected, events began to make sense.

The puzzle completed, she pushed away the empty cup. Jayel knew who was responsible.

Resolute, she looked in the mirror across the room and held her gaze.

No more hiding. I need to go home to Melandan without delay.

Aloud, Jayel swore, "He will pay if it's the last thing I do."

Chapter 21

Repairs continued around the clock, and Jayel wondered whether ICID was recovering from an attack or benefiting from a major restoration. *Probably a little of both.*

Dareck, Layon, and visitors from Onus One attended meetings tasked with unraveling the situation's complexities. At a pace rarely seen, ambassadors from Marshe and Catana accepted invitations to discuss concerns. Peace talks began.

By early afternoon the day after being discharged from the hospital, Jayel felt restless and went down to Layon's laboratory.

Brusch looked up from a monitor at the sound of the door opening. "Good to see you, Jayel, but are you sure you should be up and walking around?"

"I can sit here the same as I can in my room. I … I want to be doing something productive, get my mind off other things."

"Ah, you remember." He smiled.

No use hiding it from him, but no need to tell who shot me. "Yes, but it's behind me now. I've recovered."

"Hmm," he said, studying her face. But he didn't push. "I welcome the company. Feel up to helping with data collection?" He reached for a pad and handed it to her. "Here are some tasks. I've made significant improvements to Layon's programming. They speed the conversion of neural signals to screen pixels while enhancing details."

"Sounds great," Jayel said, relieved Brusch didn't pursue talking about the shooting. She scrolled through the list and walked to the thought imager.

Wow, no dust anywhere.

Brusch returned his attention to his monitor, and Jayel sat, eager to work. The first task repeated from the morning of the attack. She immediately noticed the programming improvements—less delay between thought to image, and details remained sharp when she imagined the tree's leaves blowing in the wind. *Can't wait until I have an imager in my house.*

About two hours later, Dareck and Layon walked into the lab.

"We bring fresh fruit from Onus One." Layon placed a variety on the table.

Brusch stood and reached for a red pome. "Do I detect good news on your faces?"

"Well, better than good. We've excellent news." Dareck produced a bottle of expensive wine, filling the glasses with an air of dramatics.

"We like excellent news." Jayel smiled, taking a glass.

Her uncle started the toast. "Let us drink to show our joy."

All eyes looked at him.

The Endowed member paused, holding their attention. Then announced, "Marshe and Catana have declared peace."

"What?" Brusch exclaimed, his smile broadening.

"Who was the supplier of the base?" Jayel wanted details.

Dareck held up his hand. "In negotiations, we must make compromises. Marshe offered immediate peace in exchange for keeping secret who supplied its military aid."

"And Catana accepted their offer?" Brusch asked.

"Without qualification." Dareck put the bottle on the table.

Brusch and Jayel exchanged surprised reactions.

Layon explained, "Don't you see, naming the supplier would've escalated the aggression, not ended it. If a named supplier came from Onus One, both systems would be openly involved in the war. By accepting the terms, Catana gives peace between the two cities, between Catana and the supplier, between the supplier and their neighbors, and among all peoples in both systems who now aren't forced to pick sides. Even General Foxtrend, who led the investigation on finding the external supplier, agreed this solution is a great outcome."

Brusch frowned. "Do you think all parties can live by this agreement?"

"Well," Dareck replied, "At the moment, their commitment is sincere. And, System One has generously offered to pay for damages inflicted upon ICID."

Jayel spoke her doubts aloud. "But the supplier of the base—they get away unscathed. Don't we have a moral responsibility to those who died?"

Her uncle shook his head. "Their anonymity brings peace for all. The Systems War Council and representatives of concerned parties find this compromise—the absence of full disclosure—saves future lives. The agreement empowers Ondre to move forward."

"I suppose," she reluctantly agreed, "revenge must yield when peace triumphs." *Words to live by, but I don't know if I can.*

"Let us drink in celebration of peace," Dareck toasted.

They raised their glasses higher in a salute and sipped the

wine.

Layon commented, "Excellent import, from the vineyards of Copea on Uamung, the best in Onus Two."

"I've more news," Layon announced. "General Eidelnim is holding a celebration tonight, perhaps the biggest and best party he's thrown yet."

"Sometimes I wonder," Jayel said, "if you only work at the RIC so you can attend the General's parties."

"I admit I look forward to them," Layon shrugged as he sniffed his wine. "But understand, living underground at ICID will do this to you."

"Face it," she laughed. "You're a hedonist."

"Not at all. I enjoy them because General Eidelnim is extraordinarily rich and extremely influential, which allows top-of-the-line food, company, and entertainment. It's not hedonism, my dear. It's snobbish taste." Layon sipped his wine and smiled.

Dareck chuckled, "My son a snob? I wonder where he gets it from?"

Not wanting to dwell on Layon's heredity, Jayel shifted the conversation. "Does peace mean we can soon leave Ondre and go to Melandan?"

The question seemed to surprise them. The three men looked at each other, perplexed.

Dareck spoke first. "Well, I admit I haven't thought this far ahead. I assumed it would take longer for investigative work to finish. But," he nodded, "the time has come to start thinking about our future and how best to proceed."

Clasping his hands, Brusch leaned forward on the table. "I joined Dareck in Quintar on Leidran for what I thought would be a short jaunt, a day or two. It's been a week now. I need to return to my home on Characta. Also, in a few weeks, there's an AI conference where I hope to learn more to work out remaining bugs in Layon's thought imager program." He looked directly at his older friend. "While I support your quest, my role ends here."

The two Endowed members exchanged smiles. Dareck sighed. "I understand. You've helped me in more ways than one, and I thank you for your support." He picked up his glass, sipped, and put it down. "I have been gone over a month from Characta. My apprentice, Ranthal, reminded me last night that I have a backlog of work waiting for me. I can only do so much long distance. I, too, want to return to Characta."

Jayel felt disappointed. She didn't want to go to Characta or incur any more delays. "If you think one week or a month is a long time to be away from home, try two standard years. I'm eager to go home to Melandan. I feel recovered from my injury and can travel alone."

"How will you get there?" Layon inquired. "From Ondre, Melandan is much farther than Characta."

"I could find transport with one of our peace delegates, or now that the war is over, I expect I could take a normal commercial flight."

Dareck looked unsure. "I don't like the idea of you going to your father's estate alone."

Jayel didn't relent. "I know what needs to be done, and I'm up for it. Thanks to your Endowed exercises, I have better mental discipline to keep my motivations hidden from my father."

After a short silence, Layon spoke. "I could go with her."

Brusch and Dareck exchanged glances.

Layon continued before they could voice objections. "I can watch over Jayel and help, if needed, to get the evidence.

Besides, I would like to see the Onus One star system. You talk of a week, a month, or two years away. Well, I've been waiting more than fifteen standard years to leave Ondre."

Dareck raised an eyebrow but shook his head. "Too risky, Layon. If my brother or General Chrysic were to find out who you are—"

"I know there are risks," his son interrupted, "but I can go in disguise…as Jayel's companion or research assistant. And it will be easier for me to contact you than Jayel could if Karsch becomes suspicious of her motives and watches her communications."

Dareck hesitated then turned to Brusch. "What do you think?"

Brusch leaned back, thinking before replying. "This plan might work. Jayel and Layon go to Melandan. After obtaining the evidence, she gives it to Layon to take to Characta for your review. Then, and only then, Dareck, do you decide what to do with it, how best to approach the Endowed. Remember, we aren't sure what the documents reveal." He leaned forward. "There may yet be other discoveries to deal with and difficult decisions to make." Brusch paused. "As you know, I'm a great believer in destiny. Layon should play a role in resolving his mother's murder."

"I suppose," Dareck said, "I could secure a fake identity for Layon to help keep him safe. Yes, I think a research assistant would work as a cover story. I'll speak to my friend Samson from the spaceport, who has connections. We might produce records for a young man from Ondre who studies neuroscience at Orim's medical university."

Layon smiled. "It's agreed, then. Jayel and I will fly to Melandan while you and Brusch return to Characta."

Layon put their wine glasses in the sanitizer. "The future

looks grand, indeed. Let's leave and get ready for General Eidelnim's dinner party. More than ever, I feel like celebrating a new start, for Ondre, for us."

As Jayel stood, thoughts of revenge gave way to looking forward to getting to know her brother on the long flight home.

Chapter 22

The silence of anticipation filled the large, crowded hall as the signing ceremony commenced. Jayel watched the two mayors, dressed in ceremonial uniforms, sit side by side for the first time in years. The Chair of the Systems War Council handed them large electronic pads. A wall monitor displayed the view from above as the mayors simultaneously pressed their thumbs on the screens and appropriately pasted their city's seals.

The war officially ended.

Loud cheers erupted.

The jubilant audience stood back from their tables as efficient staff cleared the room. The orchestra players entered. Circles of conversation formed in the interlude.

Layon, Brusch, and Dareck knew many interplanetary guests and remained in the mix.

Jayel preferred to keep a low profile and moved toward one side of the room, although if anyone recognized her, they probably assumed she was her father's representative. To maintain the illusion, Jayel didn't wear Dareck's pin tonight.

Watching the crowd, she glimpsed a man approach Dareck, lean in, and speak into his ear. The stranger wore Dareck's pin. This man pointed to an area deep within the crowd. Her uncle's eyes followed, then he spoke in the man's ear. The two men parted, and Dareck came toward her. Jayel caught a puzzled look before he erased it.

Her uncle took two glasses of wine from a passing waiter and offered her one.

Accepting it, she stated, "I saw you talking with one of your men. Is there a problem?"

"Your Endowed exercises have improved your attention." Dareck sipped the drink, savored it, and swallowed. "A hundred people in this room, and your eyes are on me. I'm touched."

His niece replied, "*All the women* in this room are watching you." *This statement wasn't too far from the truth.* Dareck's charisma diminished the attractiveness of others, even General Eidelnim, and Ondre's mayors.

After another sip, Dareck returned to her inquiry. "My man Charlo told me someone was asking about you."

"Who? Someone from Melandan?"

"I don't know. I sent Charlo to bring the person to me."

Jayel's shoulders tensed.

Dareck added, "I'm sure it's nothing to be alarmed about. Well, there's my man now. Excuse me a moment."

Her uncle walked off with Charlo. Her eyes followed until the men disappeared.

Consequently, Jayel didn't see another man approaching from the left until he stood before her.

Dorind.

Once their eyes met, the room disappeared. Dressed in formal evening attire, Dorind cut an impressive figure. His blue eyes sparkled as they met hers. As usual, his hair curled around the ears. Gone was the cold facade he had shown days before in Engineering.

Could my memory be wrong? Do I see love in his eyes?

The orchestra prepared to start the first dance of the evening.

"Dance with me." Dorind leaned close, the voice familiar and compelling.

Was it a request or a command? Jayel felt confused but wanted to dance with him, to remember the love they once shared. *If only …*

"Dorind …" she stammered, not moving.

"Shhh. Let's dance."

She put her wine glass on a table and followed his lead. The crowd absorbed them, and the music began, transforming into a slow rhythm of the *qualanza*, a dance they had rehearsed for competitions.

If the flesh has memory, then their bodies remembered, each perfectly matching the movements of the other. They danced as if not separated by years or change of heart.

It feels good to be in Dory's arms again.

They stood close and moved slowly, together swaying and turning precisely. Jayel's white sparkly dress swished with just the right amount of flourish to punctuate the steps.

She searched Dorind's face for any sign of regret. *Was the shooting an accident?* His hand pressed above her hip close to the scar. Jayel found ambiguity in Dorind's expression. She sought to enter his mind. But Dorind didn't let her in.

Time floated by as they fluidly moved around the room. But the experience couldn't undo all that had passed between and within them. While they swayed, the flame of hope was but an ember in the ashes. Both knew this would be the last time they danced together.

While they danced, Brusch and Layon stood together by the wall, watching Jayel and the stranger.

Dareck joined them. "Who's dancing with Jayel?"

Brusch shook his head. "They're having a private moment. Their minds are closed to me."

Layon looked at the Endowed members. "I know who he is."

They turned to Layon.

"Her boyfriend from medical school."

Brusch nodded. "Ah, why they fit so well. You remember, Dareck, Jayel mentioned their dancing competitions."

"Yes." Dareck squinted as he re-evaluated his appraisal of the pair. "But I would expect their reunion to be happier."

Brusch focused on the dancers. "I agree." After a moment, he observed, "That's what love looks like when it's over. They know they're dancing together for the last time."

On the final chord, Dorind embraced Jayel. Their lips met, tentatively at first, then firmly. But when they separated and looked into each other's eyes, she knew it was a goodbye kiss.

Jayel's eyes moistened. She didn't speak. Anger and love canceled each other and left her uncertain. *I can't let this be how we say goodbye.*

But then Dorind whispered, "Can we meet later and talk?"

When Jayel hesitated, her former lover pleaded, "If you're afraid, come armed. But come alone." He appeared genuinely upset she wouldn't agree to meet later.

"Dory, I …"

"The second level greenhouse. In an hour." He let go of her hand and melted into the crowd.

People milled around. Jayel turned and saw Brusch, Dareck, and Layon watching on the sidelines and joined them.

"Gentlemen, no dance partners?"

Brusch asked, "Is everything okay, Jayel?"

"Yes, of course." *It's a lie but I don't want to discuss this right now.*

Layon looked up from his pad, concern on his face. "It was Dorind Saerskind you were dancing with, wasn't it?"

"Yes, it was." Jayel looked surprised. *Why does Layon know his name?*

Dareck smiled. "Well, we'd like to meet him. Where did he go?"

Jayel looked down. "We were close once, but the years apart have changed us. I think we just said goodbye."

"I'm sorry, Jayel," Brusch replied. "I know you loved him very much."

She pushed her bangs away from her eyes and swallowed. "I wasn't expecting to see him tonight. But I … I suppose we had to meet eventually. I'm glad we had this last dance." She didn't add more.

Layon continued to attend to his pad, and a guest approached Dareck to talk with him.

The orchestra began the next song. Brusch extended his hand. "Jayel, you promised me a dance. Dareck, Layon, if you will excuse us?"

He escorted her to the floor. Jayel stared over his shoulder as he guided her around the room.

"I apologize," Brusch muttered, "for being such a poor dancer."

Jayel returned her attention to her dance partner. "What? You're a fine dancer, Brusch."

"Well, you just stepped on my foot."

Jayel stood back. "I'm sorry, Brusch. I'm … I'm more tired than I thought. It's been a long day."

"Yes, it has," he agreed.

Before Brusch could say anything more to encourage her to confide in him, Jayel turned and left the room.

"What happened?" Layon inquired when Brusch came back alone.

"Jayel said she was tired. Probably went back to her quarters."

Layon snapped, "Alone? She shouldn't be left alone tonight!" Layon quickly left, exiting through the door Jayel had used a moment ago.

Dareck, alone again, turned to his friend. "Layon seems to know something."

"It would seem so. Now that I think about it, I recall Dorind's sister, the woman I told you about who worked at *The Thirsty Boots* in Quintar, said Dorind left medical school to work for General Chrysic. Maybe Layon knows something about this Dorind Saerskind we don't."

Dareck looked concerned. "We must worry about Chrysic even when he's not here. We should follow Layon." He waved to Charlo, who rushed over.

"Our earlier person of interest, the man we saw dancing with Jayel, is named Dorind Saerskind. He may have left the hall. Find and follow him. I want to know where he goes, what he does."

Charlo nodded, and Dareck and Brusch left in search of Layon and Jayel.

Chapter 23

The strong floral scent of *elania* filled the air. Loud splashing water from an unseen fountain muffled Jayel's footsteps. Plants, pierced by grow lights in the nocturnal darkness, cast mysterious shadows throughout the greenhouse. Halfway down the rows, Jayel saw Dorind's silhouette in an open workspace.

Dorind greeted Jayel as she neared. "I'm glad you came. Good. I see you've changed your dress."

Jayel ignored his greeting. "Why, Dorind? Why did you try to kill me?"

"A bit direct, but I suppose it's necessary. Dear, dear Jay..." He took a deep breath. "I deeply regret my action."

"Action? You shot me!"

"Yes, but it was a reflex. When I saw Dareck's pin, I pulled the trigger without thinking. Why were you wearing his pin? Why? I must know."

"He's my father's brother. Why would his protection upset you?"

"Skip public knowledge crap. General Chrysic told me, at great length, of the cruelty Dareck did to your father, how he robbed Karsch of everything that rightfully belonged to him. Don't tell me you're not aware Dareck is an enemy."

"No, you're wrong about Dareck." She stepped closer. "My father hasn't spoken publicly against his brother nor has anyone else. Dory, Dareck is a member of the Endowed, sworn to justice and upholding the common good."

Dorind shook his head and stepped back, restoring the distance between them. "Damn, I didn't know you even knew him. All the years we were together, you never mentioned your uncle."

"I only met him recently." Jayel tried to read Dorind's face, but shadow covered it. She shifted her weight and pointed to a bench nearby where suspended nursery lights provided better lighting.

They sat, knees almost touching.

Dorind still wore his party attire, but he looked disheveled, no longer dashing, more like a tortured man.

Dorind swiped his mouth, then began, "After you left, I continued my medical studies. I managed well at first. I was doing surgery rotation, and the schedule was grueling—no time to miss my lover. I expected you to return from your home but never came. But General Chrysic came. He didn't believe I didn't know your location. The general didn't leave, constantly in my face, demanding to know where you were. I needed you, but you sent no word. Then, the general persuaded me to work for him."

"Persuaded?" Her brows furrowed. Jayel heard about Chrysic's infamous persuasion methods.

"Yes. You don't know what it was like. Day after day the general talked to me about you, about us. I questioned what he said at first, but then everything made sense. The general helped me see why you didn't return, how you left me only after visiting your father's estate, how you must have learned your father disapproved of me and a marriage between us. You would never marry someone your father disapproved of."

Dorind paused and looked into her eyes. "You always ran from conflict and it's why you failed to tell me your feelings had changed. You didn't dare to face me."

He paused again and swallowed hard. "Then, I saw I could gain Karsch's favor by working for the general, moving up the ranks, and showing my worth. I joined Chrysic's unit and received special forces training."

Dorind leaned in. "I am very good at my job."

Aghast, Jayel stood. "No! I told you I was taking a leave of absence from school for personal reasons. They had nothing to do with you, Dory." She sighed and sat again. "I had no idea how long I would be away. I didn't know Chrysic would get to you. You were such a good doctor, and you loved your work. I wasn't worried about you."

He moaned, "You never called. You could have sent a message, let me know where you were … let me know you thought about me and dreamed of our intimate embrace."

Jayel sighed. "I went primitive. No electronics. I needed time to work things out."

Muscles on Dorind's face tightened, and his voice grew cold. "And now you work for Dareck." He spat the name.

"I'm not working *for* him. His pin gave me protection while at ICID. Nothing more."

"Why identify with him at all? Why doesn't your father know you're here? Why are you hiding from him? From the general? From me?" Dorind's eyes were moist, but his voice was dry.

"I met Dareck on Leidran, where, by the way, I ran into your sister, Ruchelle. She told me you joined Chrysic's army, how you grew cold and mean-hearted. She's worried about you, Dory. I am, too."

Dorind recoiled at hearing his sister's name but pressed his lips together. "Chrysic ordered anyone working with Dareck should be … removed. If you wear Dareck's pin, you are a traitor, conspiring with the enemy. You betray your father."

"Oh, Dory, your voice is cold. My heart is chilled listening to you." Jayel searched the face she knew so well. "You love me. I know it. Focus on our love."

He started to reply, then stopped. Dorind rubbed his eyes as if under strain and trying to regain control.

Taking his hand, Jayel pleaded with him. "Dory, you weren't yourself when you shot me. I understand now. We can get past it. We love each other. I know it's true. Please, I want to help you. Come with me and leave General Chrysic's command."

Dorind blinked, looking past her. "No one walks away from the general. His orders must be followed." Dorind pulled back his hand, stood, and looked down at Jayel. "I need to bring you in."

She didn't like this turn in the conversation or how Dorind looked. Sweat trickled at his temple, his eyes blank. Jayel felt unsafe.

Putting her right hand in the slack's pocket as she stood, she met Dorind's eyes, pleading, "Don't go back to Chrysic. The general has no power over you anymore. This is your chance to be rid of him. Leave him, Dory, and stay with me. We'll fight him together."

Dorind spat, wiped his mouth, walked to a nearby sack of dirt, and pulled out a laser rifle. "I'm sorry, Jay. You don't know how it is. The general is powerful. He wants you. The general wanted you two standard years ago when he came to school, but he got me instead. It's not enough. He wants you. And General Chrysic doesn't take no for an answer."

Is this why you suggested I come armed? Part of you wants to protect me, not harm me.

Jayel fingered the gun in her pocket. "I will not go with you."

An uncomfortable silence fell between them, the dripping water fountain echoing in her ears. *Only a few ways this standoff could end.*

Finally, Dorind licked his lips, closed his eyes, and took a deep breath. "Yes, there is an alternative." He stepped forward, laser lowered. "If we both die here, then we would be free of him. We would be together again."

Find another way out. Jayel tried to think of words to break the general's hold over him.

A movement down the row behind Dorind caught Jayel's attention.

She looked over Dory's shoulder and saw Layon sneaking closer.

Dorind swiftly turned. He raised the rifle and searched into the darkness. A moment later his arm stopped.

As Dorind zeroed in on Layon's location, Jayel withdrew the gun from her pocket and pointed it at Dorind. She shouted the warning to stop. "Don't —"

His finger began to move on the rifle's safety mechanism.

"No!" screamed Jayel, and she fired the weapon.

Dorind's gun dropped to the ground, his body collapsing on top of it. A death rattle confirmed the fatal result.

Jayel stared motionless.

Layon ran to her, forced open the fingers around the gun, and took it from her.

Jayel's emotions churned—sorrow, sadness, loss, regret, anger, love. Tears swelled, and her knees buckled.

Layon caught Jayel as her body sagged, and together they

knelt in a tight embrace.

Jayel sobbed, but sorrow yielded to gratitude. Layon was alive.

Layon is my brother, I'm sure of it.

She gathered strength from his body, Layon's arms a comforting blanket.

At this moment, Dareck and Brusch entered the greenhouse, turned on the lights, and rushed to them.

"Are you all right? What's happened?" Dareck asked.

Layon separated himself from Jayel and answered, "Dorind Saerskind worked for General Chrysic. I recognized him at the dance from the RIC's profiles of suspects involved in the attack." Layon stood and pulled Jayel to her feet. "He was a member of General Chrysic's special forces unit, possibly involved in illegally supporting Marshe's military power."

The men nodded and shifted their eyes to the dead body.

"When Saerskind discovered me approaching, he was about to shoot me, but Jayel shot him first. She saved my life."

The Endowed members turned their attention to Jayel, who wiped tears before speaking. "In Quintar, Dorind's sister, Ruchelle told me he was working for General Chrysic. She said Dorind changed for the worse. I didn't believe her."

Layon raised an eyebrow. "So, you already knew when you danced earlier but agreed to meet him here anyway?"

"Yes."

Dareck asked, "Where did you get a weapon?"

"I had it since leaving Melandan. Never believed I would need it."

Brusch moved to Jayel's side and put his hand on her shoulder. "Dorind was the intruder who shot you in Engineering, wasn't he?"

"Yes. I agreed to come tonight because I needed Dorind to

explain, and I thought everything would be all right, but…." Jayel sniffed and looked down. "I believed our relationship was strong enough to overcome whatever the reason was for shooting me. I was wrong."

Dareck said, "I'm sorry, Jayel, truly I am. When I saw you two dancing tonight, I could tell you were in love."

"He felt I betrayed him." Jayel continued to stare at Dorind's body.

Dareck frowned then bowed his head. "Because you wore my pin the day of the attack. Your friend shot you because of your allegiance to me."

"That's what he said," Jayel nodded, "but, honestly, I don't know what Dorind would've done if I wasn't wearing your pin, Dareck. I'd probably be captured. He said General Chrysic was looking for me."

Brusch murmured, "I wonder why," but then he looked at Dareck. "Jayel's right, the shooting in Engineering wasn't your fault."

Dareck swallowed. "Well, at least we know why the general was on Leidran in Denerow Woods. He was looking for Jayel at the House of Leidra. Maybe Chrysic was doing Karsch's bidding, or the general had a personal agenda." Dareck paused. "I was relieved General Chrysic didn't come to Ondre for the peace talks. Probably didn't have enough time to make arrangements. No one expected peace so soon."

Layon moved Dorind's body just enough to retrieve the rifle and examine it. "Military issue. Do we know where General Chrysic is?"

"No," Dareck replied, "but we damaged his ship, and it couldn't go anywhere fast. I've received no reports that he found harbor."

They fell silent. Jayel took a deep breath. *A time will come when I shall have my revenge.*

Pulling out a pad, Layon stepped aside and contacted the authorities. Shortly after, he returned to the group. "It'll be a while. I suggest you three leave. I'll stay here until they come to collect the body. I'll make a full report."

Brusch offered, "I'll take Jayel back to her room. Dareck, you should return to the party to complete your official duties. There's still another hour until the fireworks begin. Your absence will be noticed. Let's regroup tomorrow."

"Very well," Dareck reluctantly agreed. Before leaving, he hugged his son and looked gratefully at his niece. "Thank you for saving my son's life."

Accepting Dareck's gratitude with a nod, Jayel didn't know what to say. *I would do it again,* didn't seem quite right, but it would be true.

"Let's go." Brusch turned and guided Jayel out of the greenhouse.

As they neared the exit, Jayel looked back at Layon. She looked forward to the day when there would be no more secrets and Layon would know she was his sister.

Chapter 24

Wrapped in a warm housecoat, Jayel took a seat across from Brusch. The shower's cool water and oil extracts helped make the transition from alarm to acceptance.

Brusch handed her a mug of hot chocolate. Jayel tried sipping it but found it too hot. She sat back and looked at her friend. Brusch had loosened his collar but still wore his white dinner jacket.

After sitting silently for a short period, Jayel sighed. "I'm now a murderer." She watched a scoop of frozen cream melt in his mug.

"It was a justified killing. You saved Layon's life."

"I wish there had been another way. I hope you aren't disappointed in me."

Brusch looked up from his mug and met her eyes. "I'm not disappointed. But I do wish you told me earlier today that Dorind was the intruder who shot you." He added a scoop of ice cream to her drink.

"I wanted to put it behind me, I suppose. Keep a focus on the future, not the past."

"You avoided telling me because you knew it would hurt." Brusch sat back and sipped the hot chocolate, a touch of cream lingering on his lips.

"Yes, you're right. Feelings of betrayal aren't easy to share." She paused, grabbed a tissue, and dabbed her eyes. "But I understand now getting shot wasn't about Dorind's feelings for me. It was about what happened to him after I left school."

"You know you can trust me. Dareck and Layon, too. You don't have to go through this loss alone."

Jayel reached out and touched his arm. "Thank you for caring, Brusch. Hard to believe we met a week ago."

"It's been a long, eventful week." He turned her palms face up and scrolled his fingers across them. "You have the hands of a healer. I know you aren't a member of the Endowed … yet … but you have an extraordinary power to give and draw strength, to stand up after being knocked down."

"I'll try to keep it in mind next time I'm on my knees wondering if I can get up."

"Good. I don't want you to retreat to your inner sanctuary and not let me, or others, in."

Jayel nodded and, stirring the hot chocolate, sighed. "I wasn't prepared for the change in Dory. … I had to see it, hear him, to believe it." She reached for another tissue. "Foolish hopes. He was never coming back to me."

Brusch waited a few moments before questioning her. "When we talked the other day in your sanctuary garden, you said you failed. Can you tell me now what you meant?"

Pausing, Jayel took a sip. "I didn't hold up my end of the relationship. Dory needed me, and I wasn't there. I knew I took the path of least resistance by leaving home without returning to school, but I did it anyway." Jayel dabbed more tears and swallowed to soothe the tightness in her throat.

"I'm sure you thought of him often while at the House of Leidra."

"Yes, but I didn't worry about him. I didn't think my absence would be a problem. See, on Melandan, friends and loved ones are often away for prolonged periods. At home, my mother's work kept her away for months, and my father was busy being governor. We think nothing of these absences. But Dory came from Orim. In his culture, family members talk to each other every day, live near each other, and long physical absences cause distress."

"Your mother is an archeologist, isn't she?"

"Yes. My father favors modern politics and my mother ancient civilizations. You can see why long absences away from each other fit their lifestyles."

"Cultural values typically affect our life choices," Brusch commented after a swallow of the hot chocolate. "Both you and Layon were raised to be independent at an early age. On Characta, where I live, we have mixed parenting customs—some families keep children at home until they're adults, as do families on Orim, and others send children away at age ten to start a career as on Melandan."

"I failed to realize Dorind would lose trust in our love because I wasn't there. I took him for granted. Lack of trust dooms a relationship no matter the culture."

"Don't be too hard on yourself. The change in Dorind wasn't your fault. You didn't know General Chrysic would intervene."

"Yes, if only Chrysic had left him alone." Jayel pressed her lips tightly. *Thoughts of revenge must wait.*

Brusch refilled their mugs. "Hindsight is much clearer than foresight. Don't you think so?"

"Yes, despite our best efforts to have keen foresight." Jayel took a deep breath and ran her fingers through her hair. "As you said, I need to stand and move forward. No more running away. I need to go home and get the evidence."

They sat in silence for a while. Jayel went to the freezer and withdrew another small carton of ice cream. As with the closet, ICID placed items in the room's refrigerator based on the tastes of the room's occupants. On the hot planet, ice cream was a staple.

After dropping a scoop into their mugs, Jayel shifted the conversation. "Did you hear from your contact who knew Neondra?"

"Yes. Marcellum confirmed the timeline. Your father and Neondra worked together before and after Neondra's marriage to Dareck. Marcellum remembered them as casual friends and didn't think they were romantically involved."

Jayel leaned forward. "I'm certain Layon is Karsch's son. The connection I felt tonight when he held me was unlike any I'd felt before. It was stronger than when I touched Dareck in the woods. An overwhelming closeness, like I would give my life for him."

"Or save it even when the cost was Dorind's life."

"Yes." Jayel looked down and sighed. "I didn't even think about it. And I would make the same choice again. Dorind didn't know what he was doing. But he had to be stopped." Her eyes moistened.

"It'll take a long time to get over your loss. Don't dismiss your grief. Give it time."

"Is that your favorite expression, 'give it time'?"

Brusch shrugged. "I suppose so. Patience helps me cope with life's challenges."

"If anything, Dorind's death makes me impatient to return to Melandan."

"For revenge?"

Jayel threw him a look and sighed. "I admit revenge against Chrysic is part of wanting to go back immediately. There are too many unanswered questions. Why did General Chrysic want to find me? Is he working for my father, or do they have separate interests? We need to know if my father murdered Neondra and why."

Brusch swallowed the last of his drink. "Answers don't necessarily bring satisfaction. For example, a friend of mine once liked a boy who agreed to go to the prom with her, but then the week of the dance he got sick and canceled. School ended, and they went their separate ways. Ezelle often wondered if this boy thought of her and dreamed of what could have been. Then one day, six standard years later, at Characta's main spaceport, there he was, in a lounge waiting for a flight. Ezelle felt, in her words, mushy inside but gathered the courage to say hello, intensely hopeful to renew their relationship. But this boy, now a man, didn't remember her. He dismissed her with a 'good day.' Ezelle said his rejection pained her more than six years of wondering 'what if.' She wished she'd never taken the risk to talk to him in the spaceport."

"And you think after we obtain the evidence from my father's office, we won't find what we hope to find, perhaps learn something worse, and we'll regret getting the evidence? Surely you don't think we're better off ignorant of what happened."

"You and Dareck believe your father murdered Neondra. But we don't have all the facts. We might be surprised by what the evidence reveals."

Jayel doubted him. How often had she relived the overheard conversation between her father and General Chrysic? No other possibilities came to mind.

Brusch frowned. "Dareck will be hurt no matter what we learn. If you are correct, and Karsch fathered Layon, Dareck loses his son."

"Yes, I'd like to be wrong, for Dareck's sake. No use burdening him with my belief until we know for sure. On Melandan, I plan to get samples from Layon and my father for a definitive DNA test."

"Good. I'm glad Layon is going to Melandan with you. I'm fond of the boy and have enjoyed mentoring his research. Siblings or cousins, you'll get to know each other. But be careful at your father's estate. Don't take unnecessary risks."

"Sound advice." Jayel sat back and yawned.

Brusch stood to leave. "Good, your body has calmed down. It's time to rest."

Chapter 25

Midmorning the next day, Jayel happily accepted Layon's invitation to join him, Brusch, and Dareck down in the lab. They planned to discuss the identity Layon would use for the research assistant cover story.

Upon entering Layon's laboratory, she found her friends sitting around the table studying documents displayed on the table monitor. They were casually dressed, and in Ondre style wore tunics with loose long sleeves.

Layon greeted her warmly. "You're here just in time to help us choose my new identity."

"Good." Jayel sat next to Brusch and reached for the pitcher of water to fill her glass.

"How are you feeling?" Brusch asked as he pushed a plate of fruit her way.

"I'm following your advice and giving it time."

Dareck nodded as he reached for the pitcher next and filled his glass. "Good advice." Her uncle turned his attention to the table monitor. "My friend Samsen sent me three profiles for our review. Each is a male born on Ondre, between 18 and 21 standard years old, registered at the University of Orim, and has taken a course in cognitive neuroscience. If anyone checks, they will find records."

"Samsen does good work," Brusch commented. "If for any reason someone on Melandan does search into Layon's background, it's helpful to find a life history to back up the identity."

They studied the information displayed on the monitor as Dareck began. "The first profile is a man who returned to Ondre from Orim about six months ago but became lost after a battle. By lost, I mean they couldn't confirm his identity among the dead. The second is a friend of a friend of a friend of Samsen's who's willing to lay low and not return to Orim until Layon completes his mission. The third is, well, a phony profile Samsen created."

"How did Samsen create a phony profile?" Jayel asked.

Dareck smiled. "Well, a spaceport controller is a great occupation for an undercover operative to watch for incoming and outgoing persons of interest. Samsen is resourceful and a trusted friend. It's not the first time he created a fictional personal history."

Layon responded, "Any of these three identities will likely work. My main concern is the name on the passport. Most names of people born on Ondre are exceptionally long, but Melandan's customs agents like to shorten them to fit into their software fields, and then this short name appears on all documentation."

Jayel's brows knitted. "Why are the names on Ondre unusually long?"

"It's the one exception to our systems' standards. As you know, our two solar systems advanced well in recent centuries because all planets accepted standard ways," Layon started his explanation. "Like how every planet uses Standard Time to maintain one date and time in both systems even though every planet experiences a different length of a day, month, and year.

The custom works well. Onus Two's satellite is calibrated to Onus One's temporal satellite. Only once every five standard years does Onus Two's satellite adjust one day and 17 hours to align the two clocks."

Brusch interjected, "Certainly comes in handy for each planet to use a universal time reference despite each planet's different orbital path and axis rotation speed. One calendar for all."

"But, despite such standards," Layon continued, "Ondre maintains one custom from the original settlers. See, the people who came here from Onus One sought new ways. They weren't explorers but emigrants wanting to start a new, different life. They rejected some old traditions and invented new customs and practices. Yet, over the generations and the increased interaction between systems, it proved more efficient to align with the standards of Onus One. However, the custom of long last names persisted. Indeed, today some families still add a syllable each generation. But when interacting with the other planets, these old-way residents typically use truncated names."

Dareck enlarged the first profile on the screen. The photo showed a man who could easily be mistaken for Layon. With another click, the name Befuddlescragmortonunderdarragh appeared.

"Absolutely not," Layon declared.

"What's wrong with him?" Jayel asked. "He looks like you and has blue eyes and dark brown hair.

"Befuddles."

"What?"

"They will shorten his name to 'Befuddles.' I cannot keep a straight face if someone calls me 'Mr. Befuddles.'"

Brusch chuckled. "True, and the purpose of having a fake identity is to deflect attention, not draw everyone to scrutinize Mr. Befuddles."

After the laughter quieted, Dareck displayed the photo of the second profile. "The hair is off, but we might be able to fix yours to match."

The group studied the face with a head of light brown, thick curly hair.

"The name. Let's see the name," Layon prodded.

Dareck pushed a key, and the name appeared. "Battersbysacketteesguilfordnesperdale."

"They'll shorten it to Batters or Battersby. Might be okay. What's his first name?"

"Cimorelli."

"Hmm. Let's see the third profile."

Dareck cleared the screen and displayed the picture of the third candidate. A blond-haired, blue-eyed face smiled over his shoulder at them.

Jayel smirked. "Looks like a model agency photo."

"Their way of hiding it's a phony person, perhaps," Layon said. "Let's see the name."

Dareck pressed a key. "Richurdsum Burngurncrunkunruhdurning."

Brusch moved his hand to his chin. "'Befuddles' could be a name we can get used to. Say it a few times, and you don't laugh as much."

Layon swallowed. "Never. Of these three, I lean towards Battersby." He turned toward Jayel. "Do you think you can get used to calling me 'Cimorelli'?"

"I would enjoy calling you 'Befuddles,' but 'Cimorelli' is growing on me. I had an elementary school friend on Melandan named 'Murtunelli.' The name has an older, classic tone to it. I don't think 'Cimorelli Battersby' will arouse attention on Melandan."

Brusch suggested, "Additives to your hair will curl it enough and give you a more youthful look. I doubt anyone will think this picture isn't you taken one or two standard years ago. Many men lose their youthful curls."

"I agree," Dareck said as he moved the second profile to the forefront for all to view again. "Well, Samsen did an excellent job selecting our candidates. A live person with complete documentation about his past is more secure than a dead man who could come back to life or a phony one which might have one too many gaps should anyone deeply check into the background."

Layon entered "Cimorelli Battersby" into his pad. Moments later, he announced, "We've transportation to Melandan, a passenger ship. It leaves tomorrow morning, ten o'clock."

Dareck nodded. "Good. Brusch and I leave for Characta tomorrow afternoon."

"How long a flight will ours be?" Jayel asked.

"Two days," Layon responded. "Dareck's private ship will get to Characta in one day. Our ship not only flies slower, but this time of year Melandan's orbit adds six more hours to the flight than if we flew months ago."

Layon handed another pad to Brusch. "I'm grateful you will continue working on the thought imager project. I started a list of equipment for you to take." They walked with the list over to a pile of boxes.

Dareck stood. "Jayel, let's leave them to their sorting and packing, and go up to the first-floor atrium by the new fountain, *Waters of Peace*, and talk."

Chapter 26

Soon after leaving Layon's laboratory, Jayel and Dareck exited the elevator on the first level. The atrium's glass walls and ceiling filtered shafts of sunbeams throughout the lounge where ICID staff relaxed. Potted plants and trees filled the area, and a large fountain graced the back wall. Cascading curtains of water rippled down smooth rock facades.

Impressed, Jayel remarked, "ICID constructed this in one day?"

The pair found an empty table in a corner offering privacy and a view of the fountain.

"You look well, Jayel." Dareck sighed as he settled in. "It's been a difficult week for you."

"I appreciate your support. I've made peace. I'm feeling strong and ready to return to Melandan."

"Good." He moved his eyes to the cascading water and paused, then returned his gaze to her. Dareck smiled. "Well, we've been together for nearly a month, and tomorrow we separate."

"The last two years seemed like one month to me, and the last month seems like two years."

"I want you to know you helped me, and I don't mean only physically." Dareck sighed again. "In recent years, I've been going through the motions without a real purpose. So much so that I didn't realize it. I thought I was coping well. But meeting you clarified my thoughts. You reminded me what it means to be a member of the Endowed and to keep focus."

Before she could comment, Dareck spoke again. "I hope you will continue your Endowed training and apply for membership."

Jayel looked into Dareck's eyes and nodded. "Because my father never suggested I train, I assumed he knew membership wasn't for me. But now I find I am interested in becoming a member. I'll certainly continue your exercises. They'll make me a better doctor, Endowed member or not."

"Yes. I want you to finish your medical studies."

"I will return to the University of Orim's medical school once I complete my task."

"I'm glad."

A worker approached and took their beverage order. Afterward, they sat in silence and watched the water. Jayel noticed the slow rhythm of the cascade calmed her breathing. She allowed the water to figuratively wash over her shoulders and soothe the remaining tension.

From a shirt pocket, Dareck took out a *borrell* and handed it to her. "Take this." He showed her how to open the pouch. "I designed it, but it can only be used once. Its energy source can't be replenished. It will aid you in contacting me in an emergency."

From the *borrell*, Jayel pulled out a small metallic object of an unusual geometric shape. Nothing about it suggested a communication device.

"If there's an emergency, hold it between your hands like this and concentrate on reaching me. I will hear you, I assure you."

"It's an amplifier of telepathy?"

"Exactly."

Jayel returned the object to the *borrell* and closed the pouch. "Hopefully, with Layon's help, we'll succeed without incident. I don't know how long after our arrival I'll be able to search my father's office, but we'll seek to obtain the documents without arousing anyone's suspicions."

Dareck leaned forward. "If at any time you need to abort the mission, do so. I've waited fifteen standard years and can stand by longer—I learned patience from Brusch. Remember, your father may read your thoughts, so always keep your guard. And avoid General Chrysic. My contacts say he hasn't returned to Melandan after our encounter, but the general remains a threat to our success."

Avoidance isn't what I have in mind. Jayel nodded. "I've made several plans, depending on whether my father is happy to see me or angry because I've been gone so long without contact. With luck, we'll have the evidence before Chrysic returns."

Dareck leaned back and watched the ripples. He sighed. "All these years and I'm still in search of peace. I need to know what happened and why. Justice will complete my journey."

Jayel felt a wave of regret and sympathy. Her uncle's future included finding out Layon is Karsch's son. She reached over and touched his hand.

He smiled. "Your hands send me strength. I cherish our connection. Thank you, Jayel, for everything you have done and are about to do."

Refreshments arrived, and they toasted their commitment to the future.

***

Layon handed his father a cup of *switchya.* They sat in Layon's quarters on two small couches facing each other, having one last talk before they went their separate ways.

"I'm proud of the man you've become," Dareck said after taking a sip. "General Eidelnim speaks highly of you and your excellent service to the RIC during the attack. He is sad to see you go."

"Thank you, Father. It's an ideal time to take a leave. ICID can return to its original research mission now that Marshe and Catana are at peace."

"Also, Brusch admires your work with the thought imager. You've accomplished much in your youth."

"Brusch is a generous mentor. I'm eager to continue our collaboration once we finish this mission."

Dareck crossed his arms across his chest. "I admit I initially felt reluctant to have you leave Ondre and travel with Jayel. But after recent events, I'm glad she isn't going alone. But, my son, you must be careful. Curb your wanderlust a little longer. Your life could be in danger if Karsch discovers your identity. Everyone thinks you died in the fire, and Neondra's murderer might want to finish the job."

"I shall be careful. I'm looking forward to traveling to Onus One with Jayel." Layon's voice lowered as he leaned closer to his father. "I want to tell you something, about what I experienced last night. Perhaps you can explain it. As I was holding Jayel in my arms, I experienced profound emotion. I felt extremely close to her. Our minds opened to each other. I experienced a love more intense than I ever felt. Like I belonged to her."

"Cherish this feeling. Not just because you're cousins, but you are two future Endowed members sharing an energy that feels like strong comforting arms binding two into one. You won't find this feeling in most relationships."

"I've always wanted a sister," Layon added. "I've begun to think of Jayel that way."

"Endowed relationships are often intimate."

Layon frowned. "You and Karsch are Endowed members *and* brothers. Yet you aren't close."

Dareck paused a long time, then said, "Well, I do love my brother. But you're right. Our relationship is very un-Endowed-like. Perhaps too many unspoken words between us."

Layon reached for a bowl on the table and took a handful of nuts. "Do you anticipate Jayel will have problems getting the evidence about Mother's murder?"

"Well, the first problem concerns the two-standard year absence. She's progressed in my Endowed training, and Karsch will notice a strengthened mind. Hopefully, a welcome change and one that doesn't make him suspicious of her motives. I'm not sure why he didn't train his daughter. I would think having Jayel in the membership would serve his public profile. And Jayel will have to explain why she didn't finish medical school. This is where you come in. You can help make a research sabbatical a feasible explanation."

"Karsch will sense only truth when we mention the thought imager project."

Dareck agreed, then continued, "Even if Jayel can avoid strict surveillance and carry out a search of her father's office, we don't know if the documents are still there after two years. It might take time to find them, and Jayel doesn't know what they look like—she only overheard them talking."

Layon swallowed his last drop of *switchya.*

His father added the last of their problems. "But assuming all goes well, you will need to get the documents to me without anyone knowing."

"I don't think these are insurmountable."

"Hmmm." Dareck looked his son in the eye. "Karsch thinks you are dead. Our cover story is thinner than you realize. I advise you to avoid interactions with him."

"I wonder what he is like. In person, I mean."

Dareck took a handful of nuts and chewed them. "You might be surprised, Layon. He's popular and well-liked. Stay on guard. Try not to stare at him or give Karsch reason to delve below the surface of the persona you present."

Layon affirmed, "I'll not betray my emotions."

"I suggest you make a plan in case you need a speedy exit."

"Already done. With the help of your friend Samsen, I reserved a small craft housed four kilometers from Karsch's estate, available on short notice for a speedy escape. It will fly us to a southern spaceport for transport to Characta."

Dareck signaled approval and stood. He hugged Layon goodbye. "I love you, my son, and wish you success. Let's hope we will be together soon."

Chapter 27

Jayel patiently watched Layon study his playing cards. His left finger twisted a hair curl above his ear.

"Down the hole!" Layon smirked as he discarded.

"Up your shaft!" Jayel threw her array of cards on the table and grinned.

"Noooooo," whined Layon. "Not again! How many wins total?"

"Twenty-three, with the last ten in a row." She entered their card values into the scorepad.

Layon leaned in. "What's the total now?"

"1,720 to 80."

"Wait," Layon corrected her. "80.5, if I'm not mistaken."

"Ah, 80.5, yes." Jayel enlarged the decimal point and digits.

Layon sighed. "My excuse is I've only just learned how to play tunnels. Give me another 500 hands … you better watch out!"

They laughed as Jayel scooped the cards and shuffled.

Layon sat back. "It's nice to see you laugh again."

"When I left Melandan for Leidran, I smuggled myself aboard a freighter. I was miserable. Now, I'm returning on a luxury passenger ship with a companion, enjoying the game room and spacious accommodations."

"This craft's enormous. I have to say it's the only way to travel. Of course, it's my first trip in space." Layon smiled, his eyes gleaming in the light. "I like the company, also."

"Even though I'm crushing you at cards?"

"Even though. I love the competition." He slapped his hands palm down on the table. "All this strategizing, however, has made me hungry. Let's go to the dining compartment and get brain food."

They left the game room and walked past the library. Through the glass door, Jayel noticed passengers lounging on comfortable furniture, their focus on electronic pads or computer monitors.

"Something wrong with this picture," Jayel remarked. "We're traveling through outer space, and people are absorbed in alternate realities. I've got an idea. Before we go eat, let's stop at an observation pod. They have telescope goggles for seeing far away objects."

Up one deck, they reached a hallway of rooms lining the port side of the spacecraft. On the first door marked "vacant," they entered a small, dimly lit, three-window-sided room and found goggles on the benches. A pad displayed instructions for how to adjust the vision. The wall's electronic monitor listed points of interest and an index of coordinates for the goggle's settings.

"Let's look at the Tree Nebula," Layon suggested. "We couldn't see it with telescopes on Ondre because of our position relative to Onus Two. I've only seen digital pictures of it."

The pair tapped the setting on the monitor's control panel and heard instructions to look left and up. A green light on the goggles' lenses showed it telescoping space until it zoomed in on the nebula.

The Tree Nebula appeared in full view. Against the blackness of space, they saw giant wisps of light spreading branches from a gray-black trunk of stardust.

Jayel squealed, "Turn on the 'artist' setting. It colors the wave frequencies."

After changing the setting, Layon exclaimed, "Wow, it's beautiful. "Look how expansive it is. And the density in the trunk. Too bad we don't have the technology yet to travel there. Space is kind of boring here between Onus One and Onus Two."

"It took centuries to move from one planet to another and then to the nearest solar system. Hopefully, one day soon, people will learn how to span the galaxy without running out of fuel or time."

"Yes. I'm out of fuel right now. Let's get food. We can come back later."

They removed their goggles and placed them on the bench. Returning to the deck below, it wasn't long before they came to the dining compartment.

Passengers occupied about half of the sixty tables. Huge electronic monitors lined the wall, and a complete bar with stools filled the opposite side.

Layon and Jayel sat at a table near a monitor showing the ship's current location and flight path. After ordering, they studied the information on the display.

Five hours into the trip, the craft had left the Onus Two solar system and was currently flying between systems. It was too large to make use of the express M corridor. Engines of passenger ships converted enough energy to surf the curvatures of solar radiation trails to travel between systems at speeds only achieved in the past century. Yet, though they couldn't feel any change in the ship's speed, the passenger ship moved faster unblocked through intersystem territory and would slow again once they entered the Onus One System in about eighteen hours.

Layon grinned. "I'm finally going to see the Onus One solar system in person. Of course, I've studied it in schoolbooks, but to be here …" He pointed to the populated planets Orim, Melandan, Characta, and Leidran. "I feel like a giddy tourist and want to see everything."

"I've been to all of them." Jayel pressed the menu and selected the orbital path view of Onus One. "As you know, Orim developed space travel first, and it has many ancient cities on its six continents. I went there on an archeological dig with my mother for three months when I was eight. Of course, I'll return to Orim's University of Mena to complete my medical studies once our task is done.

"When the Orimish discovered the planet Melandan supported life—plants and animals thriving—colonies started, and within a century, they built cities on Characta, too. As you can see, Characta's orbit allows it to come close to Melandan for a few months every standard year, so it was easy to travel there even back then when ships flew slower. It's similar in climate to Melandan.

"Only Leidran posed a challenge being rather inhospitable to life because it was so far out. But, once they put weather satellites in orbit and warmed up the planet, Leidran became the gateway to Onus Two. I believe Leidran's one city, Quintar, is the most culturally diverse of all of Onus One planets because people from both solar systems use it as a vacation and distribution port."

"Then Melandan has always been your home?"

Jayel nodded. "Until medical school, yes. I lived at my father's estate full-time until I was ten. For my advanced education at universities, I lived on school grounds with occasional trips home."

Layon drank from his water glass. "I lived in the city of Catana until I was ten and then lived and worked at ICID. Don't get me wrong, I had wonderful experiences and an excellent education, but somehow I always felt like a visitor. Once my family lineage is made known, I hope to live on Characta, my father's home planet."

"I've only been there once, for a medical conference, three standard years ago." Jayel zoomed in on the planet. "It has four main continents, so you'll need to choose which one if you aren't going to live with Dareck. Melandan has only two continents, one in each hemisphere. One nice thing about our system, there's plenty of land to go around. And Onus Two nearly doubles one's options. After getting my medical degree, I was planning to live where … Dorind would go." Her voice trailed off. A feeling of loss emerged. She looked away.

Layon reached across the table and squeezed her hand. "I know. I'm sorry."

Smoothing hair behind her ears, Jayel smiled. "It's okay. It's odd to suddenly realize those plans aren't possible anymore."

Their food arrived—Melandanian fruit, a sandwich sampler of fish, vegetables, meat fillings, and three types of bread. They each took a little of everything.

Between chews, Jayel asked, "Will you miss Ondre? Do you have a favorite memory?"

Layon cocked his head in thought, then laughed. "When I started my apprenticeship at ICID, researchers were working on designs for mountain climber gear, like tents that fit into small spaces. My new friend and I often snooped in the labs—we were ten standard years old and curious about the complex. He found a box on a shelf marked 'hot air balloon prototype.'

Now the box was no bigger than twelve by twelve inches. My friend picked it up and said, 'No way can a balloon fit in here,' and pressed the lid. Suddenly, material bulged from the box as it unraveled and engulfed him and half the room. A full-size hot air balloon was in the small box! Once we recovered from the shock, we tried to fold it back up again, but … well you get the idea. It lay across tables like hardened vomit. We couldn't hide what we had done. Got a month's punishment."

"I would like to have seen your expressions as the balloon unfurled."

"No need for a thought imager. Security cameras captured the whole thing." Layon smiled as he focused on his sandwich and quickly devoured every crumb. "RIC hired me despite the disciplinary record. I'm sure Dareck persuaded them to trust me."

Jayel turned on the tabletop's monitor, brought up a map of Melandan, and zoomed in on one area. "Our spaceport is here, about one hour away by aircar from Karsch's estate." She enlarged the view of the governor's complex and pointed at the largest building. "Family quarters on this end and the governor's rooms and offices on the other."

Layon lowered his voice. "And will I be staying in your room?"

"Not exactly." Jayel looked up and caught his mischievous smile. "My 'room' is a suite, and friends sleep in an adjoining bedroom."

"Ahh, I see." He feigned disappointment. "Do they know you're coming home?"

"Once my name and pad number appeared on the ship's manifest yesterday, the estate flagged it. The governor's executive assistant contacted me before we left this morning, and I messaged back to say I was arriving with my research assistant."

Layon smiled, then frowned. "Do you think you will be questioned or grilled?"

"Hard to know. From what I gathered, my mother is away on a dig, and my father hasn't returned from dealing with a natural disaster. See, not too long ago, a volcano erupted on the southern continent and created havoc along its east coast. It's likely why he didn't arrive with the peace delegates from Melandan."

"If he isn't at the estate, we might be able to search his office soon after we arrive."

"Fortune favors the fearless," Jayel quoted Orim's literature.

Layon picked up a red pome and took a bite. "Delicious. Any word on General Chrysic's whereabouts?"

"If my father isn't home, perhaps Chrysic won't be there either."

"I haven't heard anything good about the man."

"He's my father's Number One. They go way back." Jayel looked at the monitor. "I feel an odd mix of fear and longing to be home."

"I'm confident we can respond spontaneously to whatever comes our way."

"Strength in numbers, right?" Jayel studied Layon's confident expression. The additive to his hair created curls and lightened it. She wondered if Brusch altered Layon's appearance not to match the passport as much as to make him look less like Karsch. Even his eyes seemed a lighter shade.

Layon pushed away his empty plate. "My brain is ready for another round of tunnels. I think I figured out why you've been winning. I've conceived a defense strategy, and I predict your streak is about to come to an end."

"Game on, Cimorelli." Jayel put down her empty glass and stood.

They returned to the game room and played many hands before retiring to their dormitory compartments. The final score was 4,200 to 389.50.

Chapter 28

A voice from the loudspeaker announced, "Our craft is entering orbit. Please prepare for landing."

Today's passenger ships barely jostled with turbulence or gravity transitions when everything went well, but the potential for re-entry complications required the crew to stand by their stations. Passengers strapped in rows of seats on the main exit level. Regulations forbid loose objects, not even items held in their hands. The Planetary Orchestra entertained them on a big screen.

Jayel looked out the window when the ship entered Melandan's atmosphere. White clouds replaced the blackness of space. She marveled at how technology controlled gravitational changes. She couldn't discern when the planet's gravity took over or when outside air was pumped in. The engines made no sounds through the bulkhead, and if not for the view, Jayel wouldn't have noticed the ship's slowing speed.

Eventually, the ocean below disappeared. Increasingly closer, Jayel could make out the western cities, mountains, and farmland. Finally, Melandan's main spaceport came into view. The craft glided to land like airplanes of old. In the distance, she saw a similar parked passenger ship, its engines larger than the terminal.

Home.

After disembarking, Jayel and Layon endured a lengthy line through planetary customs. Finally, their turn arrived. The officer first examined Layon's documents and studied his face, then nodded, apparently satisfied his reddish burnt sienna curls matched the picture. A beep from the retina scanner confirmed his identity.

"Of course, your name, Battersbysacketteesguilfordnesperdale, is too long for Melandan's software fields for ID documents," the officer said. "Do you prefer Batters or Battersby?"

"Battersby will do." Layon added, "Thank you for giving me a choice."

The customs officer handed a wallet pad to Layon and motioned for him to step aside as he accepted Jayel's information. After a glance, he looked up from the screen and smiled.

"Welcome to Melandan, Jayel, daughter of Governor Karsch. You are expected. A limousine is waiting for you and your research assistant, ah Mr. Battersby, at Stand 16."

The pair left, entered the spaceport's crowded baggage claim lobby, picked up their rucksacks, and walked through the exit marked "Stands 10-20." Fresh air greeted them, and Jayel lifted her face to feel the sun on a clear, dry summer day, cooler than Ondre, sunlight stronger than Leidran.

They approached Stand 16. A woman wearing a governor's security service uniform waited next to a small black vehicle, scanning a pad's screen.

"This limo doesn't look very big," Layon said, sounding surprised.

"Sized for the two of us, so no need for the business model. At least we don't have to do the driving. Most importantly, we each get a window to appreciate the scenery."

The woman looked them over and barely smiled as she opened the back door. "Do you want these bags in the trunk or to stay with you?"

Jayel responded, "We'll keep them with us, thank you."

Layon and Jayel stepped up through the passenger door and settled in the roomy back seat. The driver closed the door and took her place in the front seat behind a panel of switches and screens. Immediately after everyone clicked their safety belts, the car silently sped away and soon elevated to the main highway. Traffic, initially heavy, soon thinned.

Although the driver appeared bored and uninterested in their conversation, Jayel closed the window between compartments. From now on, they needed to watch what they said aloud in case someone overheard.

"Thirsty?" Jayel opened the fridge, took out two bottles of water, and handed one to Layon.

He took a sip and looked out the window. Geological diversity abounded as views of green woods, occasional silver streams, and brown-patched farmland stretched to the horizon. "It's incredibly beautiful. I especially like the blue sky and white clouds. It goes well with the green and dark brown landscape. Vastly different from hot, dry Ondre."

Jayel's eyes sparkled, and impulsively she partially lowered the window. Although on Ondre she had her hair cut above the shoulders, air-pushed strands tickled her nose and eyes.

Layon laughed as he backed away from the draft. "Your short hair has doubled its volume—you look rather wild."

Jayel raised the window. "Sorry, but I couldn't resist. I found ICID stuffy."

"No apology necessary. You were underground for a week."

Jayel opened her bag, pulled out a comb, and untangled the wind-whipped knots. She groaned when hair caught in the comb's teeth, but soon, every short strand blended in place. After putting the comb away, she removed her necklace, a gift from Brusch.

Layon leaned toward her. "Why are you taking it off? I liked it." He held the pendant and fingered the embossed image of a pine tree.

"It's the custom here for a daughter to return unadorned by jewelry. This way, the parent can show their pleasure in her return by giving the present of a necklace or bracelet."

"So, if your father is happy you've returned, he'll give you a necklace?"

"Yes. The more ornate or precious the gems, the greater his pleasure."

"Can all happy fathers afford precious stones?"

"Typically, the jewelry comes from the family's collection. They can always borrow a neighbor's if need be."

Layon handed back the pendant. "I see. And if your father isn't home? What then, will you continue to go without?"

"Yes. I won't wear a necklace until he greets me."

"An interesting custom. I hadn't heard of it before." After a moment, he added, "Do you expect Karsch to be happy to see you again? I don't think I have a clear idea of your relationship."

"I'm not sure I have a clear idea either," Jayel quipped. "I think my father will be happy I've returned after being away for two years. But he doesn't know why I left Melandan suddenly or medical school. My absence may have angered him, and maybe it's why he sent General Chrysic to look for me."

"And if he did?"

Jayel laughed, nervously. "Let's play it by ear."

Nodding, Layon looked out the window but then returned his gaze. "I think once your father heard you were arriving, he speeded things up to return from the East Coast to welcome you home. It's what I would do."

"Whether home today or not, we stick to the plan. Keep a low profile. We don't need anyone too curious about you."

"I understand." Layon smiled. "By the way, do I get paid as your assistant?"

Jayel enjoyed teasing him. "Don't push it. You're getting water, at least."

"Is it too late to resign?"

"Very funny." Jayel pointed out the window. "Look, I see the property marker. We're almost there."

Both kept their attention on the view outside.

"Does all this land belong to Karsch?"

"Yes. Father owned the land before he became governor, and then he moved the government offices here. Should he retire, he'll continue living here, and the offices will move to the new governor's property."

"Where is the house? I don't see it."

"It'll be on your left. One more hill and you'll see the buildings."

Layon looked to his left. Fields and meadows gave way to gardens. Houses clustered to form a large complex of offices, living quarters, and recreational facilities. Their facade of white bricks, black window shutters, and black tiled roofs gleamed in the sunlight.

"So many flowers. The buildings appear larger than their pictures," he remarked, turning to Jayel, who also studied them. Her eyes were moist. He added, "It's a beautiful estate. I can't wait to see the inside."

"I'll give you the grand tour."

The air limousine paused and then descended in front of the main building. On Melandan, the sun set in the west, and as it lowered in the sky, the white bricks blushed yellow. As soon as the car parked, the building's massive front door opened. A small group of people stood inside.

A security officer walked from the entrance, opened the limousine door, and stood at attention. After a deep breath, Jayel stepped out, and Layon followed behind.

Pende, a man in his early sixties and top aide to the governor, stood inside the entrance. He had worked for Karsch for the past twenty standard years, starting a few years before his boss was governor. Jayel loved him dearly.

Pende smiled broadly as he greeted her. "My sweet honey, I'm pleased to welcome you home."

"Thank you, Pende. Good to see you. Are you well?"

"Yes, thank you." He motioned to a staffer to take their bags. Pende scanned Jayel's face, then looked her over with unabashed eyes. He spoke in a paternal tone. "You should've told us weeks ago you were coming. Your sudden arrival has caused much chaos."

"I'm sorry, Pende. I didn't know myself until two standard days ago."

"Well," he continued in his friendly, intimate manner, "you can imagine the uproar when we received a call from the lines regarding your imminent arrival. We've been rushing ever since to prepare."

With a slight hesitation, Jayel asked, "And my father?"

"He, too, has been rushing about."

"Has he been well?"

"Yes, sweetie. And, if I might add, though, of course, it's not necessary, he was happy to hear about your return."

Jayel felt relief but showed no outward sign. She glanced into the hallway. "Is he home from the eastern shore?"

"Yes, the governor arrived two hours ago." Pende paused. "Your father will greet you in traditional style." He turned and took a folded cloth from one of the staff. "Here is the vest for you to wear to the ceremony."

Pende unraveled the material and put the vest over Jayel's shoulders. The embroidered garment draped to her knees. He remarked, "I see you remembered to remove your jewelry. Good."

Jayel moved aside, and Layon stepped forward.

"Pende, this is Cimorelli Battersby, my research colleague."

"Welcome, Mr. Battersby. We knew you were coming and have prepared a room for you in Jayel's suite."

Layon returned the older man's smile.

Pende led them away from the bright, airy foyer, past a massive staircase, and stopped at the entrance of a large reception room. Inside, thick green carpet complimented deep brown wood furnishings.

A small group of reporters, digital recorders in hands or microphones near mouths, casually waited for Karsch's entrance. Near one corner three house staff stood. To her relief, no one looked apprehensive. The Governor's daughter's return home meant nothing more than a minor news item—a few pictures, a short column. *So far so good.*

In the front, far right of the podium, Jayel stood next to Pende and smiled for photographs. Layon stood in the back behind the press and bore a preoccupied expression. For all she knew, he truly was thinking about modifications for the thought imager.

A creak near the side door diverted everyone's attention. Silence filled the room in anticipation of Karsch's entrance.

At last, two governor's aides walked through the doorway followed by two musicians, one holding a drum and the other a minor trumpet. Behind them, several men and women from the security detail ceremoniously entered, their pace drawn out for added effect. No one minded the theatrics. Everyone waited.

The suspense finally ended when Karsch stepped over the threshold.

Chapter 29

As he waited, Layon felt more anxiety than he wanted to admit. All his life he wondered what the suspected murderer of his mother was like beyond a picture or news video. He was about to find out.

Fortunately, Dareck taught him how to keep emotions in check. Thus, he stood in the back of the room as if waiting his turn at the replimat.

After the fanfare of a small procession, Karsch entered the room. Immediately everyone else diminished in stature. The tall man walked with unassuming grace and palpable charisma. A devilish sparkle in his dark brown eyes brought smiles from everyone in the room.

He wore a light gray tunic loosely tucked into his black trousers, their legs belted around the ankles. A garment hung around his shoulders like the vest Jayel wore. The air beneath his clothing caused the material to shimmer as he moved. The way his blackish-brown hair lay on muscled shoulders added a youthful appearance to his well-shaven face.

Layon perceived the family resemblance. Karsch had Dareck's nose and Jayel's genuine smile. Karsch's hair was lighter than his brother's, a shade closer to Layon's natural color. Most importantly, the man appeared happy and relaxed.

It looked to be a pleasant reunion between father and daughter.

Was Karsch hiding his true feelings?

As Layon contemplated this possibility, Karsch turned his head and looked in his direction. Layon at once lowered his eyes, remembering not to appear too interested.

"Please be seated," a uniformed woman at the podium said. "Governor, the floor is yours."

The audience sat while musicians played the introductory passage for the ceremony.

Karsch walked on beat to the podium. Two aides stood at his side. He declared, "As in the tradition of our ancestors, parents welcome their children after prolonged absences. Perhaps we developed this tradition because words like 'it is good to see you' or 'why have you bothered to return?' were deemed inadequate greetings. We manifest our love or annoyance of their return home through gifts. Now, parents on Melandan celebrate the independence of our young and encourage them to develop their lives early. Nonetheless, we also celebrate the family unit and the joy of belonging."

Karsch paused for the traditional introduction drumroll. "After two long, silent standard years, my daughter has returned. I proclaim with sincere happiness, Jayel, my daughter! I welcome you home."

As Jayel approached the podium, Karsch turned to an aide who handed him a velvet box. Her father opened it and withdrew a silver chain necklace. As he held it up, lights caught reflections from numerous blue gems in silver settings. Layon heard pleasant gasps from the audience.

Jayel stood with her back to her father, symbolizing the trust he would not harm her. Layon realized the ritual allowed unhappy fathers to strangle or whip prodigal daughters without looking into their eyes.

Gently pushing aside Jayel's short hair at the nape, Karsch placed the necklace around her neck and secured the clasp. Members of the press murmured their appreciation of its beauty and strained to capture pictures of the jewels.

As required by ritual, father and daughter stood not yet facing each other until the trumpet player punctuated the end of the gift ritual. Once the music ended, Jayel turned around. The audience watched their facial expressions and took pictures as they smiled and embraced. The gems matched the sparkle in their eyes.

Trumpet and drum marked the end of the traditional ceremony. Karsch said to the audience, "No interviews. I'm eager to chat privately with my daughter."

As the procession formed to take their leave, Jayel whispered something to her father, and he nodded. Jayel looked at Layon and motioned for him to join them.

Karsch led Jayel, followed by Layon and Pende, to a nearby room, a lounge richly decorated in tones of maroon and brown. The decor created a stately and quiet ambiance. Layon considered the furnishings antiques but common in pictures of Onus One estates. The Governor pointed to chairs around a coffee table on their right.

Jayel and Karsch removed their vests and carefully folded them. Karsch's finger lingered a moment on the family crest before he handed the pile to Pende.

They took their seats as Pende closed the door, silencing noise from the adjacent rooms.

"Jayel," Karsch began, "It *is* good to see you again."

"Thank you for this beautiful necklace, Father."

"Your grandmother's grandmother originally owned it. It gives me pleasure to pass it on to you."

"I'm glad my return pleases you. I confess I was unsure how

happy you would be."

Karsch looked surprised but recovered quickly. His eyes moved to Layon.

Layon lowered his eyes slightly and hoped Karsch interpreted the look as one knowing his place. He felt the pull of Karsch's eyes upon him, but he didn't look up.

Jayel spoke. "Father, let me introduce you to my research colleague and friend, Cimorelli Battersby. We worked together on Ondre."

Karsch nodded at Layon but directed his question to Jayel. "You were on Ondre for the peace celebration, then?"

"Yes. We were there before, too, conducting research at ICID."

Karsch looked carefully at Jayel. "During the war? Were you safe?"

"Yes, up until the attack on ICID when I was shot." Seeing the immediate concern on her father's face, she quickly added, "But I received excellent medical attention and am doing well now."

"Hmm, I'm relieved to hear you've recovered." Karsch's eyes lingered on his daughter, then he looked briefly at Layon, and returned his gaze to Jayel, apparently satisfied.

He sat back. "I wish I could have attended the peace negotiations. If I had known you were there, I might have tried harder to get away. Unfortunately, the towns around Kistra are suffering the aftermath of the latest seismic activity from Mount Elstis. I was needed to hold a few hands and to increase efficiency in the distribution of resources."

"When did the volcano erupt?" Jayel asked.

"About two weeks ago, but the situation is still tense. Recent rains added mudslides to the destruction. Citizens are still in need of food and shelter. We're rebuilding farther away, but the soil on the mount produces excellent flowers and spices, and they want to live near where they work. Therefore, they deal with great anxiety knowing the lady could blow her top again. She smokes daily."

Layon smiled at the Melandanian use of metaphor. The inhabitants of Ondre didn't personify their volcanoes.

Karsch picked up a cold metal pitcher from the coffee table and poured three glasses of a green foamy beverage. "Some things are easier to assess or conduct in person. Nothing like a community disaster to expose weaknesses in personnel or outdated equipment."

Accepting the glass, Jayel commented, "I'm sure they appreciated your leadership."

Sighing, Karsch added, "On this latest visit, I replaced a few inept officials and restocked 3-D printers and dry goods to supplement the continent's donations. Melandan, despite its great technological comforts, must still deal at times with nature's wrath. Our people are generous with their support."

Layon sipped his beverage, finding it had a refreshingly light taste and definitely contained alcohol. He wanted to drain his glass but refrained.

Karsch responded to his reaction with a smile. "It's *svanisita.* Made from limes grown only on Melandan. Do you like it, Mr. Battersby?"

"Yes, sir. Thank you." Layon looked away from Karsch's warm inviting eyes.

After a short silence, Jayel cleared her throat. "Eh, I didn't see General Chrysic on Ondre for the peace celebrations, either."

"No." Karsch sipped his drink. "He's been busy recently on other business. The general hasn't been on Melandan for over a month, in fact. Shall I invite him to join us for dinner when he returns?"

"Absolutely not. Father, please, I dislike the man."

"Really? I thought you two liked each other."

"It's one-sided." Jayel's lips tightened.

"I see," Karsch responded, knitting his eyebrows.

Jayel changed the topic and looked around the room. "I see you've replaced the paintings."

"Noticed, did you? Good. These are recent acquisitions from modern Melandanian artists."

Layon stood to admire them and walked around the room. "These have modern themes and colors. Somehow, I expected a Governor's artwork to favor classicism."

"You will find many classic artworks throughout the estate, but I thought it best to support our local talent. For this room, I selected ones with brighter hues. If you like one picture in particular, Mr. Battersby, I can arrange for you to meet the artist."

Layon's eyebrows lifted in surprise at Karsch's invitation for friendly conversation.

Jayel walked to a painting by the window. "I like this one, a seaside. It reminds me of family outings when I was very young." A shadow crossed her face, and Jayel turned away. They returned to their chairs.

Karsch picked up his glass and swirled the foam directing his attention to his daughter. "Speaking of family, your mother wasn't happy she didn't get to see you on your last visit. You must call her soon."

"I will."

"How long can you visit this time? I'm hoping you'll stay several weeks at least."

"We aren't sure. This trip was rather impromptu. We took advantage of the passenger ship leaving Ondre after the peace signing."

Karsch picked up the pitcher to pour refills, although his was the only empty glass. "Because Ondre's war is over, there is peace on every planet for the first time in many years. The war on Ondre put a crimp in development plans of the outer planets in Onus Two."

"You are involved in exploration planning?" Jayel asked.

"I'm a member of the System's Exploration Committee," Karsch informed them. "Last year SEC named me chair-in-waiting. Not much has advanced because of the war, but now it makes sense to invest our energies. I hope to suggest policy plans at the Governors' Council in two weeks."

Layon remarked, "I hear the Governors' Council is full of pomp and ceremony to mark its infrequent gathering. Every six standard years isn't it?"

"Yes," Karsch answered. "I'll be attending for the third time as governor. Some members of the Endowed also attend the council because they advise governors."

One day I hope to attend. Layon looked away before he appeared too interested.

Jayel picked up her glass and sipped. "Where will the upcoming conference be held?"

"In the city of Salais, on the planet Characta. Perhaps you can accompany me." Karsch leaned over and refilled Jayel's glass. He waited for Layon to look up, then smiled. "My daughter's friend as well."

Layon thanked him and took a sip. To block the Endowed member from reading his thoughts, Layon focused on how to solve the problem of screen pixels taking up too much cache in his imager's program.

"I want to hear about your career, Jayel, and your research." Karsch leaned back in his chair again and fingered his glass. "I know you didn't finish medical school. Your research must be important and interesting to take you away—"

A knock interrupted. An aide opened the door and motioned for the Governor to approach. Karsch frowned, stood, and walked over. After a short exchange, he returned to the seating area.

"The lady lost her temper."

"Mount Elstis erupted again?" Jayel asked.

"I'm afraid so."

"Can we help?" She stood and Layon followed.

"Not at the moment. Pende will take you and Mr. Battersby to your rooms to settle in. Dinner will be in one hour. I'll know by then whether I must go to Kistra."

He hugged Jayel and looked deeply into her eyes. "It is good to see you again," he repeated the customary greeting. "Two years with no word was much too long. I sense there is something different about you, something on your mind, though. Perhaps something you want to ask me? We'll talk over dinner."

Chapter 30

Jayel looked out the window and waited for Layon to finish checking for listening devices in their suite. The sun hung low in the sky, casting long shadows about the room. "I've missed this view. Interesting how trees differ so much across planets. Not just their leaves, but how they are clustered and transform the landscape."

Layon put down his pad. "My program detects no listening devices in the entire suite. But I generated a white noise background signal just in case. We don't hear it, but the waves will be picked up by any sound digitizer."

He walked to her side and looked out. "Yes, the trees are different than those on Ondre. You have a great view of the gardens. So much green and color."

When Jayel turned around, the light twinkled on her necklace. Layon tugged at it. "This is nice, too."

"Yes, isn't it? More valuable than I expected. Six gems instead of one or two. Apparently, my father *is* pleased I've returned."

They walked to the sofa and sat. Pende had freshened her room with several vases of flowers and left a tray holding a water pitcher and glasses on the coffee table. Jayel poured Layon a glass and filled one for herself.

After sipping, Layon commented, "Your father isn't what I expected."

"How so?" Jayel gave Layon her full attention. *Did he feel a bond between a father and son?*

"He is so … likable."

"Yes. Most people report having a positive first impression of the governor. He has a knack for making you think you are the only person on his mind."

"I expected someone dark and mysterious, but he brightened the room when he walked in, and I swear his eyes sparkled."

Jayel laughed. "Of course, they did. The same way Dareck's eyes sparkle, don't you think?"

"Yes, now that you mention it. They are brothers and members of the Endowed." Layon paused a moment and frowned. "Hard to think he could ever do something not expected of an Endowed member."

"Yes," Jayel's voice faltered. "I wrestled with these impressions and expectations of my father for a long time. but as Dareck reminded me, the Endowed are people, not gods."

Layon refilled his glass. He was thirsty and deliberately didn't drink much of the *svanisita* because of its high alcohol content. "On the way here, we talked about being unsure what to expect. Now we know, do you think your reception was genuine? Is he happy you've returned home?"

"I think so. I didn't detect any concern beyond mild curiosity for why I left. Of course, as a member of the Endowed, he is the master of his emotions. Over dinner, we'll learn more."

"I got the impression your father is good at his job. How long has he been governor?"

"More than fifteen standard years. We live in peaceful

times, and his job is mostly the management of policies and resources to ensure a high quality of life for all on the planet."

Layon noted, "Times of low stress often make it easy to bring out our best, to be on our best behavior. We live in good times right now, with no war and plenty of room for people to find a place to meet their needs. Catana and Marshe were blips in how our cities in our solar systems manage conflict."

Jayel drank deeply, the water as refreshing as the streams on Leidran. "I agree. The future is full of exciting possibilities. Just wait until your thought imager is mass-produced. It will open more frontiers to explore."

"And the more we learn to control nature, the less we must deal with destruction. Most planets have volcanoes, and we do a decent job of monitoring and predicting their behavior. But I wouldn't be surprised if we soon learn how to control seismic stress, diffuse energies, and prevent destructive eruptions."

Jayel remarked, "Families are micro versions of planetary activities, making it simpler for us to get along when problems are dormant."

"I suppose so."

Jayel sighed. "We're fortunate the general isn't here—now there's a conflict I don't want to manage."

"I agree." Layon finished his drink.

The light in the room dimmed with the sunset. Jayel stood and turned on the lights. She noted the time, a half-hour until dinner. Before returning to the sofa, she paused at the mirror and fingered the necklace.

After a moment, Layon walked over and asked, "What are you thinking about?"

"Because of this necklace, I've decided to ask a favor from my father."

"What will you ask?"

She leaned toward his ear and whispered the answer.

When he understood what she said, he hugged her briefly. "I'm happy for you. And if he says 'no'?"

"Yes or no, our mission remains the same."

Layon nodded. After a moment, he suggested, "I won't go with you to dinner tonight. Without me present, you will be free to talk with your father and ask this favor."

"Are you sure?"

"Yes. I would be in the way." He walked over to the suite's computer. "I've enough to keep me busy. An idea came to me earlier about my thought-imager program, and I can work on it while you're at dinner."

Jayel joined him at the desk. "You can order dinner from this menu, and it will be delivered." She pointed to the screen and then at the wall's dumbwaiter.

Heading to her bedroom to dress for dinner, Jayel turned and said, "Tomorrow morning, we'll take a tour of the estate."

***

Not long after Jayel left for dinner, Layon munched on a sandwich in the suite's sitting room. *All is going well. If Karsch goes to Kistra tomorrow, we might be able to search the governor's office undisturbed.*

His thoughts drifted to the attractive blonde-haired staff member he saw at the welcome ceremony. She had returned his smile. Layon wondered whether she worked all evening or might be free to enjoy some company tonight.

He browsed the screen map for the staff quarters.

Chapter 31

"The best meal I've had in a long time." Jayel pushed away her dinner plate, satisfied. She scanned the serving dishes one last time to ensure she had sampled a little of everything. "Nothing like a meal cooked at home."

Her father agreed. "Too hot on Ondre to enjoy this game, fresh from our eastern forest, and these vegetables, grown in our estate gardens."

Karsch chewed and swallowed the last of his broiled meat, drizzled in spicy *ester* sauce. "Dessert will be your favorite, local Breyore's cocoa-bean ice cream. Melandan's cattle make the richest milk."

"Very thoughtful of you to remember my favorite flavor."

Karsch smiled, a sparkle in his eyes. "Who can forget you like to pour *switchya* over it."

"Melandan's blend is the best, too. Ondre's tasted good but weak."

"Let's eat dessert in my suite. I have a few hours before I need to prepare for my trip. We've talked about volcanic eruptions and Melandan's political elections. I'd like to talk about *you* and catch up on your activities of the past two years."

They left the upstairs family dining room and walked down the hall to the sitting area of Karsch's suite.

Jayel sat at one curve of a U-shaped sofa. "I'm relieved to know this latest eruption isn't worse than the last one."

Karsch sat a few cushions down, leaving space for a small tabletop to fit between them for their dessert. "I won't be gone long. I'll confirm recovery is going well with the latest changes I made and add assurances of my support. My Number Two and Three generals are overseeing cleanup and shelter demands. I could be back tomorrow night unless an unforeseen problem demands longer attention."

Pende came in carrying a tray of two bowls of ice cream, coffee cups, and a pot of *switchya.*

After he left, Karsch began an intimate conversation with a touch of disapproval in his voice. "You never got your medical degree."

"True, but I've only a few more courses left to take. Then I will apply for residency in neurology/brain science."

"Why did you take a break from your studies? The short letter you left on the day of your unannounced departure didn't convey much information."

Jayel paused and looked down at her bowl. She poured the *switchya* over the ice cream and concentrated on practiced explanations filled with the fewest lies possible to stay believable.

As he filled his cup, Karsch prompted her. "Did you leave because of a lover? I recall you and another student at Orim enjoyed an intimate relationship."

"You remember Dorind." Jayel stirred the ice cream and swallowed to control her breathing. "I loved him very much."

"Loved? You're no longer together?"

"No."

"I thought he might have traveled with you. He didn't stay very long at the university after you left."

Jayel looked up sharply. "How do you know?"

"I had General Chrysic check for me a few months after I received no word from you. I thought your partner might know your whereabouts. Chrysic reported Dorind didn't know where you were, and apparently, he dropped out soon after his visit."

"I see," she answered stiffly.

Karsch sipped and put down his cup. "So, why take a leave of absence when so close to finishing?"

"I needed time to make decisions concerning my future and went in search of solutions to particular problems."

"And did you find them?"

"I may have, I don't know." She took another spoonful of ice cream.

Karsch frowned. "If you needed help, why didn't you come to me or your mother?"

"My parents taught me to work things out by myself." Jayel smiled and stirred the melted ice cream.

"Good." Her father leaned back on the sofa cushion, his dark brown eyes fixed on her. After a short silence, he probed, "You've returned to ask something from me."

Jayel stood and paced to the fireplace and back. "Yes, but before I ask it, I want to preface it with another question."

Karsch reached out to hold Jayel's hands, pulling her to sit beside him.

"Ask, Daughter. I'll try not to get angry if you're about to confess something bad."

Jayel laughed. "No, I'm not confessing."

"Then ask away."

She swallowed. "Why didn't you give me, the firstborn daughter of an Endowed member, training in the ways of the Endowed?"

The expression on Karsch's face hardened. Her father sat back and looked away. "You surprise me, Jayel. Why ask now about not receiving training years ago?"

"Because I want to know. I need to know."

Karsch stood and turned his back to her.

Jayel inquired, "Why does my question bother you? Because you hoped I'd never ask for an explanation?"

He turned to answer, shaking his head. "I'm surprised you want to know, that's all. I assumed you had little interest in the Endowed. Often Endowed parents begin training early in their child's life, but I had a lot going on in your early years and thought your training could wait. Other events you know nothing about distracted me, and public service demanded my complete attention. Then, after Jonlon's drowning, you turned away from me, and, … our relationship became too distant for the intimacy of training."

Her father paused and looked deeply into her eyes, which at the mention of Jonlon, moistened. He continued, "When you refused Chrysic's swimming lessons, I inferred you lacked the desire to overcome your fears and learn the ways of the Endowed. As I recall, General Chrysic and I talked about you and Endowed training multiple times throughout your childhood. We decided if you had no interest, we should respect your decision and not pressure you to begin the training."

Did Chrysic deliberately dissuade my father from providing training?

With effort, Jayel suppressed her hatred for the general before responding. "I think, Father, you relied on the general's opinion too much. From my perspective, I felt you considered me unworthy of membership."

Her father shook his head and spoke slowly. "Actually, I assumed you confided in my Number One and told him you didn't want Endowed training, and he was doing you a favor by talking me out of beginning training. This way, you avoided a difficult discussion with your father, knowing Chrysic would be the one to tell me, and you didn't have to see my disappointment."

Karsch stepped closer and let out a deep breath. "When a man reaches a certain age, he reflects on his life and realizes he made choices he wouldn't make again if given the chance to go back. At the time, they seemed correct, but now they are regretted.

In the last two years, with you away and your mother busy with an archeological dig, I reflected much on my family. I've already made efforts to repair my relationship with your mother. I wish to do the same with you. I regret not doing more to encourage you to train for Endowed membership."

Jayel stood and fingered her necklace. "This gift shows you love me. Thank you."

"You remain precious to me."

They held each other's gaze. Jayel sat again, and her father followed, sitting closer than before.

With resolve, she said, "Which brings us to the favor I ask."

Karsch anticipated her question. "You want me to give you training in the ways of the Endowed?"

"Not exactly."

"I don't understand."

"I want induction."

"Induction!" Karsch stood and walked across the room toward the windows. "Not possible."

Jayel stood and walked to him. "It's my birthright."

"Yes, but you can't receive induction to the membership without training first."

"I already received some training, Father."

"Indeed?" He studied her face. "Yes, I understand now what I've been sensing. I detected your improved mental discipline. I assumed your doctor's education taught you to regulate feelings and modulate your responses. Endowed training by whom? Who trained you?"

"It's a long story."

"Perhaps, but I can't agree to your request without knowing more."

Jayel hesitated. She didn't want to inflame her father's anger or jealousy by bringing Dareck into the conversation.

"Would it help, Father, if I told you, in a way I have already received permission?"

"Please continue. You're full of surprises, my precious one."

"I didn't spend the last two standard years doing neuroscience research, only the last month. When I left Melandan two years ago, I went to Leidran and stayed at the House of Leidra."

Karsch stared at his daughter, eyebrows raised, lips apart.

My father didn't know, hadn't sent Chrysic to Leidran.

Then, her father's muscles relaxed, and he smiled broadly. "No one finds, let alone stays, at the House of Leidra unless invited and permission given. Your request for induction is rightfully made."

He extended his arms to embrace her. Their hands clasped, and Karsch again nodded. "Yes, you have the hands of a healer. I feel your strength. I'm glad. And proud."

They hugged, and then Jayel pulled away. She loved her father but needed to discover his role in Neondra's death before taking down defenses. She couldn't yet be openly honest with him about the reasons for her return.

Karsch walked to the desk and added notes on a pad. "I will

begin making the arrangements for the induction ceremony when I return from Kistra. All should be ready soon, perhaps before the Governors' Council."

"Thank you, Father."

"But I still have many questions to ask you."

"Yes, but they can wait, can't they? It's been an exhausting day."

"Luckily for you, I'm a patient man." Karsch pushed his hair away from his cheek. "I'm tired myself. I must leave soon to deal with another demanding lady."

He kissed his daughter goodnight.

Jayel returned to her suite, greeted by the eerie stillness of a vacant room. Dismayed, she read the message Layon left behind: "I went to check something out in housekeeping and will return shortly."

Still holding the note, she looked toward the door at the sound of it opening. Jayel studied Layon's slightly disheveled clothes, moist skin, and tousled hair. She laughed. "Don't tell me you left the suite to have sex with the hired help!"

"A perk of the mission," he grinned. "Not only did my evening provide extreme pleasure, but I also acquired something important."

He dangled a magnetic keypad in front of her questioning eyes. "A key to Karsch's office."

Chapter 32

An hour after sunrise, Jayel enjoyed a walk through the east gardens. The time at the House of Leidra increased her love for the outdoors. She couldn't live underground as Layon did on Ondre. The morning sun highlighted autumnal colors on bushes, shrubs, and flowers carefully planted along aesthetic corridors of statues, fountains, and trees.

On her way back to the house, Jayel saw an elderly man, pulled by three energetic young dogs, walking toward her. She smiled broadly as they approached.

"Chab! What a pleasure to see you. It's been a few years."

The man flipped the switch on the device in his right hand to rein in the invisible leashes and opened his arms to greet her warmly.

"My, you've grown, Jayel," Chab said, looking her over. "You are a beautiful woman."

"Thank you, Chab. You look as strong as ever. Last time I saw you, the Lennix litter, much like these pups, trampled you on their walks."

"I remember the litter. Beauties they were. These might just be their offspring's offspring."

The three pups wagged their furry tails as fast as their noses sniffed.

"They're adorable." Jayel knelt to pet each wiggling body as they competed with each other for affection.

Chab interrupted the love affair. "Well, Jayel, which one will it be?"

She stood and brushed fur off her hands. "You're a dear, Chab, but I must decline your offer."

The elderly man looked crestfallen.

Jayel placed a hand on his arm and explained, "I don't know how long I'll be here, Chab, nor where I may go when I leave. I can't take a pet right now. But thank you for trying to please me with such a tender gift."

The wrinkles on the man's face diminished, and a sparkle gleamed in his eyes. "You can't tell me your heart hasn't gone out to one of them. Because you're my favorite, I'll not sell any of them for a while. If you decide to stay—and I know your father would like it, and so would many of the staff who've sorely missed your visits—let me know, and any of these lads is yours."

Layon arrived amid a rousing chorus of barks. Chab gave Jayel a wink, flipped the switch on his handling device, and pulled the dogs away to continue their morning exercise.

Jayel turned her attention to Layon. He had showered and dressed in Melandanian fashion, his trousers belted at the ankles. Muscles around his face appeared tense. She asked, "You have news? What is it?"

"I've received a communiqué from my father," Layon responded.

"Has something happened?"

"No, but Dareck has learned Karsch will be nominated for Systems President next month at the Annual Governor's Council."

"What!"

"Dareck talked with Sissau, Governor of Characta, and she told him the majority of governors and council members favor electing Karsch."

"What an honor for my father," Jayel remarked.

Layon grabbed her arm. "Honor? We can't let Karsch be nominated. He's a murderer. We must expose him before the meeting."

Jayel's eyes lowered from Layon's intense stare. "Yes, of course," she replied lamely.

Layon didn't release her. "'Yes?' Is it all you can say, 'yes'? Have you forgotten what we're doing here? Or has the necklace which shines so brightly on your throat altered your memory?"

"Of course not. Don't look at me like that, Layon. I'm on your side."

He looked away. After a moment, he continued, "Dareck said you might be reluctant to get the evidence now that you received your father's approval."

"I admitted I've had difficulty seeing my father as a murderer. But nothing has changed in my commitment to justice. I promised to get the evidence from my father's office, and I shall."

Layon sighed, returned a smile, and offered a compromise. "I could search instead of you. I have Rissa's key."

"No. The consequences are too severe if you were caught alone looking through things. I will be the one to go through his office." Jayel inhaled deeply. "With my father away today, now is the time to search. Let's go back to the house and pretend to take a tour of the estate. If the workers finished their cleaning—they usually do the downstairs before the upstairs—we might get in the governor's office unobserved."

They walked to the house and made their way through

hallways to the governor's business suite. They found the area near Karsch's office empty and silent. *Too silent.* Jayel flashed back to walking through Engineering during the bombing of ICID less than two weeks ago. She swallowed to stifle the fear knotting in her stomach. At least this time she didn't walk alone.

When they reached the office door, Jayel muttered, "I wish my heart would beat quieter."

"It's mine you hear," Layon whispered over her shoulder.

Jayel smiled and willed herself to relax. Jayel touched the door handle and found it locked. Layon handed her the key he obtained last night. She held it near the sensor, the door clicked and unlocked, and they walked in.

This outer office provided space for visitors and staff meetings. It connected on their right to Karsch's administrative assistant's office and on their left to his private chamber. The dark assistant's office suggested he went with the Governor to Kistra. Elegant furniture filled the spacious room, including plush area rugs, several couches and stuffed chairs, a conference table, and an executive desk. Large computer monitors lined the opposite wall, powered off.

"With the governor away, the workers are busy elsewhere," Jayel said, relieved.

"Let's shut this hallway door," Layon whispered.

"Right."

After closing it, they stepped toward the private office. Jayel stopped Layon. "I think you should stay here while I search my father's personal office. Keep an eye on the outer door in case someone tries to enter."

"Agreed."

She walked to Karsch's private office door and waved the

key, but nothing happened.

Layon gasped, "Oh no, my key only works on the outer door. What should we do?"

With a mischievous smile, Jayel pulled out another key fob, waved it in front of the door, and heard it unlock.

"How?" he asked.

"Perks of childhood." Jayel shrugged. "No one ever asked for it back. I found the key last night still in my closet. Lucky for us, no one changed the signal code."

Jayel opened the door and peeked in. The dim lighting confirmed no occupants. Karsch's personal office, much smaller than the public one, contained a massive desk and three walls filled with floor-to-ceiling shelves displaying books and small art sculptures.

The fourth wall displayed classic oil paintings spaced between two doors. One door led to a private bathroom, complete with a shower and a closet full of clothes for any last-minute changes. Behind the other door, a staircase led to her father's bedroom. Only the family key would unlock it from either side. No staff allowed.

Jayel looked back at Layon who stood guard by the public hallway door. She whispered as if afraid to be overheard, "I'll leave this inner door slightly ajar so you can call out and warn me of unexpected company."

"Be careful," Layon whispered back.

"I will."

The lighting automatically increased to full illumination as Jayel entered. Her eyes moved to the familiar desk, masterfully carved in the last century's style. The well-cushioned chair behind the desk afforded comfort for a man who needed to sit for long periods, including late at night to contemplate problems or escape interruptions. A few turned-off pads lay on the desk.

Jayel glanced at some of the knickknacks on the shelves, gifts collected over the standard years Karsch served as governor. She smiled at a framed photograph of her parents. *I must remember to call Mother.*

Next to the office privy, a large cabinet built into the wall stored Karsch's documents. She went over and pulled the brass handle. It didn't open. For a moment, Jayel feared another lock, but after a second tug, the six-foot cabinet hatch opened. The thick door, like iron safes of old, moved slowly. Inside the cabinet, shelves, slots, and drawers organized the contents. *There is a lot here to go through.*

From the slots, Jayel pulled out a few folders and looked briefly through them. One folder contained letters of commendation received across the years from the System Council, planetary societies, and Melandan's cities in appreciation of the governor's services. Her father stored them rather than framed and displayed them. Another folder contained letters family members wrote generations ago, the handwritten script and language difficult to read now. The contents of the last folder caused a smile. Her father saved a well-preserved birthday card she made when three years old. *Things had been so simple then … love was so easy to express.*

Suddenly, Jayel felt a sense of urgency. She opened the drawers one by one, searching for a thick packet. Jayel remembered crinkling like an overstuffed envelope the day she heard her father talking with Chrysic about Neondra's death. After fingering through the contents of the top four drawers, all the envelopes she found only contained irrelevant information.

Jayel sighed. She promised Dareck and Layon to find the evidence, but nothing so far seemed incriminating. If only she had seen what Chrysic and her father looked at when they talked about the fire.

Bending over to open the bottom drawer and looking under an empty sack, Jayel found two unsealed stuffed 10 x 10-inch manilla envelopes bound together by a rubber band. She touched the flap of the top packet, and the band broke.

"Not good," Jayel said aloud, knowing it should be replaced if things needed to look untouched. *Where would I find another rubber band?*

Layon called out, "Did you find something?"

"No, not yet. Only one drawer left to search."

Jayel slipped a hand inside the envelope and heard a crackling sound as she remembered. Her heart beat faster. Jayel's hands trembled as she pulled out a photo. It pictured Dareck and Neondra, possibly from their wedding reception. Smiling, both wore traditional mauve and navy shrugs over tight-fitting formal attire.

These envelopes could hold the material we need. A glance at their contents revealed more photos, handwritten notes, a computer disk, and what looked like receipts.

After removing the envelopes from the drawer, Jayel discovered a wooden box in the back. She picked it up. Its light weight suggested it might be empty. Nothing moved when she shook it. The box didn't open. *Could have papers inside, I'll take it, too.*

Standing upright, holding the box and envelopes so as not to wrinkle them, Jayel pushed the drawer closed with her foot. She pulled the heavy cabinet door, and once it swung past her, leaned in and with some effort pushed it flush against the wall.

Suddenly, Jayel felt dizzy. She heard voices in the outer office.

Chapter 33

Layon, facing the outer office door, watched it open. *No time to warn Jayel.*

"Who are you? What are you doing here?" boomed a demanding voice.

A middle-aged man dressed in a military uniform, a faded bruise above his right eye, stood at the entrance. The blue light on the large gun in a belt-mounted holster indicated readiness to fire.

"Good morning, sir," Layon replied calmly. "My name is Cimorelli Battersby. I am Jayel's research assistant. We're taking a tour of the governor's estate." Layon moved slightly to his left to force the man to look away from the inner office door.

"Are you now?" The officer's eyes narrowed as he stepped into the room. "Is Battersby your real name?"

"Planetary Customs truncated it, sir." *Never give too much information. If he wants to know the full name, he'll have to ask.*

The uniformed man raised an eyebrow. "You're from Ondre?"

"Yes, sir. You know the language?"

"Hmph. No. I don't think they know it, either. They keep adding consonants to names which already have too many consonants. A person can be out of breath before they get to the end of their name."

Layon laughed in agreement. "I think it has happened, sir."

"Hmm."

Shared humor did not defuse the situation, as after a brief pause, the man sneered, "Odd you should be alone in the governor's office, Mr. Battersby. I know Jayel has returned to the estate, but I don't see her with you."

"Yes, well, we came in together, but she left to check whether her father departed for Kistra yet. I expect Jayel will return shortly."

"Is that so?" The man stepped closer to Layon. "Show me your identification documents."

Layon handed his ID to the man. Respectfully waiting, Layon fingered a curl above his left temple.

After a long perusal, the officer returned the pad, his facial expression unchanged. "I don't like you being alone in this office. Best you come with me. We'll check your story, and if you are telling the truth, no harm done. But if you're lying, Mr. Battersby," he growled in a low, slow voice inches from Layon's face, "you will find my interrogation methods extremely unpleasant."

"Yes, of course. Will you inquire after Jayel, so she knows where I am? I wouldn't want her to return and find me missing."

"Don't give me orders, lad. Do you know who I am? I'm General Chrysic, the governor's Number One. You will do as I say and mind your attitude."

The general snapped his fingers, and two aides immediately entered from the hallway.

"Take him to my chamber downstairs."

Layon displayed an innocent, unworried look while they

whisked him away. *A turn for the worse, but if I can keep the General occupied, Jayel will have time to escape.*

Turning to follow, Chrysic stopped and glanced toward Karsch's inner office, the door slightly ajar. He cautiously approached, then pulled the door completely open. The low illumination suggested an empty room, but he stepped inside to increase the lighting. Nothing seemed disturbed.

To be certain nothing was amiss, Chrysic turned the handles on the opposite wall's doors. One was locked, as it should be, and the other revealed an empty bathroom. With a grunt, Chrysic left the inner office and shut the door.

The general scanned the outer office one more time, closed the hallway door, and, smacking his lips, headed for the interrogation room.

***

Jayel stood in Karsch's bedroom. *How fortunate my father hadn't changed the stairway's security code.*

The memory of General Chrysic's voice felt like ice slowly melting down her spine, and Jayel shivered. She sighed and calmed her breathing.

Looking around, she recognized the exquisite furnishings even though many years had passed since she had been here. The room was twice the size of her bedroom. Housekeeping had already made the bed, not a wrinkle to be found in the large, tan bedspread.

Surely, finding a safe place for the envelopes and the box in her hands must be the immediate concern. To free Layon only to lose the evidence would be disastrous. If Chrysic suspected treason, or the theft discovered, he would search her suite. Where's a good place to hide these envelopes? *Plenty of options to choose from. I am, after all, in a house with a hundred rooms.*

Suddenly, Jayel heard people entering the adjoining sitting

room. A voice said, "I'll get on it right away."

Father has returned.

No time to think. Jayel hastily pushed the items under the bed and moved toward the entrance to the sitting room. *I hope the location will be okay even though under the bed is the first place to look for stolen items. But no one knows yet I've taken anything. Even Layon doesn't know.*

"What are you doing here?"

A quick study of her father's face suggested not to panic. Jayel saw curiosity and surprise, not suspicion. She removed thoughts of theft from her mind.

"How was your trip?" Jayel asked, walking into the sitting room.

"The situation is under control. Our previous plans anticipated problems from this new eruption. The temporary shelters have ample room for those who need to relocate."

"Good news, Father."

"You haven't told me why you are here."

"I'm looking for my research assistant, Cimorelli. Somehow, during our tour, we got separated. I thought he might be exploring the bedrooms on this floor."

"No one is supposed to be in my bedroom."

"I know, of course, but he doesn't. Cimorelli is an admirer of your art, and I thought he could have come in here after studying the walls of your sitting room. Housekeeping left it open."

Karsch smiled. "I see. Did you ask the staff? I will put out the word to find your assistant." When Jayel hesitated to leave, her father added, "Don't worry, Daughter. What harm can come to Mr. Battersby inside my house?"

Jayel nodded and left the suite, her father and the evidence still inside.

Chapter 34

Layon remained calm, confident Jayel would confirm his story. Upon arriving at General Chrysic's basement chamber, the aides escorted him to a circular floor-to-ceiling enclosure made of thick glass. Located in the center of the room, it could hold several people.

"Stand in this cell," ordered one of the men.

Inside, many small metal widgets pimpled the glass, floor, and ceiling. Layon was unsure what function these metal pieces served. The narrow spacing prevented his shoes from standing on solid ground and uncomfortably influenced his balance.

Not long after, General Chrysic walked in and stood behind a control panel. It angled like an orchestra's organ fitted with screens, a keyboard, and toggle switches. *A maestro about to play a masterpiece.*

Layon relaxed. Chrysic's quick arrival could only mean he didn't find Jayel in the inner office.

Suddenly, a bright light burned from above, dimming the room beyond. Layon couldn't see any details of the machinery along the walls he had noticed before.

The general's voice boomed from the shadows. "While we wait to confirm your story, Mr. Battersby, I will introduce you to my interrogation methods."

Chrysic moved his hands over the control panel. Layon heard then felt air emitted from the many metal widgets. The air around him compressed and moved like ocean waves. His body rose, buoyed by folds of pressure molded around him.

Layon no longer floated upright but rather was pushed into a reclining position, as if in a dentist's chair. The sensation was like sitting in a foam-fitted furniture bag, the support firm but frameless, and movement difficult once sunken into the folds of the bag. His arms were pinned to his side. While not painful, Layon felt exposed and vulnerable.

"Comfortable?" Chrysic asked.

"Please, there is no need for interrogation, sir. I'm Jayel's research assistant. We arrived yesterday and were touring the house this morning. She went to check whether her father had left the estate. The governor's daughter trusts me, and you can, too."

"So you said." Chrysic paused. "I will ask questions, and you will answer them. You are from Ondre?"

"Yes."

"Lived in Marshe?"

"No. I grew up in Catana and moved into ICID when I apprenticed."

"I see. Did you participate in the war?"

"Not directly. ICID is a neutral research organization. They did monitor war activity and collect intelligence."

"What kind of work did you do at ICID?"

"Research mostly. I hold degrees in computer science and neuroscience. I worked on a project aimed at digitizing a person's memories."

The general paused a long time, then replied, "I like to do the opposite, to tell people what to think and feel, where my orders become their thoughts and actions."

Layon stared into the shadows, unsure what to say. *Good, Chrysic didn't follow up with questions about Jayel at ICID, but an ominous tone colors this new direction.*

Chrysic continued, "I created the chamber you are in, Mr. Battersby. By adjusting air pressure points, I can move your body into various positions. Doing so allows me to control your feelings. If you do have a neuroscience degree, then you know how body functions and emotions inform each other. For instance, if I want you to feel afraid, I simply use this setting."

Layon felt intense air pressure from all directions bending his body with both arms pushed inward. Helpless to resist, his frame contracted into a fetal position. Layon focused his thoughts on controlling his fear.

Chrysic explained, "The principle is like how smiling lightens your mood, or frowning tells your limbic system to feel sad." After a pause, he added, "If I want you to relax, I change to this setting."

The air pushed Layon's body open, spread-eagle and tilted back. His body melded with the space around him. He found breathing easier, and his mind floated as if on calm seas.

The voice behind the light continued, "There's more I can do. I can send energy pulses through the compressed air. To illustrate, this is pain."

Moderate shock hit Layon's arms. He tried to move them out of harm's way but added air pressure now pinned them to his sides. He endured the irritating stings.

Moments later, he heard, "This is pleasure."

Massaging, rhythmic waves rolled up and down his shoulders and kneaded the back. Warmth radiated down the arms. Airwaves soothed tense thigh muscles. Layon relaxed, the previous pain erased.

"What do you think of my research device, Mr. Battersby?"

Layon answered calmly, "In the wrong hands, this device could be a torture chamber."

"Fortunately, it's in my hands, Mr. Battersby. As I said, I teach my prisoners what to think and feel."

"General, I'm not your prisoner. I'm Jayel's friend. I had permission to wait in the governor's office."

"So you say. However, I can't yet confirm your story. I plan to continue with this interrogation."

The light above dimmed, no longer blinding. The air pressure again increased from all directions preventing Layon from moving. Two slim metal arms unfolded from the ceiling and taped Layon's eyelids open. On the glass wall of the chamber, he saw images of famous Onus One buildings displayed on the enclosure's glass.

Layon moved his eyeballs up and down, left and right, but could not escape viewing the large pictures.

Chrysic's voice sneered, "With conditioning techniques, I can teach you to feel what I want you to feel. Allow me to demonstrate."

A photo of Karsch appeared on the glass. Layon felt pleasant rhythmic waves soothing his muscles. Once Layon's body relaxed, General Chrysic turned off the picture and airwaves. A short interval followed to allow Layon's muscles to return to baseline. Chrysic repeated the sequence a few times—photo, massaging pressure, relaxation.

The general lectured, "After these trials, your brain anticipates the pleasant massage and relax even when the massage isn't present—Karsch, relaxation." The image of Karsch appeared, and Layon's muscles felt warm and relaxed. "I've taught you how to feel. Karsch is the good stimulus. You like him."

Next, the general showed a picture of Dareck and sent an irritating shock to Layon's shins. Layon's body recoiled, a marionette under Chrysic's control.

General Chrysic asked, "Do you know who this man is?"

"Yes, Dareck, a member of the Endowed and Governor Karsch's brother."

"Very good, Mr. Battersby. Do you personally know Dareck?"

"Yes. He visited ICID several times and received VIP treatment."

"And—"

A voice interrupted the general. "General, what is the meaning of this? Stop what you are doing!"

Both Chrysic and Layon looked toward the door. Karsch stood bathed in the hallway light, waving an arm. The governor's voice exuded authority despite his casual clothes and rolled-up sleeves in contrast to Chrysic's military uniform.

"Release him!" Karsch commanded as he closed the door and stepped closer to the control panel.

Chrysic sighed, turned off Dareck's picture, and shut off the forced air within the cell. Layon fell to his hands and knees, the small metal widgets adding a final insult to palms and kneecaps, but they didn't draw blood. The aides opened the glass door, pulled Layon out, and held him upright until Layon could stand on his own.

The illumination in the room returned to normal.

The general pleaded as he pointed at Layon, "Governor, I found this man in your office. To gain entry, he used a stolen keypad from housekeeper Rissa Santoro after last night's sexual encounter."

"Did he? Well, he is young, on vacation, and Santoro is beautiful. Perhaps he hoped she would seek him out this morning to get its return." Karsch sent Layon an appreciative glance, then returned his eyes to Chrysic. "Nonetheless, Jayel has been searching for Battersby for the past hour. I wondered if you had taken him—the house is large but not so large for a man to disappear."

General Chrysic hesitated, but Karsch pressed, "Number One, this man is my daughter's colleague. He's not a prisoner or a spy. You shouldn't have brought Battersby here to do with what you will."

Chrysic relented and softened his features. "No harm done. Isn't that so, Mr. Battersby?"

With effort, Layon maintained composure and ignored the general. He kept his eyes on Karsch. "Thank you, Governor, for verifying my identity. I've seen enough here. May I go?"

Karsch directed an aide, "Take him to Jayel's suite. If my daughter isn't there, please find and tell Jayel Mr. Battersby waits there for her return." He turned to Layon, "You will wait there, won't you, Mr. Battersby?"

"Yes, sir. Thank you, again."

After the aide and Layon left, Karsch said, "Really, General, you must be more careful. Please don't interrogate my guests, at least not without going through me first."

Chrysic shrugged off the reprimand. "How was your visit to Kistra?"

The governor sighed. "Our repositioned ash collectors did an excellent job in limiting the damage. The west side required evacuations, though. Number Two and Number Three have things under control."

"You've done an excellent job assisting people affected by our lady's temper."

The general walked over to the desk and briefly checked a pad. "When I saw the news of Jayel's arrival—you gave her a beautiful necklace—I returned to the estate without delay. I'm eager to see your daughter again."

Karsch shook his head. "The feeling is not mutual, Number One. And, after this stunt, I expect she won't want to see you for a long time."

Chrysic frowned. "How long does she plan to stay?"

"She's uncertain." Karsch paused. "Jayel asked me to sponsor her membership to the Endowed."

The general raised an eyebrow. "Has she now? How interesting. When will you start the training?"

"She apparently received training during her two-year absence. I don't yet know the details."

"I see. Most interesting." Chrysic stared past Karsch's shoulder.

"I'm planning the induction ceremony to happen soon, perhaps before I leave for the Governor's Council."

Chrysic returned his attention to the governor. "If you need assistance with preparations, I'm here to help."

"Of course." Karsch walked toward the door and then turned around. "It is good to see you again, Number One. Come upstairs for lunch." He pointed at residual swelling on Chrysic's forehead above a faded bruise. "I want to hear what you have been up to this past month."

Chapter 35

Jayel heard a loud knock and activated the security viewscreen. In the hallway, a uniformed man stood next to Layon, and she promptly opened the door.

"Cimorelli Battersby! Good to see you." Jayel pulled Layon into the room, and with a brief nod to the guard, closed the door. She leaned a high-backed chair against the door.

Layon held up a hand to remain silent. He walked to his bedroom and returned with his pad. "My program reports no listening devices. Nonetheless, I increased the jamming background signal. Best if no one overhears."

He sat on the couch, loosened the belts around his pantlegs, and laid his head back. Small beads of sweat appeared on his forehead.

Jayel joined him and studied his face. "What happened to you? Are you all right?"

"Your General Chrysic is a very interesting man," Layon whispered. "He has a torture chamber in the basement."

Jayel's eyes widened, and her body tensed.

"My mental discipline helped me to stay detached and dispassionate, but I don't know if I could've ignored his brainwashing much longer. Fortunately, your father freed me before the general inflicted harm." Layon sighed. "I could use a drink."

Nodding, Jayel walked to the bar, mixed a pitcher of extra-strength Black Holes, and poured two glasses. Returning and handing him a glass, she suggested, "Sip, don't gulp."

Layon did as instructed and relayed his experience.

When he finished, Jayel returned to the bar and poured a second round. "I hate the man," she said, handing Layon the glass. "But it makes sense now, why Dorind behaved as he did. Chrysic's conditioning is powerful. My poor Dory." A tear escaped as emotions overcame her.

"Yes, Dorind had no choice. Chrysic conditioned him to hate Dareck. If your father hadn't intervened, the general almost did the same to me."

She stiffened. "A few days ago, I swore I would get revenge, and now look what General Chrysic almost did to you. He must be stopped before hurts another person I love."

Layon put his hand on her cheek. "You love me?"

"She removed his hand and placed it between hers. "Yes, but as family. You understand, don't you?"

"Yes, and I feel the same way. We are close, and it makes me happy."

Layon put his glass down on the coffee table. "Tell me what happened to you while I was being … interrogated. How did General Chrysic not see you in your father's private office?"

"I used a secret staircase to get out unseen. It leads to my father's bedroom."

"Excellent."

"No sooner did I arrive in the bedroom when my father walked into his sitting room."

"Oh no. What happened?"

"Well, his suite is like this one, and fortunately, he didn't walk immediately to the bedroom. I had enough time to hide the envelopes."

Layon sat upright. "Then you found the evidence?"

"Yes."

"What happened next?"

"I covered up well enough. I said we became separated during our tour, and I was looking for you."

"Was he suspicious?"

"He expressed concern about your whereabouts. He suggested I look in the staff's end of the house. I left but didn't go downstairs. I waited around the corner, and when I heard him leave, I retrieved what I hid."

"You have the evidence here?" Layon looked around.

"Yes."

"Where? Let's examine the documents."

"Not a good idea. After your experience with General Chrysic, you should leave at once. You are in danger more than ever if the general finds out you are Layon, son of Neondra, and not Cimorelli Battersby, my research assistant. Leave Melandan immediately and take the evidence to Dareck."

Layon pushed the hair away from his face. "Are you sure you found the correct documents?"

"Yes. I glanced through them. There are photos, receipts, and letters." A shadow passed over Jayel's face.

"What is it? Did you see something that implicates your father? Although he came to my rescue today, I want him brought to justice if—"

"I saw a letter from my mother" Jayel interrupted. "I'm not sure what role she played in the crime. Take everything to Dareck. Best if you go through the documents together and decide whether you have sufficient evidence to proceed with charges about the fire."

"And you?"

"I'm not safe here either, I think, now that the General has returned. I'm not sure I can hide what I did from my father should he examine me, nor do I want to come face to face with General Chrysic. I already arranged to visit my mother for a few days. I'll see if I can learn anything from her. I packed while waiting for you."

"Sounds like a good plan. I can take a small jet parked not far from the estate." Layon entered a few commands into his pad, then stood. "It'll be ready in an hour."

Jayel didn't move.

Layon sat again beside her. "What is it?"

"There's more you should know. Something you haven't been told. I don't think your father knows. However, Brusch and I talked about it. It's important. I must tell you before you start looking through these documents."

"Okay. Is it bad news?"

"Not exactly. But it may be hard for you to accept."

"After what I've been through today, I can take it. Please, tell me."

She pulled him close and held his hands. "What do you know about your mother's life around the time you were born?"

Layon thought for a moment. "Mother apprenticed as a biologist. She worked at the Bemeyers Institute before meeting my father."

"And did Dareck work there, too?"

"No, I don't think so. Even after they married, my mother continued working at the Institute. However, by the time she gave birth to me, they had made a home on Characta."

"Layon, my father worked at Bemeyers while your mother worked there. They knew each other."

"Are you saying Karsch knew my mother *before* she met my

father? I do recall Dareck said Karsch didn't approve of their marriage. Do you think Karsch disliked her?" Layon paused. "Or are you suggesting Karsch loved my mother? Jealousy could be a motive for murder."

Jayel clasped his hands and studied them. "Your hands, they are strong. Their shape, like mine." She ran her thumb across his long fingers.

Layon looked down and then back up into her eyes. "What are you trying to tell me?"

"Neondra and Karsch had an affair. You are their son."

Layon started to pull his hands away, but Jayel strengthened her grip. She closed her eyes and connected to his mind.

He inhaled deeply and closed his eyes. "I can hear your thoughts. Did Brusch teach you this skill?"

"Not exactly, but I hoped it could work. It's the first time I've tried. We'll both be members of the Endowed soon, and … we are brother and sister."

Startled, Layon opened his eyes. "I … I can't believe …" But he didn't pull away. After a long pause, he nodded and slowly spoke, "I understand now what I felt about you before, the intense caring, what I feel now." He chuckled. "Back on Ondre, I told Dareck you felt like a sister to me."

They smiled, honestly sharing the truth for the first time.

Jayel let go of his hands and took a deep breath. "I don't think Dareck knows. He believes only his brother disapproved of the marriage."

Layon stood, walked to the bar, and poured the remainder of the Back Hole mix. He drank the entire glass before he returned to the couch and sat next to Jayel. "Are you sure Karsch is my father?"

"Not a hundred percent. But I suspected the moment I saw you on Ondre. You look so much like my father at his age. I don't know why anyone else doesn't see it. And then there's the connection we feel. It's extraordinarily strong."

Both smiled.

Jayel continued, "I worried my father or General Chrysic might notice the resemblance, but changes to match your photo ID appear to have worked. For now." She paused. "If you would give me a DNA sample before you leave, a test can confirm it."

He nodded. "You will be discreet, I presume?"

"Yes. My mother's archeological site is on Melandan's Osjenkin continent. I'll tell the medical center's lab it's part of my medical studies research. No one will know who gave the two samples. We'll have the results soon after."

He smiled, the revelation sinking in. "I have a sister."

"I have a brother."

After a long pause, a furrowed look appeared on Layon's face.

Jayel asked, "What is it?"

"I just realized why you shot Dorind. You saved me because you knew I was your brother."

"Yes." Jayel choked back tears as she relived the decision in the greenhouse.

They hugged and touched foreheads. After a moment, they parted.

Layon stood. "It occurs to me, though, we don't know whether Karsch knows I am his son. Did he know I was his son when he shot my mother?"

"I don't know. Maybe neither brother knew. Perhaps Neondra didn't know, either, if she was having sex with both brothers."

Sighing, Layon shook his head. "It's hard to believe Karsch, an Endowed member, could commit murder. Especially since

I've met the man. And now you tell me he is my father."

"I know." Jayel nodded and stood. "For two years, I grappled with the idea my father committed murder. But the conversation I overheard implied the fire wasn't an accident and my father claimed responsibility."

"Let's hope the evidence will unravel the mystery." Layon brushed a curl away from his eyes, went into his bedroom, and returned shortly carrying his travel bag. "I'm ready to go." He handed her a tissue wrapped around several strands of hair and a contact lens container filled with his saliva. "Either of these should suffice for the DNA test."

Jayel placed the items in her rucksack and handed a travel pillow to Layon. "I put the evidence inside the pillowcase."

"Good thing I travel light," Layon quipped as he stuffed it into his bag.

"When you sort through the evidence with Dareck, the news of his wife's affair and his not being your biological father will wound deeply. He will need your support."

"Yes. It will be a difficult conversation. But a necessary one." Layon picked up his bag, ready to leave. "You will message me the results of the test?"

"Of course, by 20 hours, system time." Jayel slung the rucksack over her shoulder. "I'll walk you out to be certain you leave the estate without more interference from our friend, the general. Then, Pende agreed to take me to the airport."

They exchanged "good luck" glances. Layon smiled, leaned in, and kissed her on the cheek.

Chapter 36

Three hours before sunset, Jayel disembarked and scanned the small crowd in the airport's waiting area. Her mother, Mandel, waved and caught her attention.

Mandel, in her early fifties, kept a youthful appearance. Her skin remained smooth, and cropped dark brown hair accentuated a strong jawline.

Mother always said long hair got in the way of work.

Jayel smiled, walked over, and hugged her mother according to Melandan's custom—two hands on the shoulders and then one arm around the back to embrace. "It is good to see you. You haven't aged a day."

"You have matured." Mandel pushed away and gave her daughter a careful inspection. "It is good to see you. But at the same time, two years without a word? I suppose coming here one day after you arrived on Melandan partially makes up for it. You look a little tired, Daughter, but I like what you've done with your hair."

"A style from Ondre, where I had it cut last week."

"Is it where you lived all this time?"

"No, but it's a long story. Where shall we go to catch up?"

"Let's go to the Greenburge Sculpture Gardens. It's near here, and we can talk while we take in the art."

"Sounds interesting, but first I need to drop off a package at the medical center." Jayel scanned the map on her pad as they left the airport. "The gardens are near the hospital, and it will delay us only a few minutes."

After Jayel submitted the materials for DNA testing, they passed over a bridge, parked at the base of one of the city's many hills, and took the air escalator to a bluff. Overlooking the downtown, the garden displayed various artistic styles of metal and stone posed among landscaped flowers and fountains.

They used the guide map on their pads to navigate to the first sculpture. While walking, Jayel explained she traveled to Leidran after leaving medical school.

"Quintar is a wonderful city," Mandel responded. "So many cultures. I imagine the food options are the best of the two systems. I haven't been there yet, but colleagues who visited on their way to Onus Two rave about the diversity."

"An interesting place, definitely. In my free time, Mother, I wondered about how you and Father met. Tell me about the early years of your relationship."

They stopped in front of a huge scratched and broken clay pot leaning against a boulder. The sculpture, *Artifact of the Giants*, celebrated archeology.

Mandel studied the piece while she spoke. "Your father pursued me. At the time, we indulged our independence. I loved archeology and enjoyed examining remote sites and pouring over data. Your father savored problem-solving, policymaking, and meeting people. He was looking for a change from his biology research, and I think my father's political career helped to develop his attraction to me."

"But despite your different careers, you married him?"

"My parents encouraged our marriage, and," Mandel

smiled, "your father has his charms."

Jayel kept her eyes on the sculpture. "I can imagine the early years were difficult."

"Our jobs kept us busy, and so the times together seemed like vacations. Good days." Mandel paused. "We did experience some rough years." Another pause, but then she smiled. "We learned how to juggle family responsibilities and our jobs. No different than any other family on Melandan, where careers start at an early age."

They walked on to the next sculpture.

"Why do you ask, Jayel? Are you thinking of starting a family?"

"I wondered about the early years of your marriage, whether you were apart more than together."

"When your father became governor, he had General Chrysic to keep him company." Mandel laughed. "They were work and play companions."

Jayel shuddered at Chrysic's name.

Her mother continued. "Once you become a doctor, you'll find a way to do research and simultaneously raise a family. Are you contemplating starting one, perhaps with your friend, the medical student, Dorindi, is that his name?"

"No. We're not together anymore." Jayel fell silent. They stopped at the next sculpture, a bird in flight, and examined its fine details.

Without taking her eyes off the art, Jayel mentioned, "Recently, I visited Ondre, where my research assistant lives. I met Dareck, Father's brother."

Her mother stiffened. "Oh?"

"Yes, he helped broker the peace treaty." Jayel paused, then continued. "I wonder why he and Father aren't close. I don't recall he ever visited our estate."

Mandel looked uncomfortable, but her voice remained casual. "They are half-brothers and live on different planets. He lives on Characta, I think."

"I heard his wife died in a fire years ago." Jayel looked at her mother's expression, but it didn't change.

"Yes. About 15 standard years ago, I suppose. Maybe longer. A tragedy for a young Endowed member."

Mandel looked past the sculpture, then looked back at her daughter. "Was he well?"

"Yes. Seemed a lot like Father—he had the Endowed confidence and charisma."

"Hmm. Yes, well, I'm glad you met your uncle."

They moved down the path in silence.

When their conversation renewed, Mandel changed the topic to her archeological research. Jayel learned Mother supervised a staff of thirty anthropologists and mentored ten of forty students on site. Jayel's visit gave her the first time off in months.

An hour later, they returned to Mandel's residence, a modest house on the edge of the city, adjacent to the research site. The ground floor combined rooms in an open-concept style. The south side's floor-to-ceiling window overlooked a vast grassland.

When they entered the front door, a man, working on a computer at a nearby table, stood. He looked about Jayel's age, maybe younger. Tall, his red plaid shirt hung loosely around muscular shoulders. Eyes, matching his dark brown hair, color gazed into hers, and the man smiled.

Jayel returned the smile, then blushed when she realized she stared longer than she should have.

Mandel motioned to the man. "Ranthal, from Characta, one of our anthropologists. He recently arrived. Ranthal, this is my daughter, Jayel, who is visiting for a few days." Mandel looked at their mutual lingering glances and took a step back. She added, "Ah, I need to go to the site and close today's crew log. I'll be back … in a few hours." Smiling, she turned and left the house.

Jayel and Ranthal moved into the social gathering space.

"Characta?" Jayel studied the handsome stranger. *A coincidence he came from Dareck's planet and recently?* He looked both young and mature at the same time, a combination exuding confidence. *Too much confidence.* "You are a member of the Endowed."

"Yes." Ranthal smiled at the insight. His face glowed as the skin around the eyes crinkled.

"You know Dareck?" Jayel asked.

He nodded. "I'm his apprentice. I recently earned a degree in medical anthropology."

They moved to the window and took in the view. A stiff breeze ruffled the grass and created the look of ocean waves. The sun hovered just above the horizon.

"Did Dareck send you?"

"He knew you might visit your mother while on Melandan."

"A spy?"

"A resource."

Jayel smiled and studied Ranthal's face. His demeanor invited trust. She said, "My research assistant traveled to Characta earlier today."

Ranthal looked deeply into her eyes. "I understand. Your mission went well, then?"

"General Chrysic returned to the estate, and we felt it best to go our separate ways."

As he nodded, Jayel believed he knew exactly what she

implied. She relaxed. It felt good to trust him.

Jayel motioned to a pitcher of water on a nearby table, and, seeing his agreement, poured two glasses. As she picked hers up, Ranthal reached for the other glass. His arm brushed against hers.

After several swallows, Jayel said, "And what does a medical anthropologist do?"

"We examine a site to help reconstruct its history. We study people's bones and artifacts concerning their health. The current site is particularly interesting. Do you know much about it?"

"No. Please tell me."

"Four standard centuries ago, early explorers from Orim came to this continent. They found Osjenkin's land too rugged and inhospitable, and all but the first expedition settled only on the main continent. The early settlers who stayed were presumed dead. Then, two hundred standard years later, a ship filled with their descendants crashed on Melandan's main continent, near the city of Mallon."

Jayel frowned. "If I recall my history lessons, everyone in the crash died on impact."

"Yes, a tragedy. Years later, when people learned to control weather and land, they returned to Osjenkin and built cities. Although nature reclaimed most of the abandoned settlement, archeologists found abundant evidence of houses sheltering hundreds of people, streets ten miles long, and farms providing abundant agriculture. The original settlers managed to thrive."

"And what have you learned about the settlers?"

Smiling, Ranthal said, "Sex and reproduction mattered greatly to them."

Jayel laughed. "How can you know?"

"From genetic analyses of bone fragments, we determined

most women bore between fifteen to twenty children, beginning soon after menstruation and continuing until menopause. In nearly all cases, siblings had the same parents, implying life-long monogamous relationships."

"What did they die from, worn out from childbearing?" Jayel asked, half-joking, half curious.

"Drought. Sixty-seven standard years of the Great Drought, a deadly weather pattern of high heat and low humidity for this continent. It killed the crops and dried up the rivers in an already harsh land. They couldn't sustain life and eventually built a ship to abandon their settlement."

Silent, the pair returned their attention to the waving grass beyond the window. Jayel imagined life on the primitive continent and their struggle for survival. A mood of loneliness descended as the sun kissed the horizon. She turned and found Ranthal studying her.

Neither said anything. Lights automatically came on as the darkness increased outside.

Ranthal unbound his hair, and it curled as it fell onto his shoulders.

Her eyes moved from his shoulder to below his neck, to the opening of his flannel shirt.

He picked up her hands and placed them on his chest.

Jayel felt warmth travel through her body. His dry, warm palms surrounded hers, harboring, comforting, and supporting.

She searched Ranthal's eyes for meaning. "Leave it to Dareck to send you to me."

"Actually, Dareck almost chose someone else, but Brusch suggested I come. Brusch knew I recently suffered the loss of a close friend and thought you could help me."

The light in the room seemed like a spotlight on them. She

looked down at his hands covering hers. "I'm sorry for your loss, Ranthal. What did Brusch tell you about me?"

"He said you would understand my situation."

Jayel searched his face. "What is it you need?" *I already know. I need it, too.*

"To trust again. To belong again."

Nodding, Jayel remarked, "Brusch is wise."

Ranthal opened his hands and slid Jayel's hands under his shirt. When she didn't pull away, he added, "Let's not be alone anymore."

Jayel's palms felt smooth skin and strong chest muscles. They sensed Ranthal's heart beating, fast and strong. Jayel's heart increased its pace to match. Her fingers circled his breast, and Ranthal shivered.

She breathed deeply and felt the powerful switch of feeling like "running from" to "running toward."

Tilting Jayel's face to his, Ranthal kissed her moist lips, parting them. His tongue briefly explored her mouth. She responded in kind.

Their minds opened, thoughts touching, embracing.

Their bodies pressed against each other.

When they separated, Jayel murmured, "This encounter is unexpected but welcomed."

After one more passionate kiss, Ranthal said. "We have the house to ourselves. My room or yours?"

She laughed. "I don't know which room is mine—I only just arrived."

"I know the way." He led Jayel upstairs.

Chapter 37

Following a clap of thunder, a strong wind ruffled the grass beyond the window. Jayel watched two small animals scurry toward a nearby tree. It would likely rain soon. A loud voice from behind shifted her attention.

"Six days!" Karsch exclaimed.

She turned around.

Casually dressed, with slacks belted above the ankles and a loose-fitting beige top, Karsch didn't look as angry as he sounded.

Jayel maintained a face of innocence. "Yes, well, I've been busy getting reacquainted with Mother."

"I thought you might visit two or three days at most, but it's been nearly a week. One dinner with me, and then, *zam*, you left. If I didn't know better, I'd say you deliberately stayed away."

"Is it so hard to understand? After what General Chrysic did to Cimorelli, I don't want to be in the same house. Honestly, Father, I don't see how you can stand him."

Jayel thought a shadow darkened his face.

Before her father could respond, Mandel walked into the room and embraced her husband. "It is good to see you. What brings you across the planet without any notice?" She sat on the couch.

"Jayel, of course. I thought she was only coming to see you for a few days, and I grew concerned." Karsch sighed and sat next to his wife.

Jayel hesitated but took the cue from her mother that it was best to talk it out rather than leave the room. She sat on an adjacent chair and reached for a glass of water. A hard rain now fell, but no thunder or lightning accompanied the cloudburst.

"I came, Mandel, because our daughter requested induction into the Endowed membership, but it is difficult to plan a ceremony when she isn't in touch with me." He looked at Jayel. "I left several messages, but you haven't returned any."

"I'm sorry, Father," Jayel responded. "But I stopped looking at my mail. Friends who heard I'm back on Melandan clogged my mailbox, and I don't intend to reply to them until my plans are more definite."

"And, Husband," Mandel piped in, "our daughter developed a romantic relationship with one of my colleagues. Young love, you remember how it is."

Karsch's demeanor softened, and he held Mandel's gaze. "Yes, very much so." He leaned over and kissed his wife. "I'm only concerned about timing because the Governors' Council is in six days."

Jayel tried not to stare, but the outward signs of affection between her parents came as a surprise. *Father mentioned working on his marital relationship, but I didn't realize the extent.*

Karsch caught his daughter's expression and sighed. He leaned back and relaxed. "Tell me about your new friend."

"Speaking of him," Mandel gestured to Ranthal as he walked in, holding playing cards and a scorepad."

The governor stood and shook the young man's hand. "I know you. Ranthal, isn't it? I attended your induction to the

Endowed membership four years ago."

"Correct." Ranthal returned Karsch's handshake. "It's an honor to meet you, Governor."

"Skip titles, please. I understand you, ah, have become friends with my daughter."

"Yes, we've spent much time together this week … getting to know each other."

Jayel and Ranthal exchanged glances, smiling, blushing.

"I see." He turned to Jayel, "Well, I forgive you for not messaging me, this time. And I approve. Dating a member of the Endowed is excellent, just excellent."

Mandel stood. "We were about to play tunnels during my work break. Jayel and Ranthal boast of being strong players. Husband, why don't we show them how the game is really played?"

"It's been a while, but one never forgets how to play tunnels."

Jayel went to the kitchen and brought out cold beverages as they took their places around the table. Ranthal shuffled and dealt the cards.

Mandel studied her hand. "Where and when will Jayel's induction to the Endowed take place?"

"I initially thought at our estate, but it turned out the timing was too close to the governors' council to hold it on Melandan," Karsch replied. "Having to make the decision myself …" he glanced at Jayel … "the induction will happen on Characta the day before the governors' meeting begins." He paused again and added, "And I hope my daughter promises to be present."

"Yes, of course," Jayel responded. She picked up her mother's discard.

Each player took a turn before the conversation resumed.

Mandel inquired, "Have you spoken to Dareck, to invite him?"

"Not directly. However, word came to me this morning of a special meeting of Endowed members following our daughter's induction, and his name is on the list of attendees."

Jayel's facial muscles tightened, and she kept her eyes on her hand.

"I received the notice, too," Ranthal remarked. "I plan to attend this special meeting and, of course, Jayel's induction."

"Up your shaft," Jayel announced, laying down her cards.

"Down the hole," Mandel replied, displaying a stronger hand. "Round 1 to the older generation."

"Excellent," Karsch remarked. He gathered the cards and shuffled. As required by the rules, he dealt the next hand. "As Melandan's governor, I'll travel early to prepare for the council. I want everyone to leave here with me tomorrow to return to our estate, and we'll travel together."

Mandel sighed. "I can't just stop work without notice."

Ranthal picked up his cards. "Sir, if it's more convenient for the women, I can provide them passage on my private ship to Characta. Travel with me will give them four days to prepare for the trip rather than leave tomorrow."

Mandel nodded at this suggestion, "I could use the time. Plus, you always travel with an entourage of guards and committee aides. One less thing for you to worry about if wife and daughter aren't in the party."

"Oh, very well." Karsch sighed, drew a card, and replaced one from his hand to discard. "I agree it'll be easier. At least today I requested my aides stay outside."

"Thank you, Husband. I don't need armed guards watching us play cards."

"It's good your porch protects them from the rain,"

quipped her husband.

Jayel picked up her mother's discard and replaced it with one from her hand. "Is there anything I need to do to prepare?"

"Before the induction, you'll meet with some Endowed members to discuss the ceremony and expectations of membership."

On her turn, Mandel picked up a card and laid her hand on the table. "Up your shaft."

"So soon?" Jayel groaned. Neither she nor Ranthal could counter with a better hand.

Karsch smiled as he held up the high card. "And I mined gold."

"Two in a row for the parents!" Ranthal entered the scores for the win and gold bonus on the scorepad.

As Jayel shuffled and dealt, Karsch said, "I'll send you a schedule and text of the rite. You need to memorize the proper responses. And this time, Jayel, you will acknowledge my messages."

"Yes, Father." Several moments later, she asked, "Will General Chrysic go to Characta with you?"

Karsch's lips pursed. "Chrysic and I will be traveling separately. He attends the Governors' Council but not the Endowed meetings. For you, Daughter, I'll give him a chore to complete on Melandan to delay his arrival on Characta. With any luck, you two won't cross paths."

"Good." Jayel frowned, nonetheless. She noticed her mother also frowned.

Karsch drank from his glass. He added, "General Chrysic means well. He's always had my best interest at heart."

Suddenly, they heard a loud explosion, and the house shook.

The door flew open, and one of the governor's aides burst in. "Sir, an airbus crashed into a building down the street."

Immediately, the four stood and rushed outside. The rain steadily fell. At the corner, a plume of smoke rose from a pile of debris. Karsch and Ranthal immediately ran to help, but Mandel held Jayel's arm and said, "I'll contact my staff and bring blankets and supplies. Set up a triage area, and we'll come soon with supplies."

"Understood." Jayel sprinted to the scene. Five survivors, disheveled and bloodied, stumbled out of the gaping hole of the shop.

"Stay here." Jayel corralled them. "We'll help you."

A crowd gathered, and Jayel pushed through. The airbus had stopped halfway through the structure.

The upper floors appeared stable, but the craft filled the first floor. Smoke from within the building billowed into the air. The rear engine had detached and was leaking fuel, but puddles of rainwater channeled it toward the street.

Jayel saw a body pinned under the back end of the bus, away from the flames but trapped. Smoke in their faces, her father and Ranthal grabbed the bumper and lifted the metal frame knee-high off the ground.

"Quick," Karsch ordered his daughter.

Jayel crouched, reached under, and pulled the person out. A heavy-set older woman, conscious and moaning in pain, looked up at her with tears of gratitude.

"Don't move. You may have a neck injury. Calm your breathing. Good." Jayel squeezed the woman's hand, and the woman smiled a "thank you."

Ranthal and Jayel exchanged glances filled with pride in their success before he joined Karsch, who had already disappeared into the smoke-filled building.

Emergency services arrived. At the same time, Mandel came with several staff members carrying supplies. With impressive efficiency, the archeologists set up a large tent across the street.

Jayel assisted paramedics in examining the six accident victims. Most injuries were not too bad, but even those with only scrapes looked traumatized. Minutes later, two pedestrians limped in. They had slipped on foamy fire retardant which oozed in the puddles running down the street.

Soon, the paramedics had everything under control, and Jayel walked over to her mother who was unpacking a box of blankets. Mandel handed her a towel to dry off.

A loud cheer erupted. Jayel looked toward the building. Karsch, Ranthal, and fire rescuers exited the ghastly hole carrying two survivors on stretchers. The bus driver, bloodied and burned, waved a hand to acknowledge the crowd. The cheers renewed.

Somehow, everyone on the bus and the home's only occupant, the older woman trapped under the vehicle, had survived.

Jayel heard voices in the crowd express praise for her father. "Let's hear it for our governor" and "Well done, Karsch, member of the Endowed."

She studied her father. His shirt looked pitch black except in a few places where the original beige showed through the dirt, his hair dripped from rain and sweat, and his eyes displayed genuine concern for the victims. Jayel wanted to feel proud but instead felt confused. *How could this hero be guilty of murder?*

Chapter 38

En route to Characta, Jayel stared out the window of Ranthal's ship into the blackness. As the arrival time drew near, her mind grew increasingly unsettled.

The evidence she'd given to Layon had been strong enough for Dareck to call the Endowed special meeting, no doubt to bring a charge of murder against her father. The murder of an Endowed member demanded the severest of penalties.

Thoughts of justice swirled with those of impending hurt and betrayal. To add further tumult, she felt guilty because she disguised her role. Both parents believed a joyous, traditional celebration awaited, but instead, a trial would make public Neondra's affair and the horrific crime.

Jayel didn't know how Dareck reacted to the news of Neondra's affair or not being Layon's biological father. Because Layon's program detected a hack on Jayel's digital account—she suspected General Chrysic monitored her mail—Jayel's only communication was a short message to Layon—to Cimorelli—wishing him a good vacation and hoping he would see his sister soon.

Sipping *switchya*, Jayel's thoughts turned to Ranthal. She knew he admired Dareck who mentored his apprenticeship. Dareck taught him how to pilot spacecraft, like the one he did now. His apprenticeship with Dareck forged a strong friendship.

When Jayel met Ranthal, he indicated knowing her mission on Melandan, but she remained careful. She never stated Cimorelli was Layon, or the evidence he took to Dareck implicated Karsch. If Ranthal wasn't fully informed, would he feel slighted at the meeting because she hadn't confided in him?

Certainly, her attraction to Ranthal helped ease some internal tension. Comparison to former lovers ended quickly. She delighted in exploring each other's likes and dislikes, and each day they discovered new ways to express their growing intimacy. Yet, the ghost of Dorind remained. Jayel hadn't told Ranthal she killed Dory. It wasn't easy to bring up, much easier to avoid. As easy as not thinking about how a small hole in the skin of Ranthal's ship would result in her joining the blackness beyond, space so black it could envelop any unsettled mind.

"I know that face," Mandel interrupted Jayel's reverie. "What's wrong, Daughter?"

Jayel looked away from the window and regarded her mother, unsure how much to disclose. Her visit had gone well, and she never felt so close, yet there was her letter among the evidence … *best to go slow.* Jayel began, "This past week has been very confusing. The whole month, for that matter. The future isn't much clearer, either."

Her mother picked up her cup and stirred the *switchya.* "We have an hour until we land. It's just the two of us. Tell me what's on your mind."

"I'm trying to understand you and Father. I thought you two had drifted apart, but the other day you both seemed … in harmony. I didn't even know you played Tunnels together."

"We haven't played cards in a long time. And you're right. We do lead independent lives. For most of our marriage, we spent more time apart than together."

"I saw genuine love. I have to say it surprised me."

Her mother smiled. "It's the Melandanian way, to be independent. We're secure in our mutual commitments and goals. We don't need physical presence to keep the emotional bond strong."

"I always thought you stayed away from home because Father was cold, arrogant, and distant."

Mandel raised an eyebrow and sipped the *switchya*. "There's truth in what you say. He can appear indifferent to our needs when focused on political matters. When he's preoccupied, then yes, you and I move down the ladder of priorities."

Jayel looked out the window again.

After a short silence, her mother added, "Perhaps you think I was cold and distant, too. My work kept me away from the estate more than you would have liked."

"Maybe," Jayel replied looking back at her mother with a smile. "This past week has gone well, though, hasn't it?"

"Yes, but I still see a face—like you're hiding something." Mandel reached across the table and held Jayel's hand. "Is it the upcoming induction? Are you afraid of becoming an Endowed member? No need. You will live up to everyone's expectations. Your father and I are proud of you."

Jayel withdrew her hand. "It's true, at the moment I don't feel worthy of Endowed membership. I've done something bad. And I'm about to hurt people I care for—even you, Mother."

Mandel shifted in her chair. "Hurt me, how? Tell me, what have you done?"

"It's complicated," Jayel sighed, "but I'm caught in a process involving you and Father and what happened almost twenty standard years ago."

Her mother stared. "Go on."

"You must swear secrecy. You can't tell Father. What we'll talk about is between you and me."

Mandel hesitated a moment, then said, "I swear."

"It concerns Dareck's wife, Neondra."

"Oh, you know about her." Mandel poured another cup of *switchya* and sipped.

Jayel expected her mother to have more questions about what she knew. Instead, Mandel looked past Jayel's shoulder and said, "They worked together and grew close. It's true, your father loved her. But we were married at the time, and he wasn't free. Neondra married Dareck instead. The two brothers grew apart."

"Did Dareck know about their relationship?"

"Hmm, I don't know. But Dareck must have sensed his brother's feelings. It drove a wedge between them, a wedge in a gap already widening since their childhood. I'm not sure the brothers were ever close."

Jayel swallowed. "And you? Did you know Father continued his relationship with Neondra even after their marriage?"

Mandel looked down. "Yes. Your father promised he would stop seeing her. But he loved Neondra, and he couldn't let go. Hard to say it, but after she died, it became easier for him to devote full attention to our marriage. It took a long time, years, for the ghost of Neondra to disappear, but we eventually found a comfortable place."

"I think last week at your house was the happiest I've seen you two together. You do love Father, don't you?"

"Yes, very much."

Jayel glanced out the window. *Should she confide more?*

Mandel looked long at her daughter. "How did you learn

about Neondra?"

"Dareck told me."

"Dareck!"

"Yes, He confided in me about the fire. He believes Neondra's death wasn't an accident."

"What?" Her mother's eyes moistened. "Everyone said it was. What do you mean, not an accident?"

"He thinks Neondra's death was murder, that someone intentionally set the fire."

Mandel looked down and stirred the *switchya.* After taking a sip, she said, "Losing his wife and son in a fire … I can imagine it's easier for him to blame someone. The authorities declared it an accident."

Jayel paused and took a deep breath. "This upcoming Endowed meeting, before the Governors' Council starts, is about the fire."

Mandel knitted her brow. "What does this tragedy have to do with the Endowed? Is it because Neondra was a member of the Endowed?"

Nervously, Jayel pushed a strand of hair behind her ears. "Yes, Murder of an Endowed member requires the severest of penalty judgments. Dareck found evidence the fire wasn't an accident."

Mandel's face paled. "Does he know who started the fire?"

"I think so. But Layon said—"

"Layon! Daughter, Layon died in the fire."

"No. Layon was rescued. Dareck hid the boy to protect him from any other attempts on his life. Neondra's son has been quietly living on Ondre. I've met him."

Mandel looked stunned then relieved. "This is good news. Your father will be happy to learn his nephew still lives."

Jayel looked out the window a second time.

After finishing the cup of *switchya*, Mandel said, "You mentioned earlier you had done something bad. What did you do? You had nothing to do with the fire."

After a long pause, Jayel whispered, "I shot someone … killed a man … on Ondre."

Her mother gasped. "Killed? On Ondre? During the attack? Did you shoot and kill the man who shot you?"

"Yes and no. I did kill the man who shot me, but days afterward. Peace was declared, I healed, and all was going well. But then the man who shot me was about to kill Layon. I stopped him."

Mandel nodded and grasped Jayel's hand. "You saved a life, your cousin's life."

"I killed Dorind, the man I loved from medical school."

"How—?" Mandel looked long and hard at her daughter. "I know, you said it's complicated. One day you'll tell me the whole story." Mandel wiped a tear from Jayel's cheek.

"I'm glad you told me. It must have been difficult for you. But it sounds to me like a justified killing. You wouldn't be the first Endowed member who has taken a life. From what I've heard, Dareck killed many soldiers in the attack on the moon base. Being Endowed doesn't mean you step aside when taking life is justified. Being Endowed concerns focusing your gifts to make wise decisions and committing to choices."

Jayel remained silent and drank the rest of her *switchya.*

"Talk to Ranthal before you accept membership if you still have doubts about this shooting affecting your worthiness to become a member of the Endowed."

Jayel nodded. "I will. I haven't told him about Dorind and what I did. I didn't want him to think less of me."

"If Ranthal loves you, and it seems to me he does, you will find a new level of intimacy when you share your fears with him. I'm happy for you, Daughter. Ranthal is a thoughtful, intelligent young man. I can tell you're good together."

Characta came into view, and the ship slowed to enter orbit. Jayel could see the impressive ring of weather satellites that kept the planet's climate like Melandan's. *Remarkable how technology from orbit could monitor and alter atmospheric temperature and pressure to modulate climates for living things.* Without these satellites, the Orimish might never have populated the other planets.

Jayel put on the shoulder strap and closed her eyes. *May Mother forgive me for what is about to happen.*

Chapter 39

Jayel stood behind Ranthal and Mandel in the customs line and viewed the schedule sent from the Endowed Induction Committee.

"My first interview is in five hours, at the Great Hall," Jayel announced.

Ranthal turned. "Good. The Great Hall is also where your induction will take place. We have time to settle in our rooms without rushing."

"Assuming this line moves," Mandel groaned.

A customs agent approached. He looked happy and relaxed compared to his stressed counterparts at the head of the lines. "Ah, I see a governor's wife, an Endowed member, and the Endowed inductee. No more waiting is necessary. I can expedite your passport check. Please, come with me."

Mandel smiled. "VIP service. Today, I don't mind."

The three followed the agent to a side desk. In seconds, he confirmed their identity, and the customs approval seal appeared on their pads.

"Welcome to Characta." The agent smiled proudly and pointed toward the exit.

Outside, colder air than expected greeted Jayel's thin clothes, and she considered opening her bag to get a jacket.

Ranthal pointed to a hotel shuttle four cars down. "The organizers reserved the entire CHT Grand for government dignitaries, Endowed members, support staff, and families."

"Are you planning on going to your home or will you stay with us at the hotel?"

"My home is too far away for easy commuting. I'll stay in your suite."

She tugged his shirt. "I like the sound of that."

They approached the CHT Grand shuttle. Before Ranthal and Jayel stepped in, Mandel hung back, eyes studying her pad. "As I expected, my husband is already in meetings, and I'm on my own time. You two go on to the hotel. I'm confirming an appointment to meet anthropology colleagues at the university. Daughter, we can connect tomorrow morning before the ceremony."

Her mother handed her carry-on bag to Jayel and gave a nod before heading toward a public airbus further down the loading zone.

Jayel smiled at her mother's disappearing figure and remarked, "She never could sit still, except when staring at an artifact."

Mother is giving me time alone to talk to Ranthal about Dory.

As they took their seats on the shuttle, Jayel commented, "I've heard about this Great Hall. It's architecturally famous. Built about fifty standard years ago, it celebrates Orim's classic contributions from past millennia. Ten stories made of thick limestone and marble shipped from Orim. The hall's ceiling is vaulted, and the exterior windows are made of thick colorful glass. We took virtual tours in school."

Ranthal added, "The Endowed like to use the Great Hall for ceremonies—helps create pomp and circumstance for their elite rituals. It has smaller meeting rooms on upper floors around the cavernous assembly hall, ideal for meetings going on this week."

"Your induction four years ago took place there?" Jayel asked.

"Yes. Not all Endowed inductions happen on Characta, but those held on this planet usually occur in the Great Hall."

They arrived at the CHT Grand within ten minutes. When they stepped into an ornate lobby, an impeccably dressed manager immediately approached them.

"Welcome. The airport notified us you arrived. Your suite is ready. Please follow me."

Ranthal and Jayel complied and took a speedy elevator ride to their suite.

Inside, Jayel gasped with pleasure at the grand furnishings. A large window afforded a splendid view of the city. She saw two large flower arrangements on the table.

"What interesting flowers," Jayel commented. "Green petals and vibrant pink leaves."

"Rare local flowers," Ranthal explained.

Jayel read the card in the vase. "Welcome to the Membership—Brusch."

"How thoughtful." She turned to the second vase filled with familiar flowers of Melandan. The card read, *Congratulations—General Chrysic.*

A shiver ran down her spine. Jayel had hoped to escape the general's attention, but he already made his presence known. She frowned.

Ranthal inquired, "What's wrong?"

"General Chrysic." She showed him the card.

"Do you expect trouble?"

"I hope not. I know revenge is, as they say, an acid wearing away the heart, but —"

"Revenge?"

"After what he did to Dorind, Chrysic needs to be held accountable."

Ranthal gave her a long look. "I only know fragments. I want to hear the whole story."

They sat on the couch. Taking her mother's advice, Jayel shared what happened to Dorind, beginning with recruitment by Chrysic and ending with Dory's death.

After she finished, Ranthal remarked, "I understand why you dislike this General Chrysic. Does your father know about Chrysic and Dorind?"

"I'm not sure. He might. Or as governor, he may have empowered the general to do whatever was needed to further their shared goals concerning Ondre. I don't know if they worked as a team or independently."

Ranthal poured refreshments. "I advise you to let thoughts of revenge go for now. After tomorrow's meeting of the Endowed, we'll likely have a clearer picture of their relationship. As my mentor, Dareck always told me, problems often work themselves out even when we can't foresee it."

Let revenge go. Not easy to do.

"I will help you forget about General Chrysic."

Jayel looked deeply into Ranthal's eyes. *He understands my feelings. Mother was right. By sharing, I feel closer to him than ever, in a way I never felt with Dorind.*

As Ranthal tucked her hair behind an ear, he whispered, "After your painful experience with Dorind, it's not easy to trust again."

They held each other's gazes.

Their minds began to merge.

Ranthal has initiated the bonding ritual!

They stood and faced each other.

Ranthal declared, "I'm humbled to receive your love and trust. I offer you all my love in return."

After a pause, during which she expressed the desire to continue, Ranthal clasped Jayel's hands and held them tightly. "From now on, you and I will never be alone. We are one." He crossed their arms. "We are forever bonded."

Warm, delightful sensations passed from his hands through her arms and into her chest. His expression showed he, too, felt the sensations. The outside world disappeared and only they existed, entwined.

"No rust will weaken us," Ranthal continued the ritual. "Here and now, I am yours."

Jayel responded, "I lock my heart and will open it for no other. We are forever one. Here and now, I am yours."

They raised their arms above their heads, hands still clasped tightly, and pressed their bodies together.

Ranthal opened his hands and slowly slid his fingers down her arms until they reached Jayel's shoulders. She lowered her arms and ran her fingers along Ranthal's arms until they rested on his shoulders. They embraced. A long kiss sealed their spoken commitment.

A ping from Jayel's pad announced the time. They released each other, smiling, laughing.

Jayel spoke first. "The Great Hall awaits, my betrothed."

"I'll escort you to your first interview and be sure no General Chrysic intercepts."

Jayel opened her luggage to pull out a jacket.

Ranthal said, "You don't need one. We'll use the enclosed bridge to get from the hotel to the Great Hall. I, however, will go out to tend to my ship and get supplies while you interview." He placed a jacket over his arm.

As she combed her hair, Jayel suggested, "Tonight, let's

celebrate our betrothal by dancing to live music. You know Characta's sound. Pick your favorite local tavern."

"An enticing plan. I look forward to it."

Smiling, they took the elevator down to the bridge level. Before they crossed over the street, a security guard checked their identities, as today the Great Hall was closed to the public. Once across, the shiny glass and fine furnishings of the modern hotel gave way to a dark hallway marked by ornately decorated columns and crown molding. Sculptures filled in nooks—lions, dragons, and mythical nymphs. Paintings of Orim's ancient cities hung on the walls depicting centuries before space exploration, a time when the focus was on family farming.

"It's rather quiet," Jayel commented as they walked around the perimeter of the hall's second level. "I hear only our footsteps' echoes."

"Yes, we've come at the best hour when we can move around without interruptions. Cuts down on us having to make introductions to everyone we encounter. They're meeting on the upper floors."

"Can we see inside the hall?" Jayel asked.

"Yes, but entrances to the central space occur only on the ground and third floors. We need to use the elevator or take these grand stairs." Ranthal pointed ahead to her right.

Jayel saw they had reached the front center of the building and had come to an enormous spiral marble staircase. Brass handrails on both sides gleamed in the well-lit entranceway. They descended.

Jayel counted one hundred steps to the ground floor. They now stood in a large foyer. She ignored the street-side entrance and studied the interior wall of ornate brass doors ten feet tall with oversized knobs.

Requiring two hands, Ranthal turned a doorknob, pushed,

and they entered the assembly hall.

Lights automatically came on to illuminate the floor. Shadows hinted at the vaulted ceiling high above them.

"I wish I could see the ceiling." Jayel's voice echoed.

In response, floodlights came on, and Jayel drew breath. Painted frescoes of scenes from Orim's history covered the entire ceiling. Scenes depicted Orim's transportation evolution, from animals to carts to ocean vessels to spaceships. At the far end, the last scene depicted the Onus One solar system, with Orim and Characta in the foreground.

"The paintings are so vivid in person," Jayel commented.

"Two local masters, Vincelli Mickelbasteri and Armeno Unglurfer, painted the ceiling in less than six months."

Lowering her eyes, Jayel saw five rows of amphitheater-style seating along both sides, starting about ten feet off the floor. The ornate chairs, well-spaced and well-cushioned, must swivel, as not all were facing directly forward. The floor area was empty, but she imagined the space could hold thirty rows twenty chairs wide. In this intimate setting, attendees could easily see each other or hear others' speeches without the need for digital enhancement.

"Grand … such exquisite artistry." Jayel's voice reverberated in the empty hall.

"Workers will set up the floor furniture tonight. You'll sit on a stage, there, and I expect they will roll a carpet down a center aisle." Ranthal looked at his pad. "It's time for you to go upstairs. Third level. Come, I'll escort you."

"No need. You are going out anyway, and we're on the ground floor."

They went into the lobby and stood by the elevator doors. Before Jayel stepped in, Ranthal pulled her close, and they kissed. They held the kiss, then tenderly parted lips.

Jayel took a deep breath. "I feel ready for whatever comes next."

"I'll see you tonight." Ranthal put on his jacket as the elevator door closed.

Exiting on the third floor, Jayel looked to the right and saw two uniformed workers chatting. According to her pad, the interview room was located around the left corner and down six doors. She turned left, smoothing her tunic and checking to see the belt was straight.

After walking around the corner, Jayel encountered a lone figure approaching, an elderly man dressed in a black ceremonial Endowed robe, no hat. His gait was strong. Expressionless, his eyes fixated on her.

When they reached each other, the old man smiled warmly. "Jayel, I'm glad to see you after all these years. I am Harmond, son of Izarsch, your grandfather."

Chapter 40

Jayel gasped. *My grandfather? Isn't he dead?*

She studied the elderly man's face. Yes, beyond the wrinkles, she saw the family resemblance.

Harmond's smile broadened. "You probably thought I was dead."

Jayel laughed. *He can read my mind. Be careful.*

"Don't worry, I'm not a mind reader, at least not without your permission. Your expression was enough." His brown eyes sparkled. "I last saw you when you were not yet two standard years old. You're grown up now, but your smile is the same."

Jayel possessed limited knowledge of this man. He was a respected member of the Endowed but not a public figure like her father or Dareck. She remained silent, uncertain how to proceed.

"I am your first interview. Shall we talk?" Harmond turned and motioned for Jayel to follow him back down the hallway.

Nodding, Jayel took a step forward.

Suddenly, they weren't in the Great Hall. Instead, they stood in the countryside. The sun warmed the air, and she could hear a breeze bristling leaves in nearby trees.

Jayel exclaimed, "How? ...I know this place. It's my inner

sanctuary."

Harmond nodded approval as he surveyed his surroundings. "Yes. Do I hear a waterfall in the distance? Let's go and sit there and talk. I like to watch the water's ebb and flow."

"I like to watch the water, too."

They smiled at having found something in common. Jayel relaxed and accepted this reality. The grass made slight crunchy noises as they walked down the hill.

Despite being nearly four times her age, his steps were firm and steady, and Harmond spoke easily without losing his breath. "Endowed ways are diverse and complex. But we can sometimes use them for our enjoyment. I prefer to meet in a peaceful garden rather than confined by four walls, no matter how elegant the rooms are in the Great Hall." Harmond glanced around. "It's pleasant here, peaceful, welcoming."

They approached trees lining the creek.

"Where have you been these past twenty standard years?" Jayel asked.

"My wife is an oceanographer. In recent years, we've been busy cataloging marine species on planets in the Onus Two system. Time passes differently on each planet, especially the outer ones, and, well, life under the sea is its own time dimension."

Jayel understood how someone could lose track of time. Her two years on Leidran seemed like months. "Did you stay away on purpose?"

"Direct. I like that. And the short answer is 'yes.'"

Harmond paused, then explained, "Your father disapproved of my second marriage and was not pleased to gain a brother. As they aged, I watched their resentment and dislike toward each other grow. I suppose it was easier for me to stay away than to tread on their broken glass."

"Were they never close?"

"Perhaps not. Soon after Dareck was born, Karsch left home to begin his first apprenticeship in satellite communications and then completed his second apprenticeship in biology. His interests gravitated toward bioethics and policymaking for planetary terraforming. After marrying your mother, he pursued a political career and became Melandan's governor. Meanwhile, Dareck mastered piloting spaceships, married, and moved to Characta."

Harmond sighed. "Looking back, I wish I had worked harder on my relationship with each son. I focused on my work instead." He chuckled. "Just as they did. We each attended to our professions as if family didn't matter. We're exceptionally skilled at our jobs, and the resulting satisfaction rewards maintaining the status quo."

They came to a wooden bench located near the base of the waterfall. A small dam channeled a steady flow of water onto the rocks, generating gentle splashes and cascading ripples.

They sat and watched the spray and the current's journey. Troubles, like a fallen leaf, could tumble and float smoothly downstream.

Jayel considered her grandfather's words. As a medical doctor, she understood the concept of hiding pain and coping without solving the underlying cause. Patients either feared the treatment or feared life after treatment. They avoided addressing the problems. *Are my father, uncle, and grandfather in need of healing?*

Harmond's voice interrupted her thoughts. "While away, I monitored the news. Stayed clear from Ondre when the hostilities escalated. But I came to Characta for your induction—I expected it years ago." He paused. "You took your time to apply for membership into the Endowed."

"Hmm." Jayel offered nothing further. *Why mention his son never encouraged me?*

Her grandfather turned toward her. "On the day you were born, I gave you a gift—if the need arose before you were inducted, you could use the House of Leidra, the House of the Endowed."

Jayel's eyes widened. "So, you're the reason. I wondered how I easily found its location and could stay there. I suspected some mysterious Endowed force."

Her grandfather laughed and returned his gaze to the water. "I like thinking of myself as a force. Well, I did possess the power to bestow the gift." Harmond again looked into Jayel's eyes. "But know, Granddaughter, if you had decided not to join the Endowed, I would've supported your decision."

After a peaceful pause, Harmond took her hands in his. "You will be a skillful doctor whether you cultivate your Endowed abilities or not. You have the hands of a healer. I knew this fact when you were a baby. I felt your warmth and strength pass into me when your tiny fingers wrapped around my thumb."

His hands surrounded hers. The grasp felt firm and safe. She sensed genuine caring.

Jayel felt guilty thinking he was dead or stayed away because he didn't care. "Thank you, Grandfather, for your gift. I enjoyed my stay at the House of Leidra. I also learned herblore and other skills from its resources. I would like to return there one day."

"You may visit the House of Leidra as often as you like once you are an official Endowed member. As I look around at this sanctuary you created, I can see you value nature. On your walks along Leidra's bubbling brook, you drew strength, as you do here from the moving water. A life force, if you will. Remember, there are no waterfalls inside a laboratory."

"When I next visit the House of Leidra, I'll not be running away but refilling my spirit to return and share with others."

"Good." Harmond let go of her hands, leaned back, and placed his right arm behind Jayel's shoulders. Together they watched the waterfall and listened to its soothing sounds.

"Now, Granddaughter, I bestow a new gift to celebrate your membership."

"Another gift? You're most generous."

"I continue a tradition begun by my great-great-grandparents and each successive generation who obtained membership to the Endowed." He smiled and looked at her. "Perhaps one day you'll have children who also will become members and keep the line unbroken. I hear Ranthal is a fine young Endowed member."

Jayel blushed. Her grandfather seemed to know everything about her.

His voice lowered. "I was sorry to hear about Dorind. But the future with Ranthal looks bright if you don't let revenge wear away your heart."

Her body stiffened at the mention of revenge. Fortunately, Harmond moved on.

"Now, my gift. Our oldest member is the Master Librarian of Knowledge. Azala's incredibly old, over twice my age. She knows history, including everyone's personal history."

"Everyone's? It's unbelievable."

Her grandfather smiled.

Jayel knew it wasn't the first time he encountered disbelief concerning Azala.

He said, "Azala can connect facts from multiple sources faster than any digital search engine. She sees patterns when others see randomness or cacophony. She provides answers people seek, answers which help them find insight or solve problems."

Jayel remained astonished. "I didn't know the Endowed could possess such powers."

"Every group has its standouts. Azala is the exception to the exceptional." Her grandfather shrugged. "Now, my gift is a private audience with Azala. In addition to a chat, Azala will grant you one question which she will answer truthfully based on her exceptional wisdom and knowledge."

Jayel swallowed and weighed the meaning of this gift. "Only one?"

"Yes. Unless she doesn't know, in which case you can ask another. It's said Azala has never been unable to answer a question. So, choose wisely. Also, for this gift, Azala will answer only with a 'yes' or 'no.' Do you understand? She won't answer 'what,' 'why,' or 'who' questions."

"I understand, Grandfather." But questions Jayel immediately thought of took the form of "why" or "who." *It will take deep thought to generate the right question.* "How much time do I have before I meet Azala?"

"She's your next interview."

Before Jayel could express dismay, they were again walking in the hallway of the Great Hall. Jayel had no idea how her grandfather manufactured this visit. He continued walking as if nothing unexplained had just happened.

At an elevator at the end of the corridor, Harmond stopped. "Go to the fourth floor, room 423. Azala's expecting you." He folded his arms in the robe's large sleeves.

Jayel hesitated. "Will I see you again? I haven't had enough time to get to know you. Are you and Eleaneck staying at the CHT Grand?"

"No, I've accommodations elsewhere." Then he confided, "I should avoid family right now. Let's not stir unpleasant waters before tomorrow's special meeting of the Endowed."

Harmond pushed the elevator button. "I will see you tomorrow at your induction."

The doors opened, and Jayel stepped in. When she turned around, her grandfather was gone. *What did he know about the special meeting Dareck called? What did he know about Neondra's death? Did he know his grandson Layon lived?* Jayel sighed, regretting their visit had been so short.

The elevator doors closed. She pressed the pause button and focused on the present. She needed to decide on a question for the master librarian. If she asked, "Did my father kill Neondra?" and the answer was "no," she wouldn't know who did. If she asked, "Was the fire an accident?" and the answer was "no," then the answer wouldn't identify a murderer or the reason.

Jayel searched for more ideas. Perhaps if she asked, "Is the evidence Dareck holds conclusive?" and the answer was "no," then she could warn Dareck before he made public accusations. Or should she look beyond the present situation and use this unique opportunity to learn something that could help more people? For instance, she'd like to know if the newly discovered element, zelium, could be used for curing blood diseases as Professor Larzo Marzzin recently theorized.

To her surprise, the elevator doors opened. *So much for stalling.* Jayel exited and found the elevator had indeed arrived on the fourth floor. She located room 423 several doors down. Jayel knocked, but no one answered. *An ancient person can't come to the door too quickly or even hear my knock. I can stand here longer and continue to think of a question.*

The door squeaked as it opened.

Chapter 41

Jayel straightened her tunic and stepped through the threshold. The door closed automatically behind her.

As the light brightened, she noticed the room was much larger than expected, each wall longer than possible in the Great Hall. Somehow, she was in a different place, much like the interview with her grandfather didn't occur in the hallway.

Mysterious are the ways of the Endowed.

Books of all sizes lined the walls from floor to high ceiling, leaving space only for one narrow window. A sunbeam pierced thick glass, the angle low, suggesting late afternoon. In the center of the opposite wall, Jayel saw carpeted steps leading to a mezzanine filled with glass-enclosed cabinets containing rolled scrolls and ancient books. Two stylish easy chairs and a coffee table occupied the center of the room.

A noise directed her attention to the right. In the far corner, a female figure wearing a black robe of the Endowed slowly descended a metal spiral staircase.

Unhurried, the slightly bent figure walked into clear view. Brilliant silver hair draped from under the mortarboard, and though her skin was very wrinkled, her smile revealed bright white teeth, and eyes that sparkled, clear blue and warm. Jayel took an immediate liking to this old woman.

"I am Azala, Master Librarian." The woman's voice sounded smooth, not gravelly.

"I'm honored to meet you, Master Librarian Azala."

"As they all are. Harmond probably told you I'm the oldest Endowed member alive. I am wise, and I'm knowledgeable. But most of all, I'm honest. I will answer your question well." The woman paused and eyed Jayel keenly. "Relax. We aren't in a battle of wills. I'm here to welcome you to the Endowed, not scare you off. Your grandfather gifted you a private audience. Let's chat before you ask *the question*."

Jayel accepted Azala's invitation to sit in the easy chair and pointed to books on the coffee table. "These look incredibly old. Exquisite binding."

"University of Orim's archivists recently found these in a forgotten box in a closet. After their contents were digitized, I set them out here for show. My assistants bring me books, and I catalog them. I've read many, including the older ones written in different languages used before the standard language our systems use now."

"My grandfather said you know personal histories. Those aren't found in books, I should think."

"Many oral stories find their way into a written record. Also, my assistants organize digital diaries, personal logs, and auditory recordings. Others do any translation or resolution of ambiguities in the entries, and we do the recordkeeping. I have … Endowed abilities … enabling me to keep track of information. As for recent history, many minds are an open book to me."

Azala smiled as she explained, "I'm an extraordinary organizer with an ability to access vast knowledge, much like our celebrity savants who can recite any digit of pi when someone suggests the decimal place—you've seen them, no?

'Tell me digit 157' and they respond '4' without a hiccup. Only my knowledge is much more thought-provoking than an infinite stream of digits. People's lives are so interesting, don't you agree?"

"Yes, I suppose." Jayel was unsure what to think about Azala's claims. *Is it possible this woman knows everyone's history? I'd like to capture some of her memories in Layon's thought imager.* "As a cognitive neuroscientist, I'm fascinated by your abilities."

Shrugging, Azala remarked, "Everyone knows more than what's stored in their memory. How so, you ask. Think of mathematics. You know the sum of every two numbers, despite there being an infinite set of numbers. You don't "store" all possible sums. You don't store all 'what-is-not-the-correct' sums. For example, you know 271 when asked for the sum of 150 and 121. You know '127 plus 127 equals zero' is false without storing all infinite errors. So it is with my knowledge. If the answer isn't already stored, I 'calculate' it."

Intrigued, Jayel remarked, "You're like a super-linguist only with historical information instead of vocabulary. By metaphor, you can produce novel sentences or recognize nonsense wording based on what you know."

"Exactly. I gained membership into the Endowed before I reached six standard years and trained to reduce memory errors and enhance my access to remote associations. After 150 standard years of practice, I learned many tricks to discover obscure or hidden information."

"Are there other Endowed members like you?"

"Yes, but they are younger, and I consider them 'in training.'" Azala paused. "You wouldn't be the first to doubt my abilities. I understand. When I was younger, occasional visitors would try to challenge my abilities. They would find a fact hidden in a library's dust-covered book and ask me about it. Or smartasses would ask me riddles, like 'Time flies but doesn't exist nor moves in the space above us, but what does exist and moves above us but never flies?'" The woman paused and waited for Jayel's answer.

"The sun?" Jayel guessed. "We say it rises and sets, but we don't say it flies across the sky. And our moons as well."

"Yes, well, you can imagine years of questions like these. I tired of people trying to trip me up, so I reduced the frequency of interviews and allowed only one question, restricted to a yes-no format."

The old woman cleared her throat. "Harmond promised you wouldn't toy with me."

After Jayel nodded, Azala continued, "Now, you, Jayel, daughter of Karsch, son of Harmond, have had an eventful life, especially in the last month."

Jayel blushed. She felt as if this master librarian aimed a lighthouse beam into her memories, and she couldn't hide. Azala knew everything, about Jayel's stay at the House of Leidra, about Layon and Dorind, and about her taking evidence from Karsch's study. Azala knew it all. *No secrets here.* Jayel swallowed.

"What is it, child?"

"I didn't expect to feel so … exposed."

"A typical reaction. You're worried I'm judging you. Relax, I don't judge. I do learn from the tribulations of others, and empathize a bit with their triumphs and tragedies, but mostly I store the knowledge without interpreting it as right or wrong."

Chuckling, Azala added, "Do you know there is an entire branch in philosophy focused on me, debating whether Azala behaves ethically to not correct errors in common knowledge or point others in the right direction to speed progress? I observe, collect, and record knowledge but do not interfere.

Even my rule of one question only allowed generate heated debates."

Azala shifted her attention to the beverage service on the coffee table and handed Jayel a cup of *switchya.* "Your favorite."

Jayel accepted and sipped. The hot beverage tasted as if made from beans grown on Melandan, the blend flavored just how she liked it. "I only just learned a few minutes ago about this gift of one question. It's overwhelming. Do you have any suggestions or stories illustrating what is a good or poor question?"

The old woman smiled. "Poor questions: 'Will it rain tomorrow?' 'Are you more than 150 standard years old?' 'Will I give birth to three children?' I don't tell the future, and I don't know the secret to happiness."

Jayel understood. In the early days of the Endowed, society expected them to know such answers. Only when people genuinely appreciated Endowed members' abilities did they stop asking simple questions and begin using Endowed talents to enhance Orim's technological progress and speed the development of the Onus One and Two star systems.

Picking up her cup, Azala continued, "I suspect you won't ask any question about yourself. What I know of your history you do, too, so why ask me what you already comprehend best? I suggest you seek an answer which gives you peace of mind, satiates curiosity, or fills in a missing piece to a puzzle."

"But what happens if I need a follow-up question or need to understand how the answer makes sense? What if I don't know what to do with the answer?"

Azala smiled as she put down her cup. "I suppose those who are dissatisfied with my answer must work it out afterward. Life goes on whether you ask a question or not, but sometimes life goes on differently because you know the answer. But not for me. I only record and organize the information."

The old woman looked deeply into Jayel's eyes. "Your grandfather's gift is meant to be a positive, not a burden or plight."

Azala poured the remaining *switchya* into Jayel's cup. "On the other hand, no one said knowledge must make life better or easier. I'm sure you've heard the expression, 'I wish I didn't know.' Once you do know, there's no going back to ignorance."

Jayel pondered this wisdom. "Has anyone ever passed up this gift … talked with you like we are now and then said, 'no, not for me'?"

The old woman paused. "No, no one ever has. Oh, I'm scary enough, but the gift is too precious for any curious person to pass up. And the Endowed are curious people. They aspire to know more, no matter their heritage or special abilities. Knowledge is power."

Jayel studied Azala. *Incredibly old but not frail.* "And you, Azala, must be the most powerful member of the Endowed."

"The most. And here you are about to acquire some power."

Azala paused and then remarked, "We gain power not only by accumulating knowledge. We gain power when we face our fears. You could ask a question whose answer you can't accept until you have my assurance it is true or false. Once you know with certainty this feared fact is true, then you will face it rather than run away."

Azala paused, then gazed knowingly into Jayel's eyes. "I think recent events have taught you running away for two years didn't solve your main problem. Don't run away now from the answer you seek."

Jayel nodded. "Yes, I see how getting rid of uncertainty helps deal with a situation. I'm stuck otherwise, hoping the truth is false. Certainty clears the path and allows me to move forward." She put down the cup and took a deep breath. After a short pause, Jayel stated, "I'm ready to ask my question now."

Azala smiled, her blue eyes gleaming. "Ask."

***

A loud knock, followed by the door blasting open, jolted Jayel to the present surroundings. She felt a momentary disorientation.

She looked around. Gone were the books lining the room. Gone was the elegant furniture, *switchya*, and master librarian Azala. Only a small conference table and its chairs occupied this small room. The sign, room 423, on the door told Jayel she was back in the Great Hall.

A frantic young man stood at the door, breathing hard. He wore a security uniform and carried a weapon in his belt.

"Jayel?"

"Yes?" she replied hesitantly.

"I'm Tomar Shanock. I'm with the ESF, Endowed Security Force. I've been sent to escort you immediately to a secure place." He took a few steps into the room.

"Why? What has happened?" Jayel stood, her fingertips pressed on the table.

"The Great Hall is on lockdown. I've orders to see to your safety."

"Lockdown? No one may leave the Great Hall? I can't go back to the hotel?"

"Correct." The young man swiped sweat from his face.

"Take a breath, Tomar. Why is the building on lockdown?"

"I don't know exactly, as I was dispatched immediately after the alert sounded. But I heard murmurs from others before I left the command center about a murder or an attempted murder."

"Murder!"

"Yes." Tomar swallowed and took a deep breath. "But I don't know if it concerns the upcoming Endowed meeting or the Council, as both parties are in the building today. My job is to protect you, the Endowed inductee, and secure your safety."

Jayel reached into a pants pocket for her pad. "Maybe there's a message—"

"Communications are blocked, and network signals are jammed. At least until they sweep the building for explosives."

Jayel discovered her pad was missing. *Did she leave it in the library or with Harmond?* "I've misplaced my pad. I'm not sure how …"

"Come with me. I will take you to your designated shelter. We are to trust no one. Everyone is being isolated. We don't want an unknown assassin and victim in the same room."

"I doubt I'm in danger. I'm neither an Endowed member nor a political attendee of the governor's council." *What about my father, Dareck, or Brusch? Are they in the Great Hall and in danger?*

"You could be a target if someone is trying to stop tomorrow's induction ceremony." The officer motioned toward the open door for them to leave.

Jayel hesitated. "You said, 'Trust no one.' Why should I trust *you*?"

Tomar Shanock smiled and moved his security sash away from his neck to reveal the uniform's lapel. "I wear Dareck's pin."

She nodded and slowly walked around the table toward him. She trusted this young officer, yet she didn't like the idea of sheltering alone in a safe room for some unknown time.

Tomar scanned saved information on his pad. "I still see

you're reluctant. There may be another option. If you don't want to go to an Endowed safe room, as the daughter of a governor, I can transfer custody to the Council's Security Force. Perhaps you prefer their protection instead of the ESF. Melandan's General Chrysic oversees protecting council members. Shall we try to find him?"

"No, thank you! Take me to *your* designated safe room."

Chapter 42

"You're rather young for a security officer," Jayel remarked as they entered the empty fourth-floor hallway. The lighting appeared dimmer than before, enhancing the feeling of an emergency.

Tomar Shanock ushered her to the elevator. "Almost sixteen. I recently started my second apprenticeship. Although this is my first emergency, we've trained for this scenario."

"What was your first apprenticeship?"

"Natural disaster cleanup. I helped assess damage after Characta's quake last year. Interesting work but a loose chain of command. I'm learning here to work with a small group of officers in a tight command structure. I haven't decided yet which career path to choose."

"Either service path seems admirable."

"You're the first Endowed member I met up close." Shanock smiled shyly.

"Not a member yet," Jayel quipped.

After they waited a long time, he groaned, "I think the elevators are no longer working."

"Is this unexpected?"

"It could mean the risk of danger has increased." Shanock scrolled a file on his pad. "The network's down but I have a stored map. We can use stairwell C. It's usually only accessible by building staff and it's the backup for ESF when elevators are down. I don't think we'll run into any unwanted persons there, only other Endowed Security Force members."

They hurried back down the hallway to a plain door labeled with a large "C." Shanock bent down and waved his pad in the lower corner.

Jayel heard the click of the lock moving.

He turned the knob, pushed in the door, and poked his head into the stairwell.

"Do you see anyone?"

"No. I don't hear anyone, either. Let's go."

They began descending the cement stairs. The emergency lighting cast shadows against the windowless walls. Twenty steps to a landing, turn around a center post, and another twenty to the next level's door. Their descent made little noise. Jayel could hear her breathing.

Shanock moved swiftly, and Jayel followed behind, holding the inner rail. At each landing, Shanock stopped and listened, then continued.

"I expected more people in the stairwell with the elevators out," Jayel whispered.

"Yes, I thought so, too. Maybe we are the last to evacuate."

When they neared the ground floor, Shanock explained, "We need to go lower. We must continue to sublevel three."

"Why so far down?"

"The first sublevel houses working rooms—kitchens, cleaning machines, and maintenance—no secure spaces. The Governors' Council staff wanted the second sublevel. They insisted during emergency planning. The Endowed control the third sublevel."

Jayel quipped, "Politicians probably need to be the first in and first out."

"You could be right. Sublevels two and three aren't used much for normal operations. The space is largely empty. I've only been down there a few times."

In silence, they descended past the ground floor and stopped at the next landing between the two flights of stairs. They came around the center post and moved down to the first sublevel, encountering no one. They continued their descent.

Jayel heard a distant rumble, too muffled to identify. *An explosion?*

In response, Shanock slowed his descent and cautiously stopped on the landing of a flight above the second sublevel door. He held up his hand and warned Jayel to wait behind the center post until he gave the all-clear signal.

"See anything?" Jayel asked.

He called back, "No. It looks clear." Shanock took one step down.

At this moment, Jayel heard a faint click, followed by the sound of an opening door. She squatted and peeked around the post and saw a man wearing a blue uniform not in the style of the ESF standing in the opening looking up at Shanock.

Jayel moved back. *I don't think he saw me.*

"Who's there? ESF?" the blue-uniformed man shouted.

"Yes. Tomar Shanock. And you?"

"Governors' Council Security, Marsten Follop. What are you doing in *this* stairwell?"

"The elevator's out. I'm heading down to the third—" Shanock stopped.

Jayel peeked around the stairwell's post. Follop pointed a weapon at Shanock.

"Are you alone?" Follop asked in a threatening tone.

Shanock calmly replied, "Yes."

He's protecting me. He must suspect something's not quite right.

"Who do you report to?"

"What has my superior to do with anything?"

Follop spit. "I was told to trust no one, and I wasn't expecting anyone in this stairwell. Don't move until I get clearance."

Shanock sighed and pushed his hair back off his face and neck. When he did, the sash moved, and Dareck's pin gleamed in the light shining in from the doorway.

Immediately, Follop fired.

Shanock fell backward, then crumpled sideways, facing the outer wall, partially laying on the landing near Jayel's feet.

Aghast, Jayel listened for Follop's movements. At any moment he might walk up to check on Shanock. She looked at the steps behind her. *I can't run up the flight of stairs without him catching me.*

Jayel looked down at her young escort's body and saw Shanock's weapon on his hip and within reach.

Inhaling and gritting her teeth, Jayel swiftly reached out, grabbed Shanock's gun, and turned to face Follop. He was still standing by the door, not moving, and seemed to be stunned as he focused on Shanock's body. She had seen the look before, when Dorind shot her.

Then, Follop's eyes moved to Jayel, and he raised his weapon.

Jayel fired.

Follop looked shocked before falling forward, the door shutting behind him. If the shot didn't kill him, his broken neck did, as his head hit the step at a bad angle.

Jayel knelt to check Shanock. He was dead. She swallowed. *Had to be one of Chrysic's men, conditioned to kill at the sight of Dareck's pin.*

Slowly, Jayel descended the stairs, stepped over Follop's body, and continued down until she reached the third sublevel. The handle didn't turn. *Damn.*

Sighing, she climbed back up the two flights of stairs, stepped carefully over Follop to avoid the puddles of blood, and walked up to Shanock's body. Jayel searched him for his pad, found it, and descended again to the third sublevel.

Her heart pounded in her ears.

At the door, Jayel waved the pad as Shanock had previously done to get the fourth-floor stairwell door to open. She hoped the way to unlock it on the inside was the same as from the hallway side.

Relieved, she heard the click. Jayel turned the knob and slowly pulled in the door just enough to poke her head through the opening. Seeing no one in the well-lit corridor, she opened it a tad more and squeezed through.

"You there!" a male voice sounded from the end of the hall.

Jayel tightened her grip around Shanock's weapon.

A man wearing the ESF uniform rapidly approached her.

"Step away from the door," he commanded.

Her body moved further into the hallway, and the door closed. Jayel heard the lock click.

"You're Jayel, the Endowed inductee, aren't you? Where is Tomar Shanock? I've been waiting for him to bring you here."

"Yes, I was with Shanock, but he's … dead. We were attacked one floor up … by a guard from the Governors' Council security team, I think. At least he said he was. He was wearing a blue uniform."

The man frowned and studied her face. "Do you know his name?"

"Followup, I think."

"Follop? Marsten Follop?"

"Yes, that's the name he gave."

"I know Follop. He's a good man. Why would he attack you and Tomar Shanock?"

"I'm not sure. He said he didn't expect anyone to be in the stairwell, to trust no one. But … I think it was a reflex. When Follop saw Dareck's pin on Shanock's collar, he fired. A conditioned reflex. I've seen it before."

The man pressed his lips together, then ordered, "Stay here. Don't move. Keep your gun raised."

He waved his pad, opened the door, and went into the stairwell. The door closed.

Jayel stood still, waiting.

Soon, the guard emerged from stairwell C, looking upset. "They're dead. Shanock was supposed to bring you down here and use this stairwell if the elevators were out. Damn, he almost made it, too." He sighed. "I will notify my major what's happened. But first I must get you to a safe room."

They walked the length of the corridor and turned.

Jayel saw and heard no one else. "Where is everyone?"

"You're the only Endowed to arrive by stairwell C. It's a large building. Several others are using stairwells A and D located on the other side."

He unlocked a door, pushed it open, and motioned for her to enter. "Stay here. My name is Lieutenant Smitham, by the way."

"Listen, Lieutenant, you must warn the ESF not to display Dareck's pin. Anyone wearing it is in danger. I believe General Chrysic may have brainwashed his men to react without thinking."

"General Chrysic? That's not intel we've had before. How do you know this?"

"It's not the first time it's happened. You'll have to … trust me."

Smitham frowned, then nodded. "I must inform my commander."

As she entered the room, Jayel asked, "Do you know what's happening? How long this lockdown will last?"

Smitham ignored the questions and said, "I'll be back soon." The door closed.

Jayel tested the knob and confirmed she was locked in. She turned and surveyed the room. In addition to a small table and chairs, and a couple of stuffed chairs and cots, she saw a corner sink and toilet. She placed Shanock's pad and weapon on the table. Although the room had decent lighting, the wall's video screen didn't work.

At the sink, Jayel washed her hands and splashed water to cool the face. She looked in the mirror. *I've killed two people within two weeks. What next?*

As she lay down on a cot, Azala's voice came into her mind. "No."

The answer to my question. Comfort in this chaos. My father didn't murder Neondra.

Chapter 43

Jayel couldn't send Ranthal a message without her pad. Had the building not gone on lockdown, they would be celebrating their betrothal about now over dinner and sipping Black Holes. Maybe even enjoying Spiral Galaxies.

She reached for Tomar Shanock's pad. It showed a standard hour had passed since Lieutenant Smitham left. Although Jayel couldn't do much without Shanock's thumbprint or password, his screen remained open to a text window. A local network now allowed communications among ESF members. She scrolled through the recent messages.

The building continued in lockdown. Jayel saw a message to remove all pins from collars. The text didn't single out Dareck's but conveyed a general broad order. *Good, Smitham believed me, and his commander believed Smitham.* She read no direct accusation against Chrysic. *Also good*, as she suspected the General monitored ESF messages.

One interesting text, the ESF took a Governor Council's security team member into custody for trying to break into an ESF office. *Did Council's security cause the lockdown—a rogue or someone following orders?*

The messages left unclear how many Endowed members roomed on sublevel three. The strongest hint suggested most people in the building when lockdown began belonged to the council. The only Endowed business on the calendar for today focused on Jayel's interviews.

Jayel put the pad down and sat in the easy chair. It rocked and swiveled. She tried to relax. *I wonder if I have any telepathic abilities.* "Ranthal, my beloved, can you hear me? I am safe."

Nothing. *Perhaps if I focus on him.* Jayel imagined Ranthal in their hotel room, waiting for word of the end of the lockdown—his brown eyes troubled, hair pulled back revealing tense neck and shoulders, and lips closed tight, dry from worry. He was beautiful even when looking concerned.

She smiled at these thoughts and imagined him looking at her even though she wasn't there.

To Jayel's amazement, Ranthal's face brightened, and he smiled back at her. He said, "It's about time you tried."

She heard him clearly. This telepathic experience enthralled her.

He laughed at her surprised expression.

Jayel reached out and touched his arm. She could feel muscles, skin, and bone.

"Why are you surprised?" Ranthal whispered. "We are bonded now—your thoughts to my thoughts, your heart to my heart."

She kissed and hugged him. Imagined or not, his body felt wonderful, and her spirit renewed. "It is good to see you," she gave the Melandanian family greeting. "I'm in a safe room on sublevel three, under ESF protection. And you?"

"As you can see, I'm in our hotel suite. Your mother is in her bedroom. Your father is safe. He left the Great Hall with a few others for a pub break when the lockdown happened. He currently is downstairs at a command post set up in the hotel."

"Do you know what's happened, why the building went on

lockdown?"

"I'm told they found explosives hidden at the bottom of a delivery container. While investigating, they found two laywomen in the upper rows of the Great Hall removing one of the fixed chairs. They denied knowing anything about explosives but stayed mute about their own activity. The ESF suspects they were creating a sniper's nest."

Jayel gasped. "Then the Endowed are the target and not the Governors' Council?"

"It looks like it. I'm not sure anyone definitively knows yet."

"Do you think it's my induction they're trying to stop?"

"Could be or perhaps someone wants to stop the Endowed meeting afterward."

"Dareck! You were his apprentice. Can you talk to him when we finish?"

"Yes. Do you have a message for him?"

"Two things. One, you must warn Dareck that some of the Council's Security Force have been conditioned to shoot in response to his pin. They could also be conditioned to shoot him on sight. He must be careful."

Jayel told Ranthal about the incident in the stairwell. She remarked, "I don't even think Follop knew what he was doing. The man looked stunned afterward. I'm sorry I had to shoot, but conditioning doesn't yield to reasoning."

They touched foreheads and held each other in silence. *I am so glad you are with me.*

When they separated, Jayel added, "The second thing, you must tell Dareck the master librarian said my father didn't do it. He must know this before the meeting."

Jayel saw Ranthal looked confused, and she realized that Dareck hadn't completely informed him of the purpose of her mission or the upcoming meeting. Perhaps to keep anyone from finding out beforehand. She added, "Dareck will know what I mean."

A new message appeared on Shanock's pad, the glow attracting Jayel's attention. She reached for it and eagerly read the text. "Lockdown ends at seven in the morning, standard time. The Endowed meeting starts on schedule at eight."

She heard a knock on the saferoom's door. When Jayel looked away from the pad, the connection with Ranthal had broken, and she was alone.

The door opened, and Smitham entered. He carried a stack of boxes. "Hello, Jayel. I bring food and drink."

"Thank you, Lieutenant. I'm hungry, but you carry a lot of food." She pointed at the four boxes he placed on the table.

"Only this smaller box contains dinner. The others hold garments for your Endowed induction."

Jayel came to the table. "Have you news about the lockdown?"

"We aren't sure the threat is over. You must stay here."

When Jayel sighed, he added, "Security is tight due to multiple threats. It will be my privilege to escort you to the Great Hall tomorrow morning."

"Are these threats against the Endowed or the Governors' Council?"

"We're investigating both possibilities. The clues are ambiguous. Plus, your father and two others are both Endowed and Council members. If they are targets, the motivations remain unclear."

"Has anyone else been hurt?"

"No. Though two of the Governors' Council's security team have been detained."

"What about the two Endowed members I saw today—

Harmond and Master Librarian Azala?"

Smitham scanned his pad. "I don't see their names. Five other Endowed members are in safe rooms under ESF protection."

Jayel's neck stretched so she could see his pad. "Is Dareck or Brusch on your list?"

"No. However, both asked to get in when they heard about the lockdown. They were worried about you. We assured them you were safe. We're not admitting anyone into the building, even esteemed Endowed, until tomorrow morning when every member must pass through our security checkpoint along with workers and musicians."

Smitham pushed bangs from his face and proudly smiled. "Don't worry. The ESF is prepared."

Jayel opened the unstacked box and pulled out a salad, fruit, rolls, and a thermos containing hot *switchya*. She poured a cup. "Thank you so much, Lieutenant. Want some?"

"Thank you, but I must report back." Smitham turned to leave.

"Wait, did anyone find my pad? It's missing. I know we don't have communications yet, but it has my script for the induction tomorrow."

"When did you have it last?"

"I'm not sure. Maybe on the second floor, or in the elevator, or near room 423."

"I'll check. But if we can't find it, I'm sure they can provide you with a script tomorrow. I'll return before eight to escort you to the Great Hall. Good night."

Alone again, Jayel sipped the *switchya* and chewed her dinner. When finished eating, she opened the remaining boxes. They contained a robe, hood, and mortarboard.

Jayel unfolded the robe. It was exquisite. Made of mauve

velvet, the robe had large sleeves, a maroon collar, and several deep pockets inside to hold personal items. *Not black like Harmond and Azala wore.* She squeezed the pockets, laughing at herself. *I shouldn't expect my pad to be in one of these pockets.*

She tried on the robe. *Too bad this room doesn't have a full-length mirror.* The robe fitted ankle length and high-waisted, making Jayel's figure appear taller than she was, at least her reflection in the dark video screen indicated this illusion. Next, she added the hood and straightened it. During the ceremony, she would get a second hood which went inside this one and displayed her family colors.

After surveying her appearance, Jayel took off the robe and hood and laid them across the chair. They were surprisingly free of wrinkles despite having been folded in boxes. *Mysterious are the ways of the Endowed.* She wished all her clothes never wrinkled.

Jayel drained the thermos. *Decent switchya, the beans were likely grown on Characta.*

The day's events caught up with her, and feeling a wave of fatigue, Jayel yawned and lay on the cot.

Her mind reviewed an emotionally overloaded day—arriving on Characta after an intimate talk with mother, completing the betrothal ritual, admiring the beauty of the Great Hall, meeting her grandfather for the first time, talking with Azala, hurrying down to the third sublevel, and feeling the weight of killing Marsten Follop.

Many unanswered questions came to mind: What will tomorrow bring? What will Dareck say at the meeting? He had several days to study the evidence I gave Layon. I only glanced at the receipts, photos, and letters. Were there clues about who killed Neondra? If Father didn't kill her, why did Chrysic imply he had in the conversation I overheard two years ago?

If only I had more than one question to ask Azala. Did my father know who killed Neondra? Maybe Dareck would use the meeting to get Father to reveal all he knew. After all, justice was Dareck's goal, to uncover the murderer, whoever he was.

How did Dareck react to learning Layon was not his son?

These thoughts prevented sleep, but her body felt exhausted. Jayel turned onto her side. Questions and worries would have to wait until tomorrow. She drew on Endowed training and cleared her mind, focused on Ranthal's comforting arms, and, letting go, drifted off to sleep.

Chapter 44

A trio of pings on Shanock's pad at six in the morning woke Jayel, the alarm reminding him to start his shift. With effort, she set aside sad feelings for the loss of this young man who gave his life to protect her.

Jayel felt mixed emotions about what this day would bring—excited to be inducted into the membership but anxious about what would happen afterward. What would Dareck say? How would her father react?

I will find out soon enough.

Jayel rose and washed as best one could with only a sink and hand towel available. Halfway through eating a breakfast of last night's fruit, she read a text message from Lieutenant Smitham. "We found your pad. It was on the second floor. I'll bring it with me when I come, about half past seven."

Smitham arrived on time holding her pad and a small box. He found Jayel already wearing the mauve Endowed robe and hood. "Here's your pad. Let me straighten your mortarboard. The slot for your feather goes on the right."

Jayel thanked him and checked for messages but couldn't access them. "Are communications still out?"

"Yes. Temporary precautions. Helps to control threats from outsiders. The ESF did set up a network for internal use only. See here," he pointed to an icon. "There you will find the script for the induction ceremony." Smitham picked up Shanock's pad and placed it in a pouch which he tucked into his uniform's jacket.

Nodding as she glanced at the script, relieved. Satisfied, Jayel slipped her pad into the robe's pocket. "Thank you, for everything, Lieutenant. I'm ready."

"Not yet." From the box, Smitham removed a purple stole. "Inductees to the Endowed wear this around the neck and down the front." He tucked the stole under her collar and straightened both ends which dangled midway down the robe. "The symbols refer to your family lineage."

They left the safe room and encountered several ESF guards stationed in the hallway, a reminder of the recent lockdown. They saluted as Jayel walked past.

"I didn't realize the induction was such a big deal," Jayel remarked.

Smitham smiled. "Even more so during a lockdown. We've taken precautions to ensure nothing stops the ceremony."

When the elevator door opened, a woman wearing an ESF uniform greeted them from inside. She smiled but didn't say anything to them. She remained in the elevator when Jayel and Smitham exited on the ground floor of the Great Hall.

From calm silence to chaotic cacophony, Jayel walked into a lobby crowded with people wearing Endowed robes of assorted colors. Many mortarboards sprouted tall feathers. Members chatted and waved greetings to acquaintances. Musicians dressed in equally colorful suits pushed their way through them to enter the hall. The inner doors were open, but Jayel couldn't see past the crowd.

The grand marshal, who wore an enormous, pointed hat with a plume of red feathers, pushed between members and approached. She leaned in for Jayel to hear her above the din. "Glad to see you, Jayel. Come with me. As our inductee, you'll sit on the stage and proceed last. Lieutenant, thank you for your service."

Jayel turned, thanked Smitham again, and followed the marshal across the lobby to a side room. When the marshal stopped at the opening, she extended her arm and ordered, "Wait in here."

Inside, Jayel met the president of the Endowed, a middle-aged woman with long black hair and laser-piercing eyes framed by thick glasses. In addition to her adorned green robe, she wore a large gold medallion and carried a heavy ornate staff.

"Pleased to meet you, Jayel. Sorry, it's a last-minute introduction. The lockdown prevented us from meeting yesterday. I was to be your last interview. Do you have the script for the induction? Good. No need to memorize it, just read from the pad during the ceremony."

"I'm honored to meet you, President Nanyum, daughter of Pluum. My father has spoken well of your leadership."

"Most kind."

Trumpets interrupted their conversation. When silence returned, Nanyum continued, "I'm pleased you finally applied for—"

The grand marshal poked her head into the room. "We're ready to begin. Places!"

Three others in the room, who hadn't yet been introduced to Jayel, immediately stood. Their robes, like the president's, were equally ornate, and their mortarboards supported magnificent feathers. Nanyum went first, then the three, and Jayel followed.

Loud music filled the lobby as an orderly procession began.

The members' solemn cadence matched the music's rhythm.

Soon, Jayel waited at the entrance with the stage party. The Great Hall's walls enhanced the sound, the percussion reverberating through her body.

When the last members filled the rows, the music changed to all strings and trumpets. Tall flagbearers, proudly displaying ornate banners of the planets of Onus One and Onus Two, left their positions along the back wall and walked slowly in a single file toward the stage. Once the flags rimmed the platform, the flagbearer carrying the green and gold emblem of the Endowed organization respectfully paraded to the front.

The grand marshal led the stage party up the carpeted aisle. Despite the inconvenience of the lockdown, the twenty floor rows on both sides of the aisle looked filled, with about six members per row, as did both sides of the amphitheater seating. Jayel guessed over two hundred Endowed members attended. In the mezzanine above the doors, Characta's system-renowned youth choir sang the Endowed anthem, their voices sounding pure in the hall's excellent acoustics.

Jayel didn't want to look like a gawking tourist. She mimicked the behavior of the stage party and walked a slow march with her face forward. The backdrop of the stage, made of an elegant gauze-like material, allowed the beauty of the Great Hall's frescoes behind it to remain visible.

Once on the stage, Jayel scanned faces in the audience and found her parents seated near the front row on the left side. Ranthal wasn't with them. Harmond sat three rows behind, and she assumed the woman on his right was his wife, Eleaneck. Both wore brown robes with gold feathers adorning their caps.

Jayel found Ranthal with Brusch sitting together in the amphitheater rows on her left. Both looked distinguished in their black robes and blue feathered caps. The three exchanged smiles. After scanning the audience again for Dareck, she concluded he wasn't present. Some ESF guards stood along the back wall.

Black dominated the color of the robes, but many mortarboards supported feathered plumes of different colors. The seats were spaced and staggered to accommodate the puffy robes and hoods and help those in the back rows see the stage. Jayel spotted only a few non-Endowed in normal dress, her mother one of them. Mandel wore a stunning aquamarine gown, and the neckline showed off an equally gorgeous diamond necklace.

Her father, wearing a mortarboard adorned with a blue feather, initially looked distracted but then smiled when he met Jayel's eyes. He appeared proud, but she thought he looked concerned as well. His facial muscles seemed tense.

After the music ended, there was a brief pause while the choir loft emptied, and the marshal ensured late arrivals found their seats.

Then the thick doors to the hall closed. The marshal walked to the stage and sat.

The president stood, walked to the podium, and opened the ceremony. "Thank you for coming today amid our security concerns. Our ESF secured the building, and we thank you for your patience. Today, we induct Jayel, daughter of Karsch, son of Harmond, into our membership."

The marshal rose and directed, "Jayel, please stand and come to the podium."

A few refrains of music played, dominated by string instruments. The marshal sat after Jayel stood before Nanyum.

To Jayel's relief, the rite turned out to be surprisingly simple. The president first spoke a brief history of the

Endowed and underscored the importance of membership. Then the induction ritual consisted of promises to uphold the dignity of the ancient organization, to work to the best of her ability, and to serve the common good.

Holding her pad as she stood center stage, Jayel loudly spoke the proper responses and swore the oath.

Soft music played as one of the robed men on stage rose and took the president's heavy staff. Then, the vice president stood and picked up Jayel's family hood from the table and presented it to Nanyum. As Jayel faced forward, the president and vice-president placed it over Jayel's head, inserted it inside the hood she wore, and pressed the seams. The two hoods became one. Digital devices flashed, and the audience clapped. The musicians played a few measures to punctuate the hooding ceremony.

Next, the vice president carried a blue feather and presented it to the president. Nanyum tucked it into Jayel's mortarboard.

Once the applause ended, Nanyum received her staff once again and announced, "We assign our youth members a mentor who guides and helps the development of their Endowed abilities. Even though Jayel, daughter of Karsch, is much older than our typical inductee, her training began only recently, and we believe she, too, would enjoy the guidance of a mentor."

The president paused, her eyes behind the glasses slowly scanning the assembly.

The grand marshal rose from her chair and loudly directed, "Will Jayel's mentor please stand?"

Jayel looked at her father, but he turned sideways to see who would stand. She looked up at Brusch and Ranthal, but they, too, were scanning the assembly.

Then, from the right corner near the stage, Dareck emerged

from the shadows. He wore a brown robe adorned with gold embroidery. A single yellow feather adorned his cap.

Jayel heard murmurs of approval. Dareck was well-known among the assembly and well-liked, and many knew Dareck was her uncle. She glanced at her father. Both parents momentarily looked surprised but smiled when those sitting near them slapped their backs with congratulations.

The president held up her hand for quiet. Nanyum continued the ritual. "Do you, Dareck, son of Harmond, agree to help Jayel, daughter of Karsch, complete her training and provide any guidance she may need to best execute her oath of membership?"

"I do."

Uncle and niece exchanged smiles, and then Dareck receded into the shadows.

With a nod from the president, Jayel returned to her seat as did the vice president. The musicians played a short joyful refrain marking the end of the induction ceremony.

When the music ended, the president raised her hands until everyone became silent. Nanyum pushed her long black hair behind her neck. "And now, we turn to the second purpose of this assembly. I yield the floor to the one who called this meeting." Nanyum turned and sat with the stage party.

A few measures of percussion instruments marked the beginning of the Endowed meeting. Dareck appeared from the shadows once again and walked up the steps to the stage. He did not glance at Jayel but, after a nod to the president, approached the podium.

Jayel noticed her father looked alarmed. Her mother's facial expression appeared frozen. *They didn't know.*

"I am Dareck, son of Harmond and Eleaneck. Many of you know of the untimely death seventeen standard years ago of my wife, Neondra, daughter of Leondra and Relston, all three Endowed members."

Murmurs spread throughout the hall. Older members whispered into the ears of younger ones.

When the murmurs quieted, Dareck continued, "I waited these many years until I collected and examined evidence concerning her death. It wasn't an accident as publicly reported. Neondra was murdered, and this crime was then covered up." He paused. "As you know, murder of an Endowed member is rare in our history, but the punishment must be severe. Well, the time has come for justice. I ask you now to hear the evidence and pass judgment. I ask for the *Elundrite*, trial by membership."

More murmurs and gasps echoed throughout the hall. The *Elundrite* was an ancient ritual, and few in the assembly had ever attended one. It implied that one of the Endowed committed the crime.

Dareck held up his hands. The assembly quieted. "Karsch, son of Harmond, please stand."

Chapter 45

The assembly hushed when Karsch stood, a solitary figure among a sea of robes and feathers.

Jayel swallowed. *Didn't Dareck get my message? My father didn't murder Neondra.*

The tense silence broke when the Great Hall's heavy doors opened, and everyone's attention shifted to the back of the room.

Azala stood at the entrance, flanked by two uniformed ESF guards. She wore a plush black robe, and in addition to the traditional Endowed hood, a scarlet cape hung over her left shoulder and arm. Feathers of various shades of yellow decorated her mortarboard.

The musicians played the opening piece of the *Elundrite*, a haunting sonorous score played in a minor key. Azala slowly walked up the aisle, stature dignified and proud befitting the oldest Endowed member, every footstep made more dramatic by the beat of the percussion instruments.

Members respectfully remained silent, waiting, and watching.

When Azala reached the stage, two robed men placed a well-cushioned chair on the president's right. ESF guards closed the heavy doors and secured the hearing.

Once Azala sat, the music stopped. A drone bailiff, a three-foot-tall cylindrical machine, rose in the air and floated to the end of the standing Endowed member's row. Karsch stepped to the center aisle and placed his hands on its lighted ledge.

The mechanical bailiff asked, "Do you swear to answer truthfully to all questions and give only honest testimony to the best of your ability?"

In a loud, unwavering voice, Karsch answered, "I do." The light on the ledge turned off, and the bailiff traveled back to the stage.

All eyes reverted to Dareck. He removed an envelope from a pocket in his robe and placed pictures one at a time on the podium's surface. Immediately, they appeared on a large translucent screen between the stage and the audience for members to view.

"These pictures," Dareck began, "taken some eighteen standard years ago, show you and my wife Neondra together … smiling, eating out, enjoying the park, touching … Do you admit to having a personal relationship with Neondra?"

"Yes, we worked together for 28 standard months. We were friends."

Dareck nodded. "You were friends before I met her?"

"Yes."

"You remained friends after I married her?"

"Yes."

"Were you … lovers?"

After a slight hesitation, Karsch replied, "Yes."

President Nanyum lifted her staff and tapped the floor, the sound resonating through the hall.

Azala declared, "Karsch, son of Harmond, speaks the truth."

"Were you lovers after I married her?"

Karsch lowered his voice. "Yes."

Jayel swallowed and noticed her mother did the same.

Azala declared, "Karsch, son of Harmond, speaks the truth."

Dareck brought out additional papers from the envelope. "Would you describe for the membership what these are?" He placed the first two on the podium's surface.

"Where did you get those paper receipts?" Karsch demanded.

Nanyum raised her hand. "Karsch, son of Harmond, your role is to answer questions, not ask them."

"My apologies," Karsch immediately replied and took a deep breath.

When Dareck didn't speak, Jayel stood. "I found them, Father, in your private office."

Her father stared at her, and she saw his surprise turn to disappointment. Jayel lowered her eyes as she sat. *He's figured out how and when I deceived him.*

Karsch returned his gaze to his brother and took a deep breath. "They are receipt records, dated the day before the fire, from different locations on Melandan. The one on the right is the purchase of an accelerant. The other is for the purchase of a weapon and its ammunition."

"And this receipt?" Dareck replaced the papers on the podium with another.

"It's a transportation record for passage from Melandan to Characta on the day of the fire."

"And this one?"

"Another transportation receipt from Characta's spaceport to Neondra's house."

"Did you make these purchases?"

"No."

The president tapped her staff, and Azala affirmed, "Karsch speaks the truth."

Gasps among the members echoed in the hall.

"If you didn't make these purchases, why do you have these receipts?"

Karsch looked uncomfortable and shifted his weight to his left leg. "Someone else gave them to me."

"Who? Why?"

"They were brought to my attention after the tragedy because they implicated another person, someone who had the means and opportunity to murder Neondra and cover it up."

"Who do these receipts implicate?"

After a long hesitation and barely above a whisper, Karsch answered, "My wife, Mandel."

Jayel gasped. *Not Mother.*

Murmurs increased, and when members' heads turned toward each other, feathers waved throughout the assembly.

The president called out, "Silence. Be still. Mandel, wife of Karsch, please stand."

Jayel's mother stood, looking pale, walked to the center aisle, and took her place beside her husband. Their hands touched and stayed connected, but they didn't look at each other.

"Mandel, wife of Karsch, you are not an Endowed member, but by agreement with Characta's government, you are bound by the laws of our *Elundrite* to tell the truth. If you do not, the punishment is as severe, if not more so, as in our Systems courts. Do you understand?"

"I do."

The bailiff rose and floated to where husband and wife stood. After swearing in Mandel, it returned to the stage.

Dareck put the first receipt on the podium again. "Mandel,

did you purchase this weapon and ammunition?"

"Yes."

"Did you go to Neondra's home on the day of the fire with this gun?"

"Yes."

Nanyum tapped her staff, and Azala pronounced, "Mandel, wife of Karsch, speaks the truth."

The air in the room felt hot, thick with tension. Jayel forced herself to inhale.

"Did you shoot her?"

"No."

The president tapped her staff, and Azala declared, "Mandel, wife of Karsch, speaks the truth."

Dareck paused. "Did you set the fire?"

"No."

Nanyum tapped her staff. Azala pronounced, "Mandel speaks the truth."

Jayel felt relieved and once again breathed normally.

Her uncle's expression softened from anger to puzzlement. "Please explain."

Mandel cleared her throat and stated, "I knew about their affair."

Karsch raised his eyebrows and studied his wife's face.

"I visited Neondra that morning, the day of the fire," Mandel continued, eyes fixed on Dareck. "I demanded she break off the relationship with my husband."

Nanyum called for silence. Then Mandel added, "We argued, and we talked about the baby."

"What about the child?"

"I asked Neondra who his father was."

"And?"

"Neondra didn't know. She said it didn't matter to her, she

was happy to have her husband or mine be Layon's father. See, she loved you both."

Dareck paused, swallowed, and asked, "What happened next?"

"I told Neondra if she intended to stay married, then she should return my husband to me. He could never love me as I needed if she was in his life. I was angry. Neondra insisted she wasn't going to break off the affair." Mandel paused and lowered her eyes. "I admit I planned to kill her."

She swallowed and looked up again at Dareck. "But I couldn't be angry at the baby. The joy and innocence on Layon's face shamed me for wanting to kill his mother. He needed her. So, I left. Both were very much alive."

Dareck pondered this information. "And the weapon you brought? What happened to it?"

"I was upset ... I don't know for sure ... I no longer needed it. Perhaps I dropped it on the way out." Mandel looked down and quietly sobbed.

Nanyum tapped her staff, and Azala declared, "Mandel, wife of Karsch, speaks the truth."

After a prolonged pause, Dareck returned his attention to his brother. "Karsch, did you ever talk with your wife about the fire?"

Still recovering from Mandel's testimony, Karsch stammered, "No. I thought my wife had committed the murders and burned the house. I grieved for the loss of Neondra and my nephew and couldn't bear losing my wife as well."

"And I, Husband, thought you had committed the murders."

They embraced and touched foreheads. Jayel felt for them, realizing the time apart during her childhood was the result of fear and avoidance more than passion for their jobs.

Dareck brought Karsch's attention back to the trial. "Brother, how did you get these receipts? Why did you save them?"

Karsch hesitated, then sighed. "They were visual reminders of records which could be made public. He told me to do as he demanded or he would make it known my wife had committed murder, that I had had an affair, and …" Karsch choked back tears. "… I was the reason for the death of your son."

After murmurs in the assembly subsided, Dareck pressed, "Who? Who blackmailed you?"

Before Karsch answered, a commotion broke out in the back of the hall, and heads turned. An ESF uniformed man struggled with a robed figure. As the guard slumped to the floor, a baggy sleeve rose with the guard's weapon in hand. It aimed toward the center front and fired.

Chapter 46

Karsch staggered forward and fell to his knees.

"No!" Jayel cried out. She jumped off the stage and ran to her father. She immediately assessed the entry and exit points. *Good, too high to damage any vital organs. Inches higher to the left, the injury would have been to his neck or brain.* She ripped her robe's sleeve to make bandages and pressed them against his upper back and chest.

Karsch reached up and placed his hands atop Jayel's to add pressure to his chest.

Jayel passed her strength to him when their hands touched, sending warmth up his arm into his shoulder.

His facial muscles relaxed as the pain lessened. His breathing eased. Karsch opened his eyes and whispered, "The hands of a healer … I'm sorry, Daughter, you learned of my past this way."

Harmond, who also rushed to Karsch's side, questioned him. "Son, tell us who blackmailed you."

Before Karsch could answer, two ESF men brought forward the shooter.

Glaring and pulling on the arms holding him, General Chrysic faced the group. Gasps filled the hall when some members recognized the robed figure.

The president, standing now at Dareck's side, tapped her staff for silence.

The guard Chrysic assaulted made his way to the stage, straightening his cap. "I take responsibility, President Nanyum. I gave General Chrysic clearance to watch Jayel's induction even though his name wasn't on our list. He's her father's Number One, and I made an error in judgment."

Nanyum nodded. She spoke briefly with Dareck. Turning to Karsch, the president suggested, "We can suspend the *Elundrite* until after you receive medical treatment."

"No. I wish to continue, Nanyum." Karsch rose to one knee with his wife's and daughter's support and then stood.

Two additional guards assisted in restraining Chrysic, holding down his arms and legs. He eventually stopped struggling but continued to glare at the governor.

"On that fateful day," Karsch testified, "I, too, had visited Neondra. I told her I wanted to end the affair and save my marriage. We argued. She would not release me, and said I would be back because our love was special. I said our affair was over, and I left while she gave Layon breakfast. When I entered the spaceport for my return flight to Melandan, I saw across the terminal my wife arriving. I hoped her presence on Characta was a mere coincidence. But hours later, when I heard about the fire, I wondered if she was responsible."

Nanyum tapped her staff, and Azala affirmed, "Karsch speaks the truth."

Karsch winced, pressed the chest bandage, but continued, his eyes fixed on his Number One. "The next day, General Chrysic reported to me his investigations found a paper trail implicating my wife. The general showed me the receipts you saw here and told me if I didn't do what he wanted, he would publicly accuse her of murder and state I had covered it up by setting the fire."

Dareck asked, "What did General Chrysic want in exchange for your silence?"

"Political power. When I became governor, I named him First General of Melandan, and he enjoyed all the rights and privileges of the position."

Nanyum tapped her staff, and Azala affirmed, "Karsch speaks the truth."

At this moment, Chrysic wiggled vigorously and tore away from the guards holding him. He stood defiant and spat at Karsch. "You've ruined everything. You always do, leaving me to clean things up. You are nothing without me. I had to stop the affair because you were too weak to do it yourself."

The general paused as he smiled, an evil grin framing the feverish eyes of a trapped man. "See, I was watching Neondra's house that morning, waiting for the right time to execute my plans. The bitch had been a thorn in my plans for months and the time had come to stop her. Then what do I see but separately you and your wife visited the home. Each time I heard angry voices. When Mandel left a weapon behind, I saw the opportunity. I picked it up and entered the front door."

Chrysic paused and stared coldly at Dareck. "Neondra laughed at me when I warned her the affair would hurt Karsch's political career. She enjoyed having two lovers. Neondra refused to bend her will to mine. I knew if Karsch was to become governor, she must be eliminated. I'm the one who bought the accelerant, and I brought it to Characta. My initial plan was to burn Neondra alive. I wanted to hear her scream as the house burned, but I settled for killing her first with Mandel's weapon."

Dareck's face reddened with anger, and he rushed from the stage. Jayel feared he would kill Chrysic with his bare hands.

She knew all too well the desire.

Karsch intervened before Dareck reached the General, however. He pushed away from Mandel and Jayel and stood in front of Chrysic, blocking Dareck, and pleaded, "Don't. Revenge is acid on the heart."

The two brothers stood inches apart, face to face, the closest they had been in decades. A tense silence filled the room.

Dareck moved his eyes away from Chrysic and gazed into his brother's pained face. Later, Karsch would say it felt as if his brother's glance dissolved the rust on his heart. Able to open the lock, Karsch remembered a day from their childhood when he and his younger brother played in the field behind their house, and Dareck tripped and sprained his ankle. Karsch picked him up, sat the boy on his shoulders, and turned the incident into a game of playing lookout. By the time they entered their house, Dareck was no longer crying but laughing and proudly naming the trees on a far hill. A silly moment remembered with profound tenderness.

Through their mutual gaze, the memory entered Dareck's consciousness. Her uncle would also report later in this moment he felt once again their brotherly bond and suddenly had answers to questions he long asked. Peace filled his mind. Hindsight, like a beacon, enlightened him and reinterpreted their past interactions. The older brother protected the younger.

Tears appeared in both men's eyes.

Karsch continued, "I'm sorry, brother, for staying silent. At the time, I didn't know what to say or do. You were in pain, and I couldn't add more by telling you my wife had killed Neondra and the baby. Avoidance was the best protection, lest you read my thoughts. Over the years, General Chrysic assured me sacrificing our relationship was best for all concerned. I should never have listened to him."

Dareck's expression wilted from anger to regret. "Forgive me, my brother. I, too, made false assumptions and conclusions. I thought you had killed Neondra to hurt me, and I hated you for it. I understand now. You weren't jealous but motivated by shame and guilt." After a pause, sadness left Dareck's face, and he smiled. "We were both in pain, but let our healing begin. I have joyous news, Karsch. The baby lived. The housekeeper rescued him before the fire consumed the house. I hid the child so the murderer wouldn't get a second chance."

General Chrysic screamed, tugging at the guards who held him. "What? The child lived? There were bones—"

"Unidentified bone fragments," Dareck replied. "Maybe one of our pets. No one investigated. They assumed the bones were Layon's … more untested assumptions. The heat melted most of the evidence … you ensured very little was left in the fire."

"Where is he?" Chrysic shouted and spit. "Where is Layon?"

On cue—Jayel suspected a telepathic message from Brusch or Dareck—Layon entered the Great Hall and pushed through the crowded aisle. "We've already met."

Outraged, Chrysic spat, "I will kill you, Mr. Battersby." He swiftly pushed his arms down, then quickly pulled them up and broke away from the guards. The General grinned as he stepped away from them, his back to the stage, and pulled a large knife from beneath his opened robe.

Everyone froze as it gleamed in the light.

Chrysic, eyes focused on Layon, raised his arm. A blast rang out.

As the sound echoed, General Chrysic fell backward, dead.

Confusion ran through the assembly. The shooter jumped from the mezzanine and immediately was surrounded by Endowed members. They took the gunman's weapon, and ESF guards escorted the small group to the front.

The shooter turned out to be a woman.

"Ruchelle!" Jayel exclaimed. *Dorind's sister.*

Dressed all in black, Ruchelle stepped toward Dareck and peered into his eyes, speaking without regret. "Justice is served. General Chrysic destroyed my brother's life. And from what I heard just now, yours too."

"You did what I wanted to do," Jayel voiced. "Justice for Dory. Justice for Neondra. I, for one, am grateful."

"As am I," Dareck sighed as he observed Chrysic's body and then focused on his brother. "What has happened cannot be undone, but perhaps now we can transform our pain into resolve to replace fear and anger with love and prosperity."

Karsch regarded Layon whom he had met previously as Cimorelli Battersby, his daughter's research assistant. "My son?"

"Yes, brother," Dareck confirmed. "The DNA test proves it so."

Jayel studied her uncle and knew it had pained him to learn the truth, but the brothers' reconciliation eased the hurt. She looked at Layon, publicly her brother now. Jayel felt his thoughts. He liked belonging to two fathers and a sister.

Karsch moved aside to let Layon meet his wife. "Mandy, I'm sorry about the affair. But I swore the day Neondra died I would be a better person and dedicate my life to public service."

"And you have, Husband. For the first time in seventeen standard years, we are free now to love each other without fear of unspoken deeds. And it feels wonderful." She touched his left cheek and wiped away a tear.

Medics arrived, and the aisle cleared. Karsch reluctantly agreed to move to the stretcher.

A young man ran in and called out, "Brusch? I'm searching for Brusch."

Brusch stepped forward. "Over here."

The lad paused to catch his breath. "I ran over as soon as I heard. They approved your patent for the thought imager. Everything's happening fast, and I mean solar wind fast. Contracts for mass production await your signature. You and Layon are nominated for the prestigious Elesh Prize in Medicine." The man turned to Jayel, "And they approved a research grant for you to use the thought imager for stroke patients. The university wants you to return to Orim immediately to finish your degree."

Nanyum approached the podium. "Let us come to order and complete the purpose of this meeting. Dareck?"

"We learned the truth, and I'm satisfied."

"Very well." The vice president leaned toward Nanyum's ear. Nanyum nodded and announced, "Would Layon, son of Karsch, approach the podium?"

Karsch held up his hand and stopped the medics from leaving the hall. "Wait. I already missed nearly twenty standard years of my son's life. I'm not going to miss his induction into the membership."

The musicians began the induction ceremony music. The assembly watched as Layon put on his Endowed robe, hood, and mortarboard. He borrowed Jayel's pad to read the ritual responses, swore the oath, and received the Karsch family hood. Brusch accepted the role of mentor.

Jayel slipped her arm around Ranthal's waist, smiling. She

was happy for her brother. *Layon can finally acknowledge his identity.*

Nanyum declared the meeting adjourned, and the musicians played the *Elundrite*'s closing piece. The flag bearers removed the banners and strode down the aisle. Azala stood and walked out first, followed by the stage party. Expeditiously, the grand marshal ushered out the members.

After the musicians left, only a handful remained inside the hall. Dareck and Ruchelle talked quietly by the stage near Chrysic's body as they waited for the authorities to arrive. Jayel noticed they stood physically close, their attention focused intently on each other. *It appears Dareck has found more than peace. I'm happy for them.*

About ten rows down in the center of the hall, Brusch and Layon eagerly chatted about the thought imager and their next steps.

Ranthal, scrolling messages on his pad, stood by Jayel's side. "Communications are back to normal. The reception tonight for you and Layon is back on schedule. Mandel reports your father received treatment and will attend."

Looking forward to the future, Jayel turned and kissed her betrothed.

The End

www.ingramcontent.com/pod-product-compliance
Lightning Source LLC
LaVergne TN
LVHW010538160826
845677LV00013B/2914